Murder at Cold Creek College

Christa Nardi

CHRISTA NARDI

.

CONTENTS

CHAPTER 1

Traffic was slow and crazy, and the semester hadn't started yet. I'd need to remember to leave earlier. With the fall semester starting next week, the population increased at a rapid rate as students returned to campus. I liked to see the hustle and bustle, the excitement of the new academic year. Cold Creek wasn't a big city with major traffic problems, even with students. Cold Creek is a small town, nestled between other small towns. It has a single main street with access to various cross streets. Although not bad by city standards, the traffic noticeably increased when students came back.

My impatience wasn't due to my job. I didn't punch a clock or anything. Faculty members at Cold Creek College came and went at different times. Work hour flexibility topped the list of best things about being faculty. Faculty pretty much dictated the hours they worked by when they scheduled their classes, held office hours, or had meetings. The impatience was just about me. I got more done and felt better if I got ahead of the game. I hated being behind and rushed.

As I approached the campus and parked, I noted lots of activity over in west campus. The excitement seemed to be near the rec center. Cold Creek College isn't known for its athletic program any more than any other small private college. In recent years, the alumni and the trustees donated funds to expand the center to foster a healthy life style. The increase in the student fees helped to keep it up-to-date. My best guess was that the hoopla was a publicity scene with one of the bigger donors. As a private college, famous and successful alumni often visited the campus. Not giving it another thought, I parked, grabbed my files, and went up to my office.

The central quadrangle of the campus was pedestrian traffic only. With about a five-minute walk from the parking lot, I arrived at the Humanities building. My office is one of several in the psychology department, located on the third floor of the Humanities Building. Sociology occupied the other end of the floor. The History and Language Departments are housed on the second floor.

I took the stairs in an effort to get some exercise. With the position of an Assistant Professor, I spent most of my time sitting in an office in front of a computer. I tried to find opportunities for exercise as part of my daily activities. As the years crept up on me, so had the weight along with a seemingly endless battle to keep fit. I considered getting one of those computer bracelets to alert when I sat still for too long. I walked toward my office and saw the door ajar. I noticed that Terra and Ali were in my office, looking out the window. As I walked in, I asked, "Hi, what's up?"

"Oh, hi! Sorry to be in here, but you've got the best view of the rec center, and we're trying to figure out what's going on over there. Any ideas?" Terra asked. As staff for the department, she and Ali pretty much kept track of everything in and out of the department. Although not always the bearers of good news, they managed the budget, payroll, and purchases. Ali smiled and then went back to watching. Surprisingly, although Terra was the younger of the two, she had seniority and, as the administrative assistant to the Department Head, she had more responsibility than Ali.

"I saw a lot of activity over there. I figured it was some kind of publicity shot or something," I answered with a sigh as I put my stuff down. As I glanced out the window, I realized that I truly did have a great view of the rec center with the fountains in the quad turned off. I found myself standing and looking out and trying to figure out what was happening along with the two of them. "Is that the fire department over there? And the paramedics?" I asked, pointing in the general direction of two vehicles, lights flashing, as they moved from the back of the rec center to our vantage point.

"I wonder if there was a shooting?" Ali asked. Ali wasn't prone to extreme responses, but the news of late had been detailing school and college shootings. As a small college, the administrators had resisted any kind of alert system. The trustees disagreed and an alert system was installed, but had yet to be used.

"No, that would be on the news already. Dr. Hendley, did you hear anything on the radio as you drove in?" asked Terra. As I shook my head to the negative, she continued, "Probably somebody got hurt in the rec center, you know fell or something. We can pull up the news in our office."

"I guess, but I gotta get to work here. Classes start next week and I still need to finish my syllabus. Then I'll check with the bookstore to make sure the order didn't get messed up. And I still have to get the on-line components set up," I lamented, partly because it was true, and partly as a hint.

"Okay, we get the message!" Ali said with a laugh. "We'll keep you posted if we get the scoop on what's happening."

"We're working on registration and payroll. I guess everyone wants to get paid. We all know the ones who will be the first to complain if something goes wrong!" Terra added the last comment with a shake of her head as they both left my office and went back to the department office. And, yes, it was always the same faculty to complain about everything and anything. No matter where you were, there seemed to be a complainer and a whiner. Thankfully, there were also some good people. I imagined the same personalities existed in large universities and business, but in small colleges like Cold Creek the squeaky wheels stood out.

I spent the next hour or so plugging away on my computer and trying to upload all the support materials for my two classes. I teach introductory psychology and research design, two sections of each. I also had an honors seminar this semester. In the end, it would be mostly freshman in the intro courses, juniors and seniors in the research courses, and a mixed group for the seminar. I made good progress and kept plugging along. When I'm in the groove, I don't notice most other activity in the hallways, and this day, I was definitely on a roll. In fact, I was so engrossed I almost jumped when Kim flew into my office.

"Sheridan! Did you hear? Something happened at the Rec Center – an accident most likely. I was working out in the cardio suite, and the police wouldn't let me leave. And I'm not talking about Security either, Sher. Cold Creek Police are over there. They asked for my ID. They wanted to know when I arrived at the center. Had I seen anything unusual? Who had I talked to? They wanted to know how often students or faculty worked out alone, how often I used the center, who I usually worked out with there. Lots of questions for an accident, don't you think?" Kim rattled in her usual excited manner until she seemed to run out of steam.

Kim Pennzel was my colleague and a good friend. She often lived up to the stereotype of red heads being energized and emotionally reactive. We were both in our forties, both entered the academy after working in the field as psychologists for several years, getting divorced, and needing a change of scene. We had become fast friends over the past four years. While I tended to be more of an introvert, Kim was definitely the social butterfly and extrovert. She tended toward the vibrant colors. I stuck to more subdued shades of blues and grays. I like that the blues accented my blue eyes. She engineered anything spontaneous we did, while I tended to be the one who took care of the details. We complemented each other and that worked well.

Laughing, I responded, "Chill, Kim, they just need to check it all out to establish liability if someone was hurt." Changing the topic, I asked, "You all ready for the semester? You know if we don't have our paperwork in on each of the classes, Jim will be on the warpath."

Jim Grant was the department head. He had been the department head since I started here four years ago. He was average height, and like many of us, a little above desired weight. His hair was cut short, and white as snow. The occasional strand revealed that he once had very dark brown hair. In his 60s, it was rumored that he would be retiring soon, maybe as soon as they offered a retirement bonus. In the meantime, he was an okay head. He did what he could and worked to make sure the status quo was maintained. And part of that meant he policed and evaluated whether the faculty did their jobs. The down side, of course, was that he didn't make waves or consider changing the way things were done. He definitely didn't deal with any conflict. He liked the status quo. Despite his foibles, it could be much worse.

"Yeah, I'm working on it. You know me, I'll get it in just under the wire," Kim said as she shrugged and smiled. "You'll share anything you find out, right?" I nodded my head in response.

"Guess I will go to my office and get to work," she added as she turned to leave. She no sooner got out the door, and I heard her say, "Hey Terra, Ali, how are you? What's got you in such a tither?"

"Oh, have you heard what happened at the rec center? I don't think we ever had a murder on campus before!" Terra exclaimed. With that announcement, I abandoned my computer and joined them in the hall. I am nothing if not curious.

"Murder? I thought there was an accident?" I asked. I wondered if Terra exaggerated the situation a bit.

"Nope! Joe just called me from the paper. He's on his way over to get some background information for the paper," Terra stated. Her husband Joe worked for the Cold Creek Gazette. I often wondered if it was a natural consequence of his job that Terra seemed to have a pulse on everything about everybody. It wasn't like she was a gossip, but she seemed to have the scoop on what was happening. On the other hand, she was very sociable, like Kim. So it might not have anything to do with Joe.

"Murdered? Who? How?" I asked, still not completely convinced. I thought of the childhood game of telephone when the same sentence was repeated to a series of people. One after the other, the story repeated. The meaning was very different by the time it reached the last person.

"Oh, my god, I was there. I could have been murdered too!" Kim exclaimed, hands to her mouth. She didn't have any trouble believing what Terra said. Not knowing the details, I guessed it was a logical leap that she was in the same place and could have been a victim as well.

"Joe didn't say who, only that the scene was being treated as a murder scene. He's been assigned to get backfill for the story. He said he'd be over to talk to faculty and staff in a bit. We turned the news on in the office, but so far haven't heard anything. They may not be saying yet. You know, maybe they haven't notified next of kin or something," Terra continued with a shrug. Her nonchalance was a stark contrast to Kim's response. Ali hadn't said anything, but shook her head. Like her name, Terra tended toward being down to earth and that gave some credibility to the idea of a murder.

"Kim, was there anything this morning that looked suspicious?" I asked thinking back to her comments about the questions she'd been asked. The questions and police presence were making sense if this was a murder.

"Sher, you know me on the treadmill. Headphones on and zoning out for five miles. I couldn't even tell you who came and went while I jogged. When the police interrupted us to ask questions, I think there were a few students and a man. I think I've seen him over in the administration building a few times and at college functions. I don't remember his name though," she related, shaking her head slightly. "Maybe if I paid more attention I could have stopped it...," she added as she clapped her hands to her face again.

"Don't be ridiculous! Unless it happened in the cardio suite, there's no way you could have done anything," I assured her. "I'm sure you would have done something if you could have."

"She's right, Dr. Pennzel. I bet it's some random thing. You should be glad it wasn't you – we certainly are," Ali chimed in. "Come on Terra, we better get back to the budget and payroll before this place becomes more of a zoo than it usually is. I bet Joe won't be the only one asking questions. And I bet the phones will be ringing like crazy once this hits the news. You know we'll need to field the calls." Normally, there would be student workers to answer the phones, direct calls, or take messages; but the semester hadn't started so no students were on the job yet.

Terra nodded somewhat reluctantly, and she and Ali left. Kim and I stood staring after them until I finally echoed Ali's comments. Kim retreated to her office and I returned to my computer. My prior high level of concentration had disappeared. Though I tried to focus on the e-lesson set up, I was not making the same level of progress as I had before. Frustrated, and a bit curious, I searched for the local television station, KCCX. I scanned for a heading of "breaking news". I checked my phone to see if a campus alert had been sent, but nothing yet.

I decided to leave the KCCX site up on one monitor, while I worked on the other. I can't imagine what it was like to not have two computer monitors to work from simultaneously. It sure made multi-tasking a lot easier. I enabled KCCX's alerts feature so I would get their breaking news alerts on my computer. Usually, the frequent beeps would be distracting. Today I wanted to be informed about the situation. Maybe just my idle curiosity and love of mysteries, or the psychologist in me, but I sensed the potential need for crisis intervention. One of the keys to crisis intervention and dealing with trauma is to have information. It helps if that information dispels the fear of continued trauma. Like that they caught the person who did

11

it.

Alert on, I went back to preparing materials and e-lessons. I no sooner got going and "beep". I shifted my attention to the KCCX screen, fully expecting it to be something minor. Instead I saw the headlines, "Foul play and not fitness at Cold Creek College Rec Center". I stuck my head out of my door and yelled to Kim, "KCCX has the story!" I continued reading. I had gotten through the where, when and what by the time Kim joined me and was reading over my shoulder. Almost immediately, Terra and Ali joined us.

'At 7:47 this morning, the Cold Creek police were notified by College security that someone had been hurt and was not responsive at the College rec center. Police and EMS responded to the scene and the man was pronounced dead at the site. The identity of the man is being withheld pending notification. Cause of death is indicated as "suspicious." Sources close to the investigation suggested that this was not accidental, nor did it appear to be random. KCCX will continue updating this story throughout the day.'

I leaned back and Terra let out a sigh. Ali mumbled something that resembled "wow." Kim was silent. In fact, for a few minutes, we all were silent, almost as if mourning this unknown man. Once again, there wasn't much to say. While we digested the announcement, the alert arrived on my phone, and the phones of the others. Better late than never, I guessed. Terra and Ali went back to their office, and Kim went back to hers. I re-read the release, shook my head, and went back to work. It was already mid-morning and I hadn't accomplished all that I had hoped yet.

Try as I might to concentrate, I kept wondering who had died. Cold Creek College is a small private college with about 1600 full-time students and 120 faculty members, including the part-timers. If it was a faculty member or student, it was probably someone I knew or at least had interacted with at some point. The downside and upside of a small college, like a small town, is that you know just about everybody.

The Humanities building had originally been a dormitory. In some ways, our offices still resembled dorm rooms, thankfully fairly good sized rooms. The bottom floor that had once been parlor, dining, and such, were redesigned as classrooms, each able to accommodate 10 to 25 students. There was a small café where the kitchen had been. It was an old building, renovated for its current purpose. What served as the departmental office had previously been one of two lounges on the floor. The departmental office for Sociology was at the opposite end of the floor where the second lounge had once been. It had a homey feel to it and murder didn't quite fit.

I took a walk around our floor and more or less did a head count. I could at least eliminate some of my colleagues as the victim. Psychology had eight full-time faculty, including Kim and me, plus Jim as Department Head. As I walked toward the department central area and reception and Ali and Terra's work area, I noted that Jim's door was ajar. I cocked my head at Terra, and she said, "Yeah, he's in. He's on the phone with the Dean who's been on the phone with the Provost and so on. Everyone is trying to do some damage control without any information. Everything is very hush hush." She shook her head and shrugged.

I nodded and continued my walk. I stopped at the next open door and said hello to Doug Sanders. Doug had his radio on and commented, "Crazy," and shook his head. Doug was about my age and specialized in experimental psychology. He was particularly interested in neuroscience and the effects of environment on people's behavior. He was one of two experimental psychologists in the department. Unfortunately, as a four-year college, faculty didn't have a lot of time for research. Most of us really weren't interested. Tall, thin, balding, and very quiet described Doug. I don't remember ever hearing Doug speak a full sentence unless it was part of a lecture. Doug was not particularly social. He was fairly predictable, right down to his khaki pants and polo shirt. Today he wore pale blue.

I nodded and then checked the next open door. Unfortunately, it was Max's office. I knocked. He swiveled around, his black hair somewhat uncontrolled and in need of a cut. I must have startled him. His brown eyes opened wide.

"Sheridan, you wouldn't believe. I 'm trying to get this experiment going, and somehow the materials I ordered haven't come in. Terra told me I didn't have enough money in my account, and that's not right! I don't know what her problem is," was his opening tirade. Max was the other experimental psychologist and the most interested in research of the faculty in the department.

"Yeah, well, Terra and Ali do the books. They would know. Maybe you didn't figure right what you had in your lab account. I bet they can give you a full accounting," I suggested. Max tended to have these tantrums a lot. He was relatively young and had come to Cold Creek straight from graduation the year after me. He had big dreams of doing enough research to get to a better university.

"You doing okay otherwise – you know with the rec center and all," I asked.

"Oh, I gave up on the rec center last year. Too crowded. I joined a private club where I don't have to deal with the students. At the rec center, they always tried to talk to me. Are you looking for a place to work out?" he asked, oblivious to the excitement on campus. But that was not unusual for Max. Unless it was going to directly affect him, he didn't seem to know about it. Now, if he had wanted to work out today, he might have been more interested.

"Uh, Max, someone died at the rec center this morning," I offered as gently as I could.

Jumping out of his seat, he proclaimed, "I knew it, I knew there were safety problems. I knew those students would wreck something! See what I mean?"

"Max, someone was murdered. It wasn't an accident," I added. I wondered at the fact that he hadn't asked the obvious question of who? It was certainly the question I wanted answered.

"Oh. Well, it better not get in the way of

my lab work. I'd love to chat with you Sheridan, but I have work to do," he responded. With that, he sat back down and turned back to his computer. Good thing or he would have seen me shake my head in disbelief. It was also probably a good thing that he did research with rats or mice, examining their use of cues, learning, and such. He sure didn't seem interested in people and didn't always pick up on social cues. I made my way back to my office with a wave at Kim. I also quickly let her know that it wasn't Jim, Doug or Max who was murdered.

CHAPTER 2

I got back to work. I planned to finish at least one class set-up before lunch. The next thing I heard was the knock on my door and I looked up. I was a bit taken aback by the officer, as well as Joe, waiting for my attention. Joe looked excited and reminded me of a live wire. He about bounced around the 6-foot plus man in my door. The man sported a badge, but not one I recognized. He was not part of college security or Cold Creek police. Before I could register which branch he was, , he filled in some of the details for me.

"Ms. Hendley?" he asked, with a glance at the name plate on my door. "I'm Detective McMann with the State Police, ma'am. If I could have a few minutes of your time, it would be appreciated. The Department Head, uh," he paused looking at his note paid. He continued, "Jim Grant, said you would help me with speaking with the faculty and the rest of the staff. Before Mr. Janis, here, interviews them." This last part was said with some disdain and directed more at Joe than at me.

"Uh, certainly. Glad to help. What can I do?" I asked, not sure what I could offer. But I wasn't surprised that Jim pawned him off on me. It happened a lot.

"Do you mind if I come in and ask a few basic questions, as a start?" he answered. He glanced around my office. I immediately jumped up and moved my bag off one of the two chairs in my office. I always dropped whatever I had in my hands on the closest chair when I came in and then had to move it.

"Sure, have a seat," I answered having cleared off the seat. He came in, and with a look at Joe, emphatically closed the door.

He then must have had second thoughts, and asked, "Do you mind that I closed the door?" It occurred to me that detectives had as much trouble trying to balance the need for private conversations and the potential risk of being accused of inappropriate behavior as psychologists.

"Not a problem, Detective," I responded.

"Okay, Ms. Hendley, about what time did

you come on campus this morning? What did you observe?" he asked as he flipped the page of his notebook and began writing. I told him what I could, but I hadn't been near the rec center. I didn't think it would help much. As he made notes, I noticed that he had good penmanship for a man. His nails looked almost manicured. This was a sharp contrast to my image of law enforcement as macho types.

On the other hand, he was at least 6 foot tall and muscular. He obviously was someone who worked at staying in shape. That was much more in line with my mental image. He wasn't in uniform, other than his badge and gun that is. I assumed that he had a sports coat somewhere that normally would have hidden the gun. As I ended with finding Terra and Ali in my office, he looked up. I noticed that he had hazel eyes with long lashes. I held his gaze for what seemed like forever. Such nice eyes, I almost had to shake myself. This man was definitely hot.

"So, you came in and they were looking out the window?" he asked as he stood and moved toward the window. "You do have an unblocked view of the rec center here. Did you notice anything else?"

"Nothing other than that there were emergency vehicles over there. We assumed there had been an accident," I answered with a shrug. It didn't seem to me that I could help much. I smoothed out my slacks and straightened my top. I was suddenly a bit self-conscious about my appearance.

"Okay, so you saw Terra Janis. That would be the wife of Mr. Janis, correct? And Ali Bough, correct? Who else have you seen this morning?" he asked.

I had nodded to the first two questions. I responded to the next, first with Kim's arrival from the rec center. Then I related told him about my checking and finding that Jim, Doug and Max were in their respective offices. He asked more specific questions. I assumed he was trying to get a timeline or confirmation of a timeline for when each of us had first been seen.

"Thank you, Ms. Hendley. This is helpful. Mr. Grant said you could take me around to each of the faculty offices. He said you would make introductions and generally help me out. Would you mind?" he asked, making eye contact again. He had beautiful eyes.

"No problem. Let me save my work here. It'll be just take a second." I clicked and saved and then stood up. I should have been irritated, but I was also very curious. Besides he was good looking. "Did you have any order in mind?"

"Whatever works. I'll have to talk to each of you sooner or later," he said, almost with a sigh. It occurred to me this was likely the more tedious and boring aspect of his job. As I opened the door, Joe about fell in. I had to smile. He looked embarrassed, and the detective looked a bit perturbed. He shook his head at Joe as we left my office. I went down the hall and figured that I would take him along the hall. We stopped first at Kim's office. She wasn't there, so we continued to Max's office. Unrelenting, Joe trailed behind us.

I knocked on the now closed door. Through the window in the door, I could tell he had two students in there with him. One of them opened the door. Max bellowed, "How dare you interrupt me! This is an important meeting regarding my research! Whatever you want will just have to wait." He then turned and signaled to the student to close the door. The detective managed to slip his arm around me and blocked the door from closing. I slid over and out of the way, but not before I noticed that he smelled good. His arm had been warm as it moved past my shoulder. The brief contact aroused feelings I hadn't felt in some time.

"Mr. Bentler, this will not wait," stated the detective with emphasis. His jaw tensed and his back seemed to straighten if that was even possible.

"It is DOCTOR Bentler, I'll have you know. And I have important work going on here," Max stated in his usual emphatic tone.

"Dr. Bentler, then. I am DETECTIVE McMann with the State Police. I don't care how important your work is. I need a few minutes of your time and of theirs as well." His tone did not brook any argument or sway from my perspective.

In a final effort to assert himself, Max stood and tried to look impressive. His effort was somewhat futile given that he was obviously shorter and less in shape than the detective. "Fine, detective. Our meeting should be over in about 30 minutes."

"Dr. Bentler, we will speak now. If you decline to speak now, I will consider obstruction of justice charges. Do you get my point, SIR?" the detective added as he stepped a bit closer to Max, who immediately sat back down. It would have been somewhat comical if not for the seriousness of the situation. The two students sitting there now looked quite terrified.

"Janet, Wesley, why don't you come out in the hall with me for a few minutes? Let the Detective here speak with Dr. Bentler," I suggested with a quick glance to the detective.

The detective moved slightly to allow them out. He stated more softly, "Please do not discuss the situation or allow Mr. Janis to speak with them" as he closed the door.

The three of us, and Joe, stood in the hall. The two students still looked terrified. They muttered about how mad Dr. Bentler was going to be with the delay. They were both seniors and Max was their thesis advisor. It was pretty clear that they were intimidated by him and his blustering manners. Sometimes it seemed that Max pushed the envelope with the students. We each had our own style and he was more bluster than bite. As we stood in the hall, at least once I heard Max's voice raised in indignation. I imagined he was being his usual arrogant and hot-tempered self. His voice got so loud at one point that Janet blanched.

I suggested to the two students they might want to have a seat in the break room. I wasn't even sure they knew anything had happened. I didn't know if they knew why a detective was here and would be questioning them. The break room was catty-corner from Max's office. They could at least sit down while they waited. And maybe not hear Max. Joe asked me if McMann had told me anything. I shook my head to the negative. Joe and Terra were good people. I liked them, especially Terra. She had sometimes made me laugh.

The door opened and McMann came out. He looked in my direction and I pointed to the break room. He went in there and closed the door. He still looked a bit irritated. That isn't often the case after an interaction with Max. Max shut his door forcefully with a scowl on his face without saying a work to Joe or me. Joe and I waited. I hoped the detective would be a bit more subdued with Janet and Wesley.

Janet and Wesley came back out, McMann behind them. They were smiling and so was he. I found myself relaxing a bit. I also noted that he had a great smile to go with those hazel eyes. The students went back into Max's office. McMann looked at me, pointedly ignoring Joe, and said, "Where next?"

I decided we should go back and see if Kim was back in her office. That interview was likely to take the longest since she had in fact been at the rec center. As we approached her office, I saw her flit out. She looked at me with a puzzled expression and said, "Be right back. Gotta grab something off the copier!"

"That's Kim Pennzel. She was at the rec center this morning," I offered to McMann.

"And would that be Dr. Pennzel? And should it have been Dr. Hendley?" he asked looking a bit sheepish.

"Yes to both, but please, just call me

Sheridan. I'm not as hung up on the "Dr" thing as Max is," I added.

"Sheridan, huh. Irish?" he asked. He let some of the official demeanor drop while we waited for Kim to return. His expression softened with a hint of a smile. I was a little surprised at his interest. It was usually Kim with her long red tresses and cute figure that garnered men's attention.

"Aye, it is." I answered with a smile. I considered asking about the 'McMann', but Kim came back. The light mood seemed to disappear almost as quickly as it had appeared.

"Kim, this is Detective McMann. He needs to talk to you," I offered by introduction. Kim looked taken aback and very wary. I wasn't sure if she was thinking about the murder or if she was remembering every speeding ticket she had ever gotten. She definitely paled, every freckle on her face standing out in contrast.

"Dr. Pennzel, this will only take a few minutes. Can we talk in your office please?" McMann said as he moved along with her into her office and shut the door. I sighed as I realized that I would be spending the rest of my morning waiting on him while he talked to everyone and anyone who was around. While McMann was in with Kim, Joe took off down the hall. He probably went to hang with Terra and Ali. He'd probably get more from them than from McMann. The hall was pretty quiet for approaching mid-day. That wasn't all that surprising considering the semester hadn't started. I also suspected that word had spread quickly that McMann was going to talk to all of us. That meant anyone who was around probably was trying to be invisible.

Standing there waiting for McMann, I found myself thinking about him. He was definitely a nice looking man – tall, muscular, hazel eyes, dark curly hair, and great smile. Hmmm. He seemed pleasant enough, polite at least while doing his job. My mind started to conjure up other interactions. Then I reminded myself of all the stereotypes and statistics related to police officers and military. I ticked them off – authority complexes, high divorce rates, high suicide rates, aggressive tendencies. I also reminded myself that he was probably married. Not to mention, I would probably never see him again. I sighed. About then, the door opened and McMann came out.

"Thank you Dr. Pennzel," he said to Kim. "Restroom around here?" he asked me. I pointed down the hall. With a "Be right back", he walked off in that direction.

"You okay, Kim?" I asked. She still looked very pale.

"Yeah, I'm okay. I've never been interrogated before or by so many different officers in the same day. Why didn't I pay more attention? I feel so bad," she said. She was wringing her hands and biting her lip. I gave her a quick hug.

"Kim, you didn't know what was going to happen. There's nothing you could have done." I tried to reassure her. She was very sensitive by nature.

"He wouldn't tell me anything either. Does anyone know who it was? Was it random? Why are the State police involved?" she asked me.

"Don't know, Kim. We may not know for some time. There's nothing we can do. All I know is that Jim told him I would help him," I answered with a grimace. I glanced down the hall. McMann was on his way back.

McMann and I went around to Doug's office. That interview lasted about five minutes if that. Knowing Doug, he may not have said more than five words. We moved down the hall and found Katie in her office. Katie's interview took a little longer, but then she would enjoy the male attention. That was her style, a little flirty with the males. With McMann so good-looking, I was not surprised as the time ticked by.

As I waited on McMann, I realized I didn't know much about Katie. I only saw her at department or college functions. She was probably my age and she had aged well. She was the petite athletic type who probably never saw a diet. She managed to have curves in all the right places. She also dressed to show off her curves, with her skirts a little short, her pants a little snug and her tops low cut and clingy. The thing was, on her it looked good. She had long blonde hair that always looked good. She seemed to use her feminine wiles and the stereotypes of blondes to her advantage with the men. But she was no 'dumb blonde' and seemed to hold her own on the academic side. She had received a number of awards for teaching and students seemed to like her.

I was getting hungry and I wondered how much longer I had to play 'escort'. Opening the door to Katie's office, McMann thanked her and closed the door again. Running his hand through his curly hair again, he asked, "Is there some place to grab a coffee and something to eat around here?" Obviously, he found this as tiring as I did, possibly more so.

With a smile, I explained there was a coffee shop on the first floor that had reasonable coffee and a light fare. He waved me forward and we made our way to Georg's Café. The café was nothing fancy. It catered mostly to students and the occasional faculty member who didn't leave campus to get something for lunch. Thankfully, the café reopened before classes started, but with lighter menus, shorter hours, and less staff. Once we got our beverages and sandwiches and sat down, McMann asked if I could describe the campus and history for him. He explained that he was not very familiar with the college.

As I explained to him, the campus originally was home to a private school. It catered to the wealthy who wanted a boarding school for their children from kindergarten through high school. As the popularity of the 'boarding school' education declined, it was established first as a two-year college in the 1960s. Later, it became a four-year college in the 1980s. With the cost of attending Cold Creek well above the state college or university, it still catered to those who could afford it. There were a few scholarships available for promising students who couldn't afford the tuition. But not very many.

Cold Creek College wasn't a key player in any specific area, but prided itself on its offerings in technology and horticulture. The college hadn't made it to the top 25 of private colleges, but the education students received was generally believed to be good. That was what the website and the administration boasted. From my experience it was true. Of the students I'd seen go through with a major in psychology, they usually were able to get into graduate school if they went in that direction. More importantly, they were admitted into competitive programs. The future goal of the trustees, though, was for the college to make it into that elite 25.

I continued to relate the history of the college and to describe the campus. Although years later, the campus still looked much like it did in the days when it was a boarding school. Most of the buildings had been renovated and updated to accommodate Wi-Fi and other modern conveniences.

All the buildings line up to form a quadrangle with major buildings at the apex. The Recreation and Athletic Center or rec center was directly opposite the Administration building at the southern point of the campus proper. To the east, at the apex, was the Student Union. At the western apex, the library was surrounded by gardens that lead into an arboretum.

With the murder at the rec center, the McCann asked more questions about the structure. The original building had served as the entrance with offices and a small laundry facility. The rest of the building had been added about 10 years ago. To preserve the aged appearance of the campus, the structure and materials were chosen to match the entrance and the other buildings. The rec center was available for various fitness activities to students, faculty, and staff. It had much of the same equipment as any private gym.

The college required that all students take three semesters of physical education, so there was a traditional gymnasium that was used for basketball, gymnastics, dance, and so on, as well as a pool. Behind the rec center were additional venues for softball and volleyball. The college did not include golf on its campus, but instead had an arrangement with the Cold Creek Country Club for those students who wished to take golf. Of course, this was at an additional cost for those students who were not already members of the country club set.

The remaining buildings were the academic buildings, and all had a similar set up. All lined up along the four sides of the quadrangle. The Humanities building stood to the east of the Administration building. Normally, if the fountains were operating, they would obstruct the view of the rec center.

As I described the campus, the detective had drawn a rough sketch that pretty much captured the campus. He sighed and offered, "I'm sorry to say that although this college is probably on our map, I never knew it was here. I was transferred to the Appomattox office last month. I haven't quite gotten my bearings," he explained.

Leaning back, and thinking it through he added, "I'm a little surprised colleges like this can thrive and compete with the major state universities. UVA and Virginia Tech are good schools."

"There are lots of advantages to the big universities. They have more options, more athletics, more of everything. But not always good things, even though the cost is lower than a private college," I explained. "At Cold Creek, most of the students are from nearby. They come from here in Cold Creek. Some come from North Shore or Alta Vista or some of the other smaller towns not far from here. Some may even live at home instead of in the dorms. The rest are from Roanoke, Lynchburg or Appomattox. For many of them, their parents think this is a safer setting. In some cases, for their kids, they don't see any advantage of the larger university. Many of the freshmen don't have a clear idea of what they want to do with their lives. They might get lost at a larger university. You might say that for many students Cold Creek College provides an opportunity for them to try living away from home and making their own decisions before they pursue a career or graduate school. Unfortunately, for some of the girls, this is something to do before they get married."

"So, Sheridan, how did you end up here?" he asked with a raised eyebrow. He again dropped the official demeanor and seemed to relax a bit.

I laughed before answering, a little surprised, and even flattered with the shift in conversation. "I was getting burned out in my position as a psychologist at a residential center for troubled youth. I needed a change. I didn't want to take up private practice, so I looked for an academic position. With no research behind me, the big universities weren't an option. I think I also would have been trading stressors. This position came open at the right time, and here I am." I added with a smile, "Most times I like my job, some days I think I am still dealing with troubled youth."

I didn't belabor the fact of a marriage that ended badly as a contributing factor to the change in my life's direction. I left it up to him to decide if the 'troubled youth' I referred to were the students or other faculty.

He chuckled and our gazes locked again. But then he shook his head, sighed. The official demeanor slipped back in place. I was once again escorting him through the Psychology

Department. Mitch and Jack were now in their offices. Mitch was probably the only faculty member older than Jim Grant. He also was the most down to earth of us all. He was a clinical psychologist and still did some pro bono work in the community. He and his wife Dora had been a lot of support to me when I arrived in Cold Creek. He took efforts to make everyone feel worthwhile. He greeted McMann like an old buddy. He acknowledged up front that he had heard about the detective. Other than an eye roll in my direction, he took it all in stride. But that was Mitch.

Jack also didn't seem to have any issues with McMann. McMann, however, looked a little puzzled by the preschool decorations of Jack's office. Jack was a developmental psychologist and he played the part. He was mostly interested in preschoolers and his office reflected that. At times, he tried to be 'cool' right down to the long hair he sported, tied back with an elastic band. No one else was around so it was time for McMann to move on. By then, it was after 2 and I turned him over to the staff in Sociology.

CHAPTER 3

As I walked back to my office to try to get some work done, it occurred to me that of the Psychology Department, only Mandy, Priscilla, and Adam were missing. That meant only Adam could potentially be the victim. It suddenly dawned on me that McMann and Joe starting with our department suggested that might be the case. Coming to me this late in the process, I felt a bit stupid for not realizing earlier that it was one of us.

I tried to think of everything I could about Adam Millberg. Adam, like Kim, tended to teach the abnormal psychology class and then specific other classes on perception, learning, memory, social psychology, or such. In effect, he pretty much only had the psychology majors in his classes, and then usually in their junior and senior years. About my age, he was attractive in a beach boy sort of way. He was blonde, hair a little longish, and dressed casually but with style that showcased the time he spent working out, an easy and contagious smile. He had a kind of charisma about him that was hard to describe, but his presence was palpable when he entered a room. He was what some would call a "chick magnet".

As I thought about it, the likelihood that it was him became even stronger. He was one of those men who seemed to think that every woman obviously was interested in him and would welcome his arm around them or his hand strategically placed. I had been surprised when Kim confided to me that when she first came to Cold Creek, she had dated Adam for a while. I think that was between wife number 3 and number 4. I recalled that he got divorced again, but wasn't sure if he remarried. I also remembered hearing that he and Ali dated at some point. That was also before my time and also ended badly.

He came on to me as well, but I declined multiple times, and very bluntly. Since then my interactions with him were always stilted. It seemed to be a constant effort on my part to let him know his advances were not welcome. I didn't feel I could ever let my guard down around him. I just didn't trust him in my gut.

There were also rumors from back in the days before sexual harassment was defined and monitored. Some said his behaviors toward female students were not always the most appropriate. Policies on faculty-student relationships were pretty clear these days. I wasn't so sure that his behavior changed all that much, but no complaints had been filed. It was certainly possible that he had pushed a little too hard or managed to make someone mad.

I sighed and tried to get back into setting up everything for my course. Murder or no, I was pretty sure I was going to have to teach next week. I wanted to get at least one week's worth of the classes finished before I left for the day. I opted to focus on the introduction to psychology class. The intro course was truly the most challenging. It was the foundation for all other psychology classes. It also was a core Humanities requirement for all students in the college.

I managed to upload podcasts and a couple of video clips to supplement the lectures for the first week, when Kim came by. She seemed a little calmer if not yet back to her usual upbeat self. She glanced at my computer and commented that she was doing the same thing for her abnormal psychology class. We complained a bit about the latest online support system and the approaching semester. Both of us seemed to be avoiding the subject of the murder. I wondered if she'd seen Adam at the rec center and so I asked in my most casual voice, "Kim, I didn't see Adam today. Have you seen him around?"

She immediately responded, and a bit on the defensive, "No, why do you ask?" I noticed that she seemed a bit more on edge than a few minutes ago.

"Oh, Kim, you're not seeing him again are you?" I asked, feeling that this was not going to be a good thing. Their previous relationship hadn't ended well. Actually, I don't think he was affected one way or the other. She hadn't fared as well, feeling a fool.

She shook her head and opened her mouth, but didn't immediately say anything. "Okay, so I went to dinner with him a few times. At least this time I know he's not serious. I know the game, but I like the attention and the company," she said with a sigh.

I sighed along with her. Cold Creek is not exactly a hotbed for singles unless you happen to be a college student or in that age bracket. Because of the college, most of the social venues also catered to a younger crowd. Because it was predominantly students from the surrounding areas, any other social venues were family oriented. At one point we'd both tried one of the on-line dating services, but the nearest potential matches ended up being at least 1-2 hours away. That put them in Roanoke to the west or Richmond and Petersburg to the east. The distance was not exactly convenient for beginning a relationship or even having a date. Even Appomattox would have been closer, but no matches from there.

Adam was one of the few male faculty members who was not married or gay, other than Doug that is. We'd joked about a date with Doug, but neither of us could imagine such a thing. There were a lot more single women faculty and staff than men, as Adam had discovered. Even in the community, and with the universally high divorce rate, there were few available males.

I dated the dentist in town a few times. Wayne was nice enough, but basically boring unless you wanted to discuss the terrain of your molars and the crevices while you ate your dinner. Kim dated one or two men she met through community groups, but never more than once. Somehow, among the society set, it was still a man's world, and women were supposed to know their place. More importantly, well-educated women didn't seem to have a place in their social circles. And then there was the fact that we were both psychologists.

"Then why do you seem defensive?" I countered, picking up on the underlying emotion that didn't match her words.

"Because I knew you'd give me a hard time, and tell me how stupid I am," she responded with a smirk. We both laughed and that seemed to break the tension. Kim left, and I was back to my online supports for classes. I looked at my watch and it was after 4, and I was at a good point to stop.

At least the first week of classes for intro were done for both sections, and I could tackle the research design class next. I shut down my computer and gathered my belongings, taking some articles home with me to read for the seminar. All at once, I sensed that someone was at my door. Turning around, Detective McMann stood there, leaning against the door jam and looking great.

"Getting ready to leave for the day?" he asked. When I nodded to the affirmative, he added, "Mind if I take up a bit more of your time?" I put down my bag, waved to the chair, and sat back down.

He cleared his throat, and then, with very little emotion, said, "The victim this morning was Adam Millberg. Now that his family has been notified, I need to ask you some more specific questions about him."

I nodded and said, without realizing it was out loud, "I knew it."

"Excuse me, did you say 'you knew it'? How?" he countered, now looking a bit confused and possibly even angry.

I shrugged my shoulders and explained that it was process of elimination. Adam was the only male not accounted for. And there had to be a reason for a detective to be in our area so soon in the investigation, when we weren't the closest to the rec center. He seemed to relax a little. I realized his first reaction might have been to think that I had withheld information earlier.

"Good deductive skills. What can you tell me about Millberg?" he asked. I noted that he seemed to mean the compliment, rather than being condescending. I certainly didn't tell him how long it took for me to figure it out.

"I think he's been on the faculty for about 10 years. I seem to recall he got a 10-year pin last spring. He's from somewhere in the Midwest I think. I always got the impression he came from money. He was always well-dressed, driving expensive cars. He certainly never seemed to lack for money, and the salaries here aren't that great. He teaches mostly the upper level classes with psychology majors.

I guess that should be 'taught'." I shrugged, and realized that I was actually very hesitant to talk about Adam. I especially didn't want to talk about his relationship with Ali or Kim.

"Sheridan, was he well-liked? Anyone have a grudge against him that you are aware of? Ever hear anyone threaten him? Any arguments?" McMann asked, looking a little frustrated with my rather minimal and academic description of him.

"Um, uh, I don't remember ever hearing anyone threaten him, no. He could get into it with any of us over which classroom his class was in or what time, but if that was motive for murder, most of us would be dead."

With a sigh, I continued, "Was he well-liked? Depends on who you ask I guess. And when. I don't mean to speak poorly of him when he can't defend himself, but truth be told, Adam was a class A jerk and a womanizer. I don't think he ever made eye contact with a female. His gaze was always chest level. He was very smooth and played to people's weaknesses.

Lots of women, including his multiple wives, as well as possibly a few husbands and fathers could hold a grudge." I knew that I could have been more explicit, but I wasn't lying. I had to figure out how to help eliminate both Ali and

Kim as suspects.

"Sounds like a real great guy," he responded, sarcasm evident. He was making good eye contact, almost exaggerated. "What about you and Millberg?" he asked. I could tell he was clenching his teeth in reaction to my description and waiting for my answer.

"My first introduction to Adam was when I interviewed and they held a reception for me. I noticed him when he walked into the room. He had a way of drawing attention without being loud or obnoxious. It was part of his charm. Very smooth. Fortunately, I watched him as he worked the crowd. Talking to the men, hands roaming on the women. By the time he was introduced to me, I wasn't sure I even wanted to shake his hand. But hand shaking wasn't his style, and I got pretty good at avoiding his advances or very purposely moving his hand."

I paused and then added, "This used to be Doug's office, and I was in the office Doug is in now, next to Adam's. The tension was such that Doug offered to switch offices with me so I wouldn't be such a convenient target. So I guess I could be a suspect as much as anyone."

"I will have to reconsider my impression of Doug. He wasn't particularly talkative, but if he stepped in to help you out, that's a point in his favor." He cleared his throat, and asked,

"Anything else I should keep in mind about Millberg?" He was obviously ignoring my comment about being a suspect. He neither denied nor affirmed it.

I shook my head, and then he went back over the notes from this morning on when I arrived, that Terra and Ali were already here, when Kim arrived, that Max, Jim, and Doug were all here. He also made it very obvious that I couldn't provide anyone an alibi for when the murder occurred, including me. He asked about Mandy and Priscilla since he hadn't met them, first in general and then in relation to Adam.

I couldn't offer much by way of information on either of them. They were newer faculty, only hired within the past two years. Both were married and in their thirties. They tended to socialize with each other because they had similar interests and kids the same ages.

Mandy was the second person in developmental and carried the history of psychology sections, while Priscilla covered some of the same courses as Adam. That would give her more opportunity or occasion to interact with him. On the other hand, Priscilla almost bristled with tension, not particularly social.

As I told McMann, I didn't think their being married would have stopped Adam, but I had no reason to believe that either of them had been involved with him. In fact, though I didn't mention it to McMann, I didn't think they were his type. Besides being tightly wound, Priscilla was a brunette. Although he did hit on brunettes, his preference was for blondes or red heads. Both Priscilla and Mandy had one child the same age, Priscilla's youngest and Mandy's oldest. Mandy's two-year old meant that most often she was only here when absolutely necessary. That alone would have limited Adam's contact with her.

He asked about Katie, with a hint of a smile. I felt a flash of jealousy that she had impressed him. I told him that I didn't know if Katie and Adam were ever involved, but that it was likely based on all I'd heard about his relationships before I came to Cold Creek. McMann also asked about the male faculty, but I couldn't tell him much there. As far as I knew, Adam only was interested in women and the men didn't comment on his exploits to me.

I hadn't ever observed him socially with any of the male faculty. It was after 5 when the detective finally closed his notebook. Running his hand through his hair again, he offered to walk me out. It was pretty deserted and we didn't run into anyone as we left. I noticed there was still a lot of activity near the rec center, and shot him a questioning look.

"They are still working on the scene. They should be done tonight, but I'm afraid the rec center will probably be closed for another day or two. You work out over there?" he asked.

"Only if it is too hot or too cold or too wet to walk in the arboretum." I pointed in the general direction. "I'd rather walk outside and there is a mile long track of sorts." He nodded, and as we reached my car, he made like to tip his hat, except he wasn't wearing one, and commented that he'd probably see me in the morning. As I pulled out, I noticed him walking toward the rec center. I wasn't sure why the State police were involved for a local murder. It didn't make any sense.

I drove home, still thinking about the murder, Adam, and the possibility that sooner or later someone was going to hone in on Ali, or more likely Kim, since she was at the rec center. Yup, of the two, Kim would be the one person other faculty would describe as highly emotional, hot-headed, and dramatic. She also worked out regularly and was competitive, at least in sports. She was involved with him in the past and present. At some level, she had motive and opportunity. Not knowing how he was killed, I wasn't sure about the means. But I couldn't see her actually killing someone, or if she did, not screaming about it. Keeping secrets was not one of Kim's strong suits. She'd get excited, start talking, and so much for secrets.

It sometimes amazed me that she had been in a private practice, doing counseling. She obviously was much better about compartmentalizing the counseling she did and being careful to ensure confidentiality. Every once in a while, she would talk about the practice, the ups and the downs of it, and the clients, most dealing with adjustment issues rather than severe pathology. But she never mentioned names or anything that would have breached confidentiality. She was capable of keeping other people's secrets, just not her own.

I suspected that she liked the practice, but catching her business partner with her husband resulted in the breakup of both partnerships. A bit fragile and not coping well, she ended up here at Cold Creek the year before I did. It was during that vulnerable time that Adam had befriended her, and she rebounded right into his hands. That was right up until he showed up at a college function with wife-to-be number four and barely spoke to her.

Months later when I came to Cold Creek, there was still some pity talk about how he used her and humiliated her. We became friends and I knew she hadn't dated or even considered dating for almost a year.

If she hadn't started seeing him again, it would be easy to argue that if she was going to kill him, why would she wait 4 years? That reasoning wouldn't work though given Kim's admission that they were again seeing each other. Probably someone had seen them out together. Cold Creek was a small town, and even if they went over to North Shore or AltaVista, the two closest towns, for dinner, they'd likely run into someone one of them knew. And Adam being who he was, anyone who saw them would have mentioned it to their friends, and so on.

Ali also had dated him for a while and almost quit her job because of him. I never heard the details of that romance. She did not have a positive thing to say about him. On the other hand, she never said anything negative either. Her favorite response was "I'm not gonna go there – leave me out of it" and then she'd walk away. But, like Kim and I, she lived alone, so no built in alibi. But like me, she rarely used the facilities at the rec center.

Ali was a hard worker, in her thirties, and generally quiet and reserved. I found it hard to imagine her with Adam, but then she may have been putty in his hands given his charm and manipulative style. She was blonde, fairly slim, except in the right places. She tended to dress very conservatively though, unlike Katie. It was easy to see why he would have been interested in her. And he may have seen her conservative side as a challenge. I sighed as I pulled my car into my driveway.

After greeting my dog, Charlie, and letting her out in the backyard, I made myself some dinner and pulled out the articles I'd brought home. For the seminar, my goal was to try to get the students to think about things a little differently, so the articles were not connected, but rather reflected some new perspectives. I read the same article three times, and didn't remember what I had read. Usually I enjoyed reading the articles and deciding which ones would work for the activities I'd planned, but tonight that wasn't happening.

I finally gave up, pulled out a blank piece of paper, and put Adam's name in the middle. Then, like I was doing a story map or brainstorming, I added the names of all of us in the department. Then I drew a line from Adam to each of us and marked it as positive, negative, or neutral. I obviously was only guessing on some of the lines. I tended to err to neutrality if I didn't have evidence for positive or negative.

When I was done, I had negatives by Kim, Ali, Max, Doug and me. As much as I might want to believe it was Max, given his overbearing attitude, I couldn't see him killing anyone unless they messed with his research. To him, his research was paramount. It was his research that was going to get him national acclaim and hired onto one of the coveted universities. Doug didn't strike me as having enough emotional get-up-and-go to kill anyone. Then again, no one thought Ted Bundy was capable of being a serial killer.

I sighed for about the hundredth time because I was right back where I started and no closer to alternate suspects instead of Ali and Kim. I had one circle not connected, representing students. It was possible that some parent found out that Adam had been inappropriate with his daughter or used his power as a faculty member to coerce her in some way.

Alternatively, maybe there was a husband out there Adam royally pissed off so I added another circle for unknown husbands. And, of course, there were all those ex-wives, each of those got their own circle. My musings were interrupted by the phone ringing.

"Hi Sher. It's me Kim. Did you see the news tonight? It was Adam." She sounded like she'd been crying and was having a hard time holding herself together.

"Oh, Kim, I'm sorry. Are you okay?" I asked, as I flipped open my lap top and pulled up

KCCX so I could see what information was released. I realized I hadn't jumped the gun and told her because I was afraid of her reaction.

"I can't believe it. I don't want to believe it," she sobbed. I read the story, which was very short. It basically identified the victim as Adam, indicated that foul play was considered likely, and the investigation was ongoing. He'd been found in the weight room by another faculty member, Dr. Scott Hickson in Technology. The story also included Adam's position on the faculty and that he frequently worked out at the rec center.

"Sher, did that detective tell you anything? Who they might suspect?" Kim asked with a catch in her voice.

"Not really, but I'm sure he'll be back tomorrow asking more pointed questions about Adam. Kim, you need to be honest with him, but you don't need to tell him all the details," I cautioned her.

"I know, I know. It wasn't me, Sher. This time I was using him as much as he was using me, honest. And I have trouble killing spiders."

"Kim, I believe you. But you know the first people to be considered are the ones closest to the victim. In Adam's case, that would include whoever he was seeing and his ex-wives first, and then the rest of the faculty," I offered, trying to put it in a realistic frame.

"But that puts me in the pile twice! He was seeing me AND I work with him. But then, I'm not the only one in that boat," she added. I assumed she was referring to Ali, but when I asked her, the response threw me for a loop.

"Not Ali, Sher. Though I guess she would fit as well. But their dating didn't last long enough to matter much. I was talking about Katie. She was Adam's second wife. They came to Cold Creek together 10 years ago, got divorced within the first two years, and he was onto wife number three. I don't remember number three's name, but she worked in Fine Arts and left after the divorce. And you know about Misty, the admin assistant to the Provost, who became number four. I heard she was dating someone in Health and Kinese these days," rambled Kim.

"Kim, how do you know all this? Katie?" I asked, incredulous at her knowledge of Adam's relationship history. And a little worried about how Kim's knowledge of Adam's relationships might seem to McMann or any other detective.

With a sigh, she explained, "Well, when I dated him the first time, Katie tried to warn me about him. I didn't believe her, and said some not-so-nice things to her. I was so sure that with me, it would be different. When it was over, every time I saw her, I felt like she was giving me that 'I told you so' look. Of course, she is a big flirt herself. Possibly that was one of the things they had in common. Did you know she dated Doug for a while? Can you even imagine that?"

I was totally blown away by that piece of information and told her so. I also pointed out to her that she shouldn't offer any opinions to the police. She should stick to the facts and not elaborate, like if she were being deposed in a case related to her practice. That seemed to at least generate discussion of her practice and the few times she had to be deposed either in relation to divorce, battering, or damages.

As she finished talking about those cases, I again admonished her to follow the same guidelines when McMann or anyone else asked her about Adam. I was pretty sure someone would be talking to her first thing in the morning. I was a little concerned about how good my friend would look as a suspect.

After we hung up, I went back to my relationship map, and adjusted the picture so that Katie was number two wife as well as colleague. Then I made that one negative. I also added Misty's name to the number four wife spot and noted that she was seeing someone in Health and Kinesiology. He could potentially have a motive as well. I didn't envy McMann given this tangled mess. I was fairly sure, with my limited interactions with Adam, and what I learned in the last half hour, that there were more circles than I had on my piece of paper.

Charlie nudged me and I let her outside again. Then I turned on the news to get the full discussion and not the capsulized version I had accessed online. Charlie back in, I decided to make it an early night, and headed for my bedroom and my book. The phone rang, and from caller ID I knew it was Terra. It was odd she would be calling me at home, this late at night.

"Dr. Hendley, this is Terra. I am sorry to bother you at home, but could you make time tomorrow to talk to Ali? I just talked to her and she's very upset. She's afraid that detective is going to talk to her tomorrow, this time more specifically about Adam. Joe thinks so too. Maybe you could help her relax, talk to her and help her to see that she needs to talk to the detective?" she asked. She sounded very earnest and I empathized with her concerns.

I assured Terra that I would come in early and talk to Ali. I also pointed out that what Ali told the detective or anyone else was her choice and her business. Ali tended to be a private person. I didn't see that she would confide in me. But I also wanted to make sure that Terra knew I wasn't going to share anything Ali said. Terra agreed and expressed her concern that Ali was likely on the 'persons of interest' list and that she was worried about her. I told her I appreciated that. After not much hesitation on my part, I had to ask who else she envisioned on that list.

"Well, I would guess that is going to be a long list, Terra. Katie may be at the top of the list, don't you think?" I asked.

Terra chuckled, and said, "Katie, Kim, Misty, Ali, and a few of the women in about every department on campus! Not to mention a few who have left because of him. You're about the only single woman who didn't fall for his lines, you know. Yeah, that is going to be a long list, but I would rather Ali wasn't on it. I don't think she has a lot of friends or a strong support network. She doesn't go out much and never did."

Terra and I chatted for a few minutes, but I didn't get any more information. I reassured her I would talk to Ali, though I wasn't sure what good it would do. I went back to my relationship map and looked again at all the possibilities. Given that Adam targeted single women, unless they were seeing someone else, all of them likely did not have an alibi. That included me.

I didn't know Katie hardly, but felt bad that she too would be a suspect. It occurred to me that probably one reason Katie and I had never become friends was the animosity between her and Kim. It also struck me that for a psychologist I hadn't been paying a lot of attention to the people I worked with.

As I started to get changed for bed, the phone rang again. I looked at Charlie and she rolled over. Most nights, most weeks, my phone doesn't ring hardly at all. My sister calls usually over the weekend to complain about her life and criticize mine. Every so often Kim calls or texts to see about going to a movie. Three calls in one night? Definitely a record. I answered the phone noting from caller ID that it was Wayne.

"Sheridan, how are you? I saw the news. It must be so shocking," he offered solicitously. I imagined he was shaking his head in disbelief.

"Hi Wayne, yes, it is shocking. Did you know Adam?" I asked, figuring that even Adam had to see a dentist once in a while.

"Not really, but here in Cold Creek, everyone knows everybody. I was concerned how you might be taking it. Maybe we could go to dinner this week. You know, take your mind off this awful situation."

"Thanks for thinking of me, Wayne. I do appreciate it, but I think I'll pass on the dinner. With this hanging over our heads, and the first week of classes looming, I think I'll keep a low profile," I offered as a tactful decline to his invitation. This was not the first time, and would likely not be the last, that I was declining his invitation. He was consistent though. His invitations were always to take my mind off something like the rain or the heat, or to celebrate something. He was, if nothing else, persistent. He wasn't a bad guy and he wasn't unattractive, but his conversation skills were limited. More importantly, there was definitely no chemistry. Even with my brief brush with McMann, I knew there was more chemistry there than with Wayne. We finished the phone call with me again thanking him for his concern. I wondered when he would give up.

I shook my head and glanced at the phone again, about daring it to ring again. I finally managed to put on my nightgown and get ready for bed. Charlie jumped up on the bed with me as I curled up with a novel. Reading helped to stop my ruminating over the day's activities. At least the novel pushed them out of consciousness. Then lights out.

CHAPTER 4

As I promised Terra, I was on campus early. I parked my car in the faculty lot and looked toward the rec center, which was relatively quiet. I couldn't see any obvious signs that someone had been murdered there. There were no official vehicles sitting there and I couldn't see any crime tape or such. Everything looked deceptively calm and peaceful. I took the stairs to my office and put my bag down before I went to the main office.

"Hi ladies, how are you doing this morning?" I asked directing the question to both Terra and Ali. I noticed that Jim hadn't gotten in yet, so they were the only ones in the office area.

"Hi yourself, Dr. Hendley. Be right back," Terra answered as she made a hasty exit, leaving

Ali and I alone. Ali smiled and shook her head.

"Subtle as a sledge hammer, Terra is. She asked you to talk to me didn't she?" Ali asked. She smiled but the smile was not reflected in her eyes. Her eyes seemed pained.

"As a matter of fact she did. Ali, Terra is worried about you," I said with a sigh. "Anything I can do to help?"

"I know, I know. I'm really okay. I don't see why she is so worried. All water under the bridge," she answered with a wistful look that belied her words.

"Ali, you know that the detective or someone will be in to talk to you about Adam, if not this morning, then some time, right?" I asked.

"Yup, and I was worried about that at first. But I didn't kill him so I'm not going to worry about it," she said with a shrug. Her puffy eyes told a different story, but I wasn't about to argue with her.

"Okay, that's a good attitude." I hesitated before saying anything else. "Ali, do you by any chance have anyone who can vouch for where you were Sunday night and yesterday morning when they found Adam?" I asked, knowing I was pushing my luck.

Ali chuckled and said, "About as good as you do! My cat can vouch for me, and I bet your dog can vouch for you!" I smiled and nodded. Not the most often voiced problem of being a single, but obviously being single left us without an alibi.

"Touché! Feel free to come by if you need to talk, Ali." I smiled and went back to my office. I hadn't even gotten my computer turned on and gracing my doorway was McMann. I sighed as I realized I wasn't likely to be getting much done today, or tomorrow.

It occurred to me that spending the day with a very nice looking man whose smile seemed to heat up my world could be a good thing. On the other hand, it wasn't so good when it was limited to talking about Adam and all the people who might have killed him. Including Kim and Ali, who I liked. And I still had my classes to prep.

"Good morning Detective," I said, with less enthusiasm than the words implied.

"Good morning, Sheridan. I brought you a cup of coffee," he added as he offered me the coffee with a smile.

I thanked him, waved to the chair he'd occupied yesterday, and waited. He explained that he had some additional questions, most having to do with Adam and his relationships. To cut to the chase, I showed him the relationship map I'd drawn the night before. He studied it, nodded and then looked at me as if to say, 'and you did this why?'

"I kept thinking about it and decided to draw the relationships I knew about. When doing family therapy or systems therapy, I'd do this kind of drawing to help me keep track of what I thought I knew, and then update it as more information came up in therapy," I explained with a shrug. I had often used these drawings when trying to figure out the why of various behaviors in the residential treatment center. Sometimes it was truly the patient, sometimes it was a staff member, or sometimes a visiting member of their family. Sometimes it helped. Sometimes it didn't, but it always made me feel like I was doing something.

"I see. This is helpful. I don't recall you mentioning that Katie van Anst was an ex-wife when we chatted yesterday," he added, his brows knitted.

"I didn't know that when we talked yesterday. Of course, everyone is talking about Adam after it was on the news last night that he was the victim. That came out in conversation. I also added Misty in as number four. So far, nobody has mentioned to me the names of one and three," I explained. McMann was looking at me very intensely. If he was trying to intimidate me, it was working. The warm feeling I had left with yesterday was fading quickly.

"Sheridan, okay, so you drew this for what reason?" he asked. The careful wording made it seem like he was attempting not to sound threatening.

"Just trying to make sense of it all. It's a fairly human reaction, detective," I answered a bit defensively.

He laughed, looked away, and then back at me. "Yes, I suppose it is. And I assume there will be a lot of talk going on. Please do keep me posted if you happen to find out anything I should know. But please, do not try to play detective."

"Like I said, trying to make sense of it. I'm a psychologist. Studying behavior and relationships is what I do." I almost felt guilty about not telling him that I also wanted to make sure neither Ali nor Kim was arrested for this murder. I did find our interactions today a bit more tense than yesterday. That made me a little less comfortable sharing information.

"Okay. This drawing answers most of the questions I have. I notice there are a number of these, like the lines from Adam to Priscilla, Mandy, and Terra that are marked 'neutral'. How come?"

"I don't know of a positive or a negative relationship, so I left them 'neutral'." I shrugged. "And I don't know who the 'husbands' or 'students' would be. And I suspect that there are more relationships that I haven't heard about."

"Hmm. Sheridan, I have to go talk with a number of these people. I hope it's alright if I come back and bounce some ideas off of you? Perhaps for lunch?" he asked as he raked his hand through his curly hair. I was beginning to think that was a behavior that indicated his fatigue or despair. If so, it was awfully early in the day for that kind of emotion. I nodded and he was gone. I felt like I'd been through a wringer, and I wasn't sure why. I had to admit, as tense as the interactions had been, he was still one nice looking man.

I spent most of the morning trying to work, but found myself checking in with Terra or Ali or Kim to find out what was happening, and what they had heard. Joe was still around and trying to get people to talk to him, but so far he'd steered clear of me. Terra told me that McMann had been in with Ali for a long time, and neither had looked happy when he left. She also said Ali wouldn't talk about it.

I continued to walk around the area, and checked on who was in and who wasn't. I told myself that I was just checking to see how they were doing, but if I were honest, I wanted to see how everyone was reacting. Jim wasn't in his office, but Terra said he was on campus somewhere and checking in regularly given the current situation and focus on the department. Katie hadn't come in today.

Priscilla and Mandy were both in. They both looked nervous, and not particularly talkative. Priscilla alternately clenched and unclenched her hands. I wasn't even sure she was aware she was doing it. Doug shook his head, rolled his eyes and threw up his hands. I didn't bother checking with Max, but he came by to complain about being interrupted by the rude detective. He also complained that the students working with him were upset and not able to get their work done.

I obviously didn't have any solutions and didn't understand how important his research was. I checked in with Kim a couple of times and each time she was more nervous and concerned that she was a 'person of interest' than the previous one. Joe's presumed list of people of interest seemed to come up everywhere. And so far it was a short list of Ali and Kim.

Late in the morning, Joe stopped by my office to get my reaction to Adam's murder. I told him I thought it was unfortunate, sad that his life had ended violently. I got the impression he had a litany of questions aimed to get me, or whoever he was talking to, to say something sensational that would make his story.

I didn't give him a chance. I asked him if he knew who the next of kin would be and if he had heard any more about the crime itself. He didn't know who was listed as the emergency contact. He didn't know how Adam had been killed or the estimated time of death. He didn't know if they had retrieved a murder weapon. He also didn't know why the State police were involved. The more questions I asked that he couldn't answer, the more frustrated he got. It wasn't an intentional tactic on my part, but the end result was a good one. Joe didn't hang around very long and nothing I said was going in the paper.

I finally went back to work. Adam's murder aside, classes would start next week. It occurred to me that someone would have to cover all of his classes, and that would likely mean additional class prep for one or more of us. I set up the skeleton for the research methods course, and then started to work on the first class.

Over four years of teaching that class, I had learned that I had to give a pre-test to each of the sections to determine if the students in both sections were at the same level, as well as to figure out where to start in terms of covering the basics. The same applied to the two sections of intro.

If I was lucky, I could use the same lecture, class activities, and assignments for both sections. Otherwise, I tailored the content to meet the level of individual sections. Needless to say, I had to come up with some assignments that differed and create two different midterms and finals. I was about to start on the next task when McMann was at my door once again.

He looked tired and his attempt at a smile was pretty feeble. He asked if I was still able to join him for lunch. He said he wanted to get my perspective on some of the information he had gathered thus far. I agreed and we were back in Georg's Café once again. He asked what I had been working on, and I gave a brief description. This seemed his version of small talk today. After he finished his sandwich and refilled both of our coffees, he sighed.

"Okay, what can you tell me about Ali? Has she ever talked to you about Adam?" he asked. He looked befuddled for some reason.

"Not really. If anyone ever mentioned Adam, she pretty much avoided taking part in the talk, and usually went back to her office. I honestly don't remember her ever saying anything about him, good or bad. Other than that, she is generally pretty quiet and stays to herself. If the conversation is about theatre or sports, however, she usually joins in. She's an avid tennis player. Does that help?" I asked, not quite sure what he was looking for, and not willing to share the rumors I'd heard about her involvement with Adam.

"Okay. It means she isn't just stonewalling me, but apparently is stonewalling all of you about Adam as well. I'm assuming from your drawing and the negative on that line that you know they dated and it didn't end well. I thought maybe she wasn't keen on complaining about him because he was dead, but it sounds like that is just her response," he mused.

"Did you ask her directly?" I asked, quite sure that he must have. It would be hard to avoid a direct question.

"I did. Quite directly. She told me that she was not able to discuss Adam or her relationship to him in the past, and provided me with the name and number for her attorney. Each question I asked her, she gave me the same response." He shook his head, not able to get a handle on this. I also suspected he was checking to see my reaction to her response. It certainly wasn't typical police practice to reveal the contents of an interview of one possible suspect with another unless the intent was a fishing expedition. And her response did seem odd.

"Well, I can't help you. I never asked her directly, but she has never responded to a comment or question about Adam that I am aware of. Guess you will have to call her attorney," I answered, a little befuddled myself.

What would have transpired in that relationship that would have involved her having legal counsel? Or had she gotten legal counsel this morning in anticipation of being a suspect? Ali was definitely a planner and sometimes on the pessimistic side in terms of anticipating future events. If she obtained legal counsel this morning, that was probably not going to be seen positively. On the other hand, it might be a good idea for her to be on the offensive.

"You said she was into sports and tennis. Did she play golf, too?" he asked.

I couldn't imagine what that had to do with anything, but answered, "No. Around here to play golf you have to be a member of the country club. That pretty much excludes faculty and staff. Well, except for Adam, at least."

We chatted a little more. He didn't ask any more about Ali and didn't ask about Kim. Mostly McMann tried to validate his impressions. He mentioned that Doug had verified the office switch with me. Doug also told him that I was professional but assertive in telling Adam to buzz off. It was also clear that McMann's opinion of Max hadn't improved with his most recent interaction. I chuckled as he recounted his trying to get Max to answer questions instead of ranting about his research.

He asked me what Joe was asking people and that opened the door for me to repeat the questions I had asked Joe, but this time of him. He somewhat reluctantly acknowledged that the cause of death was blunt force trauma to the head, but he said he couldn't tell me what had caused the blunt force. He said the time of death was still being determined. He asked if Chief Pfeiffe or any of the Cold Creek police had been by to talk to the faculty or staff. They hadn't, which seemed odd, and I told him that. He sighed.

When I asked why the State police were involved, he sighed again and leaned back in the chair. Ultimately, he explained that 'someone' requested the assistance of the State police in the investigation, and that the 'someone' was not with the local or university police. He was following orders, but his being here was apparently not well received by all. I asked who the 'someone' was, but he politely shook his head. I asked him if I was still a suspect, half joking, half serious. He smiled and seemed to relax a bit before teasingly telling me that for the time being I was in the clear.

We chatted amicably while we finished our coffees. I found myself looking forward to his occasional smile. I noticed he didn't wear a wedding band about the same time I realized that I liked this man. He was easy to talk to and I reminded myself that being easy to talk to was probably an important trait in a detective. Much as I might like him and appreciate his good looks, I needed to be careful what I shared with him. I could tell he was doing a pretty good job of breaking down my defenses. We went back upstairs, his professional demeanor and my defenses back in place.

I started back to work and Terra came in and shut my door. She was worried about Ali. Joe apparently told her that Ali was seriously being looked at in the murder. She also was concerned that ever since McMann talked to her, Ali had holed up in her office. She hadn't even gone out for lunch.

There wasn't anything I could say to reassure her, other than that hopefully the person responsible would be identified sooner rather than later. I truly did empathize with her. I was equally as worried about both Ali and Kim. On the other hand, Ali's behavior was looking more suspicious all the time. I didn't mention her comment to McMann about her lawyer.

She sighed and then asked me what I thought of McMann. I told her I thought he was very thorough and she made a crack about the rising color in my face. She also said Joe told her he saw us in Georg's having lunch and that it looked more social than business. Obviously, he saw the end of the lunch rather than the beginning. She teased me some more and then went back to her own office.

I chuckled to myself at the wonders of the small town. I remembered that after someone saw Wayne and I having dinner at Perky's Restaurant and then at the Steak House, it was pretty much assumed we would be getting married. If two meals meant an engagement, then McMann and I were at least an item, if lunches counted. I chuckled again as I realized I didn't even know his first name! Shaking my head, I went back to work.

About an hour or so later, I saw Mandy in the hallway. She continued toward my office, obviously following office numbers. Mandy is slim and petite and no one would guess that she had two kids to look at her. I remembered when she interviewed she was obviously at the end of the pregnancy, very pregnant. Less than three months later, she was back on campus and didn't look like she had ever been pregnant.

I only wished I could blame my few extra pounds around the waist on a pregnancy. The size 10s were getting a bit snug and that meant it was time to watch the diet and get more exercise.

"Hi Sheridan. You really are hidden back here, aren't you?" Mandy asked when she reached my door. Her office was more central and nearer to Adam's.

"Yeah, I kinda like being out of the way. It usually is pretty quiet back here, though I am handy if Jim needs anything," I answered. In effect, when Jim ventured out of his office, I was the first faculty member he saw. Being convenient is not always a good thing. Sometimes I wondered if that was Doug's ulterior motive in switching offices and Adam's tormenting me was a convenient excuse.

"Do you have a few minutes?" she asked. "I'm getting creeped out by this whole thing. Adam murdered, that detective asking everyone questions, and the reporter asking more questions. Now there's someone from Cold Creek police in the main office. He'll probably be around asking questions now, too. I know there were some issues with Adam, but he was a good teacher and a good colleague."

"Sure, have a seat. It is certainly not our typical week before classes start. Hopefully everything will settle down by next week," I offered by way of reassurance. "Anything in particular bothering you, Mandy?" Even after being out of clinical work for four years, when people were distressed, I shifted to therapist mode.

Sighing she said, "I don't want to offend Terra, but I don't think Joe should be asking us all questions. I told him to go ask the detective and closed my door on him. I don't want to be part of his story, but I am afraid Terra will be offended."

"That's certainly your right. You probably don't have much choice about talking to McMann or the Cold Creek police, but you don't have to talk to Joe. And I wouldn't worry about Terra. I suspect there are lots of times when Joe has been refused. But don't hold his behavior against her either. He is, after all, doing his job," I said.

Mandy and I talked for a few more minutes, with her again acknowledging complaints by students and faculty alike. She immediately insisted that Adam was a very good teacher and colleague. I wasn't sure if she was saying this because she thought the opposite or if she refused to see the down side to situations or people. She didn't say anything that indicated a direct interaction. She mentioned she had watched one of his classes that had been recorded and was available on the web page.

The conversation seemed awkward because we don't usually socialize with each other. In an effort to get her to relax some, I asked about her two boys and her husband. Other than that her husband was outraged that a murder happened on campus, she said everything was fine. I asked about her courses and being ready for the semester to start. She said she was all set and she was looking forward to the semester starting. She made a comment about all the students being enthused and excited to learn. She said she looked forward to the start of the semester and the students all dressed nicely, to impress.

I wondered about and envied her optimism and idealism. Our students are good students, strong, and quite capable, but they weren't always interested in what we were offering. These days, all the social networking, gaming, and such made it hard to keep their interest sometimes. I applauded her organization and made noises about needing to get back to work. She took the hint.

I realized she hadn't said much about Adam at all other than proclaiming him a good teacher and colleague. I again concluded that she probably had managed to avoid his attentions by being pregnant and having little ones. Of course, she may have been protesting a little too much, but I doubted it.

Mandy no sooner left, and Mitch came in and sat down. He rolled his eyes and made a comment about the status of the zoo. We talked for a while, and Mitch volunteered his opinion that Ali and Kim would probably warrant a bit of attention from McMann and local police. He also commented that he saw the Cold Creek policeman, Officer Hirsch, in the office and then going into Ali's office. His comments made me think that he might know more about what happened with Ali, but he didn't volunteer any specific information. I told him I couldn't imagine either of them killing anyone, and he agreed.

He said something about a weight being used to kill Adam, but said he didn't know if that was true or just an assumption because Adam had been found in the weight room. It certainly would be the logical conclusion. He also talked a little about Chief Pfeiffe. He played golf with Barney on occasion and said he was generally a good man, but that investigating a murder was definitely not something he was prepared for. Chief Pfeiffe, like Mitch and Jim Grant, was in his 60s and looking to retirement. Mitch said he would feel the Chief out and see if he could get an idea of the direction the investigation was headed.

Unlike most of the faculty, Mitch and I discussed some of the issues that would have to be addressed with the students. Having an act of violence on campus would, at least initially, mean that students might be a little fearful. Being questioned by various police would inevitably add to their anxiety. We discussed providing some basic safety precautions to all students. This would include always traveling in pairs, trying to stay in well-lit areas, and being alert to individuals who looked like they didn't quite belong. Now, all of these applied more if the killer was a stranger to the campus. We would also let students know that they may be asked questions, and they needed to help out the police as much as possible. That and we would be let them know they didn't have to talk to the press.

Then there were the students who would be more directly affected. Specifically, since Adam worked with only psychology majors, most of them had him for one or more classes. He also was one of the faculty members more likely to be their thesis advisor if they elected to go that route. Ultimately, of the 50 or so juniors or seniors who declared psychology as their major, at least some of them would be upset because it was Adam, and not because the death was violent.

Mitch said he would let Jim, Ali, and Terra know that we would be available for any students who needed to talk to someone. Usually, Kim would have been our third musketeer, but with her involvement with Adam, that was not going to happen.

I wondered aloud how popular the rec center would be for the immediate time, but Mitch poo-hooed me and argued that people who worked out would get past it in order to keep working out. His argument was that working out was pretty addictive and they'd need their exercise 'fix'. It occurred to me that Kim probably fell into that category. I would have to ask her when she would be going back.

As usual, Mitch mused about how being a faculty member was a pretty good job, given that your whole job centered on topics you were interested in anyway, and you had some flexibility in your hours. Of course, immediately after that, he complained about the new online system and talked about maybe retiring in a year or two. This was a frequent theme with him when it came to technology, and I teased him about it. He laughed and then left me to try to get back to work.

I checked in on Kim again and she was actually quite calm. More impressive, she was working on getting her courses set up. When she explained that Jim told her she would likely be picking up Adam's section of abnormal, I understood her current activity level. I suggested we get dinner and she agreed to meet me at the Grill around 6. That would give me time to get home, deal with Charlie, and get changed into shorts. I also remembered to ask her if she thought people would avoid the rec center. She said she wasn't sure about others, but she was going to take this week off. I guessed Mitch was right.

I stopped at the main office to check with Terra and Ali. Terra kept looking at Ali's closed door and confirmed Mitch's comment that now the local police were talking to Ali. I went back to my office and worked until a little after 4 before I decided to call it a day. I hadn't accomplished as much as I wanted, but I was spent. As happened yesterday, just as I was ready to leave, McMann was at my door. I smiled when I saw him, though I wasn't sure why I found seeing him again so pleasing.

Exaggerating a look at his watch, he commented, "Leaving already, Sheridan?"

"Yeah, that was the plan," I responded, still smiling.

"I hate to do this, but can you hold up a few minutes? I promise not to keep you too long," he asked, hands spread.

"No problem." I waved him to the chair, and he shut the door after giving me a questioning look and getting a nod. I did like his style. He sighed, sat down, and looked like he was beat. His hands went through his hair again.

"So how has your day been? Learn anything new?" he asked.

"Other than that you're not the only one who isn't thrilled with Joe Janis asking questions," I said with a bit of sarcasm, "I have discovered that I probably don't know some of the faculty I've worked with for the last few years very well."

"Full of surprises? Any related to Adam Millberg or his murder? Anyone confess by any chance? Any changes to your drawing I should know about?" he countered with a smirk.

I chuckled, and answered, "Afraid not. And how has your day gone? No offense, but you look tired."

His response was to sigh again. After some hesitation, he asked, "So which residential center did you work at?"

Not quite sure where that came from, and a little surprised he even remembered, I answered, "Children's Place, in Pennsylvania. Why? What on earth does that have to do with Adam's murder?" I must have looked very confused. I certainly felt that way.

Now it was McMann's turn to chuckle. He explained, "I think I now understand your comment about sometimes feeling like you're still working with troubled youth is all." He shook his head and asked, "Does anyone ever tell that Bentler guy to shut up? Does he think he is royalty or what?"

"Uh huh, you had yet another conversation with Max." Now it was my turn to laugh. "Unless you want to hear about his research or something outrageous that happened to him, you are probably wasting your time. I suspect he only knew Adam was on the faculty because he had to fight him for a preferred classroom with all the bells and whistles. Or maybe which student's thesis he would chair."

"But he does seem to be explosive. He was bragging how much he could press and what great shape he was in." McMann's expression showed how little he believed in Max's prowess. He continued, "Is Max married or is there any chance he might have been jealous of Adam's uh various relationships?" He wiggled his eyebrows as he asked the last question.

Sighing, I explained, "That would require that Max be aware of Adam's relationships first of all, and unless there was a scandal or such, I don't think Max would be interested. He is married. Stella, his wife, must be a saint. He's brought her to a couple of the department functions, and she smiles at him when he looks at her. I asked once, and they don't have any children. As for his being explosive," I paused to think about it before continuing. "He is explosive, but verbally. I've never seen him throw anything or even take a stance like he might be aggressive. Honest? The closest to that I've seen was his attempt to stand up to you yesterday, and he probably did that to save face."

"Okay, but I don't like the guy. On the other hand, Mitch seems to be a pretty good guy, a straight arrow, and seems to call it likes he sees it. His description of Adam's philandering was a bit more extensive than yours." It wasn't a question, but it felt like a question and his expression certainly suggested that it was a question.

"He was just murdered, and some of his philandering as you put it was with some people I care about. Not to mention that Mitch has been around a lot longer so he probably knows a lot more of the history. Hell, I didn't even know Katie had been married to Adam until last night!" I knew I sounded a bit defensive, but it couldn't be helped.

McMann chuckled again, and then got serious. "Sheridan, I know you're friends with Kim Pennzel, and I hope that it ends up that she is innocent. In the meantime though, as your drawing suggests, there are a lot of people to eliminate. Unfortunately, she's the only one so far who happened to be at the rec center and was seen with him socially recently, not to mention having a history with him. Sorry."

I just shrugged. There wasn't much else I could say. Saying I didn't think she could kill someone seemed kind of lame. He watched me, and I shrugged again.

"Well, I stopped by to see if you by chance had found out anything that would help in the investigation. I am heading back to the field office in Appomattox tonight to file reports and such, and probably won't be back for a day or two. Well, unless something breaks. Here's my card, and if you think of anything or anyone confesses, please give me a call." He handed me his business card, and I noted that his first name was Brett. Standing up, he added, "Walk you out?"

"Yeah, sure," I answered, feeling somewhat deflated. I wondered how I was going to cheer up Kim after he had just told me she was a prime suspect. I guess that meant Ali wasn't as high up on the list.

As we walked to my car, McMann asked me a couple more questions about the grounds and the arboretum in particular. At my car, he looked over in that general direction, and then with a smile, suggested that maybe I could show him the arboretum some time. I was taken aback by his comment, but also pleased by the prospect. In fact, his parting comment made me feel a little better. I only hoped I hadn't blushed too obviously. At least I had a tan so maybe it wasn't too obvious.

I drove home and took care of Charlie, changed my clothes and was off to the Grill. Kim got there ahead of me and she already had a table. I joined her, trying to be as upbeat as possible. She also seemed to be trying to be upbeat. After we ordered, I asked her how she was. She commented that one of Cold Creek's finest stopped by to tell her he needed to talk to her and she had put him off until tomorrow.

She seemed to visibly crumble and said that McMann had been to see her late in the afternoon. He had gone through all his questions again about where she had been Sunday night through Monday when Adam's body was found. He also asked her about her prior relationship with Adam. Then to her surprise he asked her about a few occasions they had been seen together recently.

"How did he know where and when we ate? It was unnerving, Sher," she commented, eyes wide. She picked up the bottle of steak sauce. It was brand new and she carefully took off the plastic seal.

"Oh, Kim, haven't you figured out that any time you go out with anyone, whether it's here in

Cold Creek or in North Shore or AltaVista, you are bound to run into someone you know? You may have been so focused on Adam that you didn't notice them, but obviously someone, or more than one, saw the two of you," I told her, wondering at how a bright, intelligent woman hadn't expected this. But then, this was the same bright, intelligent woman who got involved with Adam not once, but twice. I remember a saying my grandma told me – 'fool me once, shame on you; fool me twice, shame on me'. I guess Kim's grandma never shared that adage with her.

"I guess I didn't think about it. My personal life should be my business, not the whole towns. Anyway, he asked how the relationship was going. He asked if we had a disagreement lately, when was the last time we saw each other, and so on. I'm so scared, Sher." She was usually very energetic, but tonight even her long strawberry blonde hair seemed to lack its usual luster and bounce.

She shook her head and then shook the bottle of steak sauce to mix it, but the cover flew off and steak sauce went flying everywhere! She nailed the waitress and most of the booth. I started laughing and so did she. She and Zoe, our waitress, were now well 'sauced'. Kim's hair had brownish red streaks and it was dripping over her shirt.

We laughed until we were both having trouble breathing. Zoe came over with sponges and towels. Kim took one of the towels and made for the rest room. Zoe shook her head and I helped her move us and our food to an empty booth. She then followed Kim to the restroom. Kim came back first and had on a shirt about three sizes too big for her, her sauce decorated one in her hand. At my questioning look, she explained that Zoe had brought her the shirt. It belonged to her daughter. We settled down and ate. Zoe came to check on us after a bit and I noticed she didn't have the waitress shirt on anymore. We were going to have to tip her real good tonight.

"Kim, think back to Sunday night. Can you think of anyone you talked to on the phone? Sent an email to? Anything you did on the computer that would have a time stamp?" I asked. These were the only things I could think of to help give her an alibi or show she was at home.

"Umm, let me think. I always call my mom on Sunday nights. Around 7 or 8 before she goes to bed. We talked for probably 30 minutes. She was going for tests this week and was worried. We talked about the options if she had a problem on the stress test and needed an angiogram or surgery," she shared.

"Oh, Kim, I'm sorry to hear that. Did she

have the stress test yet?" I asked. Kim and her mother were close, and if her mother needed surgery, Kim would want to go to Florida to be with her. Not likely to happen if she was a prime suspect in Adam's murder.

"Yeah, and she did okay." Kim shrugged and then added, "It was routine, I think. Her blood pressure was higher than normal, and with her age, she is at increased risk for heart problems."

"Okay, so you talked to your mom – on your home phone or your cell?" I asked.

"On my cell, of course, why?" she countered.

"Well, you can prove you talked to your mother at that time, but not where you were when you called her. Did you take any other calls or make any other calls? Did you talk to Adam Sunday night?" I asked.

"No, I didn't talk to Adam on Sunday night." She sighed, and added, "We were together Saturday night, and he didn't leave until after breakfast on Sunday."

Seeing her hang her head at this admission, I pointed out, "Kim, you are an adult, and you have every right to have a sex life. Did you get all guilt-ridden when you told McMann this?"

"Well, actually, I didn't tell him. Just like if

I was being deposed or testifying in a hearing for a client, I only answered his direct questions. He didn't ask about Sunday morning or Saturday night, so I didn't tell him, Sher."

"Okay, that makes sense. Can you think of anyone else you talked to Sunday night? Pizza delivery? Talk to your neighbor?" I knew I was pulling at straws, but anything that would help her establish her whereabouts would be helpful in eliminating her.

"I don't remember. I cooked. I talked to my mother. I watched some television. I read a book. This is bad, isn't it?" she asked, looking beaten.

"Maybe you'll remember something. If it makes you feel any better, I can't prove I was home on Sunday either, Kim," I said, trying to be reassuring. Then Zoe came back with our check. We ate here often enough that Zoe knew us and after tonight she'd certainly not forget us. She leaned against the table and asked how we were doing with the murder and such. We sighed and gave the 'as well as can be expected' answer. Zoe shook her head and went to wait on her other tables.

I asked Kim what time she got to the rec center, who she saw, if she had even gone into the weight room, and if she ever went into the weight room. She told me McMann asked her the same questions. She had gotten there about 7 or so, did her warm-ups and then the treadmill. She said she hadn't been in the weight room at all that morning, and rarely went in there at all. One of the trainers tried to get her interested, but she preferred the treadmill, rowing machine, and elliptical, usually doing one or the other each day. All in all, the good news was that if a weight was used, and if they were able to get fingerprints, at least they wouldn't be Kim's. Of course, that assumed he was killed with a weight.

We haggled over who would pay the bill and I prevailed. I gave Kim a hug and went home. I was still thinking about how to exonerate Kim and then remembered what McMann had said about Ali and her attorney. Very odd. I remembered I had his business card and checked to be sure I hadn't misplaced it. I went to sleep thinking about his comment about the arboretum and thinking what a nice, and nice looking, man he was. It had been some time since I went to sleep thinking about a man, other than in anger.

CHAPTER 5

I no sooner arrived at my office, and Terra and Ali descended on me like vultures. They looked distressed. I only hoped no one else had been murdered or that Kim hadn't been arrested.

"Dr. Hendley, did you see the email from Dr. Grant?" Terra asked, not pleased. I answered to the negative and she quickly saved me the trouble of pulling up the message.

"He sent a message announcing that there will be a memorial service tomorrow for Dr. Millberg. Joe said the body hasn't been released yet, but even when it is released, he understood there would be no funeral. So the memorial is being held here on campus instead. Apparently it will be between the fountains and the arboretum," Terra explained, shaking her head.

"Huh? Here and not at a funeral home or

church or other place of worship? That seems a bit odd. Wonder who decided all this?" I asked. The question that occurred to me was who was Adam's next of kin? And it did seem strange that it would be secular, though I honestly had no idea what religion, if any, Adam practiced. Not to mention a bit odd to have a memorial service on campus. It wasn't like he was the President or anything.

Ali shrugged and added, "From what Dr. Grant said there will be a lot of the big wigs from the board of trustees. He said they hired the local wedding service to set up the reception because they would need chairs, and such. This place is going to be even more of a zoo than it already is." She shook her head as well. At least this must be providing a distraction. She certainly didn't look distraught over Adam, the investigation or the Cold Creek policeman from the day before. Not to mention that it somehow seemed pretty ironic that Adam's memorial was being planned by the wedding service given the number of wives he had.

I wondered if all four wives would be here for the service. We chatted a little more about the various types of services that we'd each been to when someone died, and then I excused myself to get some work done. I still needed to finish setting up everything for both research

91

design sections and the seminar.

First thing I did was pull up my email, and aside from some junk email and listservs, I had emails from Jim and from Cold Creek's President, Dr. Harrison Cramer. I pulled up Jim's and then Dr. Cramer's, finding that Jim's was passing along Dr. Cramer's with the added sentiment that as Adam's colleagues, he expected that we would all attend the service. Dr. Cramer's text read simply:

> 'The Cold Creek College community has been shaken this week by violence against one of our faculty, costing him his life. Dr. Adam Millberg served on the faculty for 11 years and was a respected and contributing member of our community during that time. His untimely death is surely felt by all who knew him, faculty, staff and students alike. Tomorrow at 11:00, there will be a memorial service to celebrate his life and his tenure here at Cold Creek College. I would encourage all to attend this service so that the College community can begin the grieving process and start the semester next week with this incident behind us. The service will be held outside the administration building, between the arboretum and fountains. Please join us.'

It struck me as a rather stark message, but then it didn't have any information. In fact, it didn't even mention the department. Mostly, I was struck with the notion that Dr. Cramer might think that this would put the incident behind us. Funerals did have the goal of bringing closure, but closure didn't seem likely unless the police were able to solve the case. It also implied that having a memorial would mean that the grieving would be over by Monday. I doubted that would be the case for those who had been close to Adam. It occurred to me that McMann probably would want to know about this, and pulling out his business card, I forwarded Dr. Cramer's email to him.

I shook my head, and began working. I worked pretty steadily for about an hour or so, until I was interrupted by a knock on my door. A student was standing in my doorway, obviously upset. She was blonde, attractive, well dressed, and looked to be a junior or senior rather than a freshman. I didn't know her so I guessed that Mitch followed up and let the front office know we were available, and someone had sent her my way. She looked about to cry.

"Why don't you come in and sit down," I suggested softly, and closed my door as she stepped in. She immediately started sobbing and it took some time before she calmed down enough to talk.

"I'm Dr. Hendley and you are?" I asked, keeping my voice quiet and calm.

"Rachel," she answered and tears started again.

"Rachel, can you take a deep breath for me? Are you a student here at Cold Creek?" She took the deep breath, and nodded affirmatively. I figured she was a student, but I wanted to stick to what might be safe.

"So what year are you in? And your major?" I asked, again trying to stick to facts.

"Senior. Psy..." and she became hysterical sobbing again. I suggested she try breathing again. With her major being psychology, I was pretty sure that this was in fact related to Adam's death. I sighed. It looked like the dam was about to break with student reactions.

"Rachel, we are all upset about Dr. Millberg. It's hard sometimes when death is sudden," I said, hoping she would find my words supportive. I added, "There will be a memorial service tomorrow for him. Sometimes participating in a memorial helps."

"You... you don't understand. Adam and I were in love," she said, and then she started sobbing again. I had been standing near her to be able to keep my hand on her arm for reassurance, but I sat down, and waited for her to calm down. I needed her to stop crying long enough to talk. While I waited, several thoughts went through my mind beginning with 'oh my God' to wondering if their romance was in her mind or real, and finally to hoping she wasn't pregnant.

When she took another deep breath and looked up at me, she said, "I can't believe he's dead. I thought we'd get married when I graduated." She seemed to be cried out for the moment, and I decided to try to get some more background and then work up to her relationship, real or perceived, with Adam.

Asking questions, I found out that she had transferred to Cold Creek at the beginning of her junior year after deciding a large university wasn't for her. A friend of her family had gone to Cold Creek, and recommended it. As a junior and majoring in psychology, she was assigned to Adam's advising load. She was in all his advanced psychology classes, and in order to figure out which courses would and wouldn't transfer for her major, she'd met with him several times. He had told her she didn't need to take my research design class for the major.

The transfer and his saying she didn't need to take my class - it was a required course - explained why I didn't know her. I sighed and she continued with her story.

She went on to talk about how he told her how pretty she was, and how he told her he liked it when his female students wore short skirts. She smiled as she explained how when she was in his sensation and perception class, he demonstrated various sensations and how different parts of the body were more sensitive than others. She looked embarrassed at this point, blushing a bit with a smile instead of tears. I opted not to get the details.

She said that was when they started 'hooking up'. I asked her about when that was, although I could have looked up which semester, and from the syllabus determined which week. She indicated that it was spring semester, March 22nd. She remembered the day. That, together with her description, seemed to give credence to the reality of more than the usual student-advisor interaction. This didn't seem to be a school girl crush and fantasy relationship. It occurred to me that at least I wouldn't have to report him to Jim, or the provost, but that was the only silver lining to this scene.

I talked to her again about how hard it is to lose someone you were close to. I pointed out that she needed to grieve, but also to take care of herself. It was probably a cheap shot, but when she talked about not being able to go on, I asked her if she thought Adam would want her to quit or would he want her to finish and graduate. Cheap or not, it worked, and she sat a little straighter.

We talked a little more about the memorial, and how some of the College administrators would be talking about Adam and his years here. I suggested she try to keep busy and focus on her studies and her future. When she hadn't broken down in over 10 minutes, I suggested she might want to go to the ladies room and wash her face. I also told her that she could come back and talk if she needed to. I didn't tell her that if she continued to need support, I would be referring her to counseling services or to someone outside the college.

She left, and I closed my door, something I don't do when I am alone in my office. I needed time to process what she'd told me. More than that I wanted a shower. I decompressed a bit and wondered idly what was going to happen to Adam's advisees. It occurred to me that whoever ended up being Rachel's advisor was likely going to give her a rude awakening on required courses. Hopefully, my class was the only one he told her not to take. It made me wonder if he thought I would figure it out if she were in my class. I'm a good psychologist, but I'm not psychic. I wondered if her parents realized what had been going on and just how angry a father might get. I suspected Adam's behavior might provide a motive for murder.

I thought about sending McMann another email, and decided to hold off. At this rate, maybe I should wait and write one later on. Thinking about the detective, his smile, his hazel eyes, and the way he raked his curly hair with his well-manicured fingers, made me feel a little better. I sighed, opened my door, and decided to take a quick walk through the arboretum to clear my head.

The arboretum was one of the best things about Cold Creek College. It included about two miles of a walkway with various options for shorter routes. Each path was decorated liberally with flora native to the region and well maintained by the Horticulture department. Someone with an artistic flair, as well as knowledge of horticulture, had designed several coves with cascades of color and water features. I found these spots to be very calming and activating at the same time.

My plan to head for the arboretum was derailed when I walked out of the building. There were multiple vans, and people setting up tents, chairs, and tables. College security and Cold Creek police, as well as many of the trustees who provided the funds for the college seemed to be congregating already. And, I suspected, each had an opinion on how this memorial would come off. Instead of calming, the noise and bustle was mind-numbing. I sighed, resigned that the arboretum was temporarily not an option, and settled for Georg's.

Again, it was pretty quiet in the Café. Getting a coffee and the same sandwich I'd had yesterday reminded me of lunch with McMann. I found myself smiling again, and trying to figure out some tactful way of determining if he was married. Maybe I could say something like his wife must miss him when he is out of town for days at a time. Or maybe ask if the move to Appomattox was to accommodate his wife's career. Both were possibilities, but I'd have to wait for an opening.

"Sheridan! Where's your buddy? Did you run out of secrets to tell him about us? Your friends? I feel like you are betraying us all!" Max's yelling interrupted my reverie. It also attracted the attention of the few others in Georg's.

"Hi Max. Care to join me?" I asked. I kept my voice low and tried to diffuse his anger by not taking the bait. I felt everyone looking at me, but tried my best to look bored. This approach had often worked to de-escalate kids in the center, and I hoped it would work with Max.

Max sat down, and then whispered, "I hear you've been spying on us so you can tell that detective what we're doing. When Joe interviewed me and I asked him what you said, he told me that you were too busy talking to the detective to talk to him. What have you told him about me, Sheridan?"

"Max, the detective asked me questions like everyone else. He is doing his job. Jim told him I would help him with finding faculty members and getting him oriented. I didn't tell him anything about you. Is there something about you and Adam I should have told him? Did you kill him?" I asked, quite sure that he hadn't and that asking him would send him into a tail spin again.

"Oh, my God, Sheridan, of course I didn't kill him. I would never do that. I never had anything to do with Adam. He didn't know anything about research, or learning or memory. Why would I talk to such an incompetent?" he said, his voice louder as he continued.

"Well, then I guess you don't have to worry about anything, do you?" I asked. The other people in the café shook their heads at his latest outburst and quickly found something more interesting. Max relaxed a little and then excused himself. His research was waiting. I sometimes wondered what he was actually researching, but dared not ask for fear he would tell me.

After Max left, I ate my sandwich and drank my coffee. I realized that what Max said wasn't all hogwash. I was giving McMann information. It occurred to me that maybe that was why he was so attentive. I consoled myself that I hadn't shared anything about Kim with him. From what Kim had told me, someone else certainly had. Thinking about Kim made me realize that I hadn't seen her today, at least in part because I was distracted by Rachel.

On the way back to my office, I first stopped at the main office and asked Jim what the plan was for re-assigning Adam's advisees. He shrugged and said he hadn't gotten that far. He thanked me for being available for students, mentioning that a few had been in already. I nodded, and then went to Kim's office. She was working diligently and seemed pretty reserved and quiet. I asked her if she was okay. She again lacked her usual high energy and optimism. She said she was keeping busy so she wouldn't think about Adam, the memorial, or the fact that she was likely to be arrested any time even though she hadn't killed him.

She said that the officer from the Cold Creek police, Hirsch, was waiting for her this morning. He asked all the same questions over again, and had a copy of all the answers she gave at the rec center on Monday. I sat down and we talked for a few minutes about the memorial and the fact that the memorial made his death that much more real. Like Rachel, I told her to give a yell if she needed to talk to anyone. I teased her about the steak sauce spray the night before and at least got a smile. I went back to my office I wondered when Officer Hirsch would be by to see me, and sighed.

I managed to make progress on my course prep with only a few interruptions. A few more of Adam's students stopped by, but thankfully none were as devastated as Rachel or mentioned a relationship other than student and faculty. I felt for one very serious student, Jerry. I remembered him from his freshman and junior years. Jerry was mostly concerned about what would happen with his honors thesis that Adam was supposed to be mentoring him on.

Jerry was applying to doctoral programs and the thesis would make him more competitive. I tried to assure him that it would still happen, but obviously with someone else, and no one was sure who that would be yet. Others were dealing with the violence and death of someone they knew. For some of them, it was the first time death hit close to home.

Deciding I needed to stretch, I stopped in the main office to check in with Terra and Ali. They both seemed to be holding up and were a little less distressed than earlier this morning. Surprisingly, Ali actually looked relieved. Terra was the more distracted, complaining about the extra calls and information she had to chase down for Jim. Joe sauntered in at one point, and asked how students were doing with the murder.

I shared with him that Mitch and I were available for any students who needed to talk. I also noted that the reactions were varied and in some ways dependent on their experiences with death. I asked him what his impressions were, and if he had any ideas on who murdered Adam. As with our previous interaction, my asking questions seemed to effectively end the conversation. He went off to find someone else to interview. Looking at Terra as he walked away, I noticed that she smirked and shook her head. Ali also seemed a bit amused. I sighed and went back to my office to see what I could get done.

Toward the end of the day, Mitch came in looking tired. He shook his head while rolling his eyes if that is possible. He mentioned he had several students stop by and asked if I had been around this morning, mentioning that my door was closed when he came by. I told him I had been, and met with students as well. He nodded, realizing then why my door had been closed. I asked him if any of the students he had seen seemed overly upset or mentioned anything that seemed inappropriate.

He sighed and mumbled something that sounded a lot like "not again". Without revealing who the student was or the details, I confirmed what he was obviously thinking. We discussed sexual harassment and the potential for that in a college setting. We talked about the memorial and how stressful that was going to be for everyone. Reminding me that I was going to need to be rested to deal with the fallout, he left. Mitch was a big teddy bear and curmudgeon all wrapped up in one. Someday I'd have to ask him why he was a professor and not in private practice.

I finished up a few things, and then checked my email. McMann had emailed me back to say thanks, and that he would definitely be back for the memorial. He also asked if anything else important had come up. I emailed him back that I didn't know if what a student said was important to the murder or not. I could let him know when I saw him or he could call me. Leaving my cell number, I pushed send, shut down the computer, and left for the day. I noticed that Kim had already left. I made a mental note to call her later on and make sure she was alright.

Walking out, I ran into Priscilla. She seemed even more out-of-sorts than usual. She complained about the memorial and the to-do for Adam, when as she put it, "everyone knew what a jerk he was." Obviously, Adam was not a topic that she and Mandy agreed on. When we exited the building, the grounds over by the administration building and arboretum were crowded with people – security, media, students, faculty, and community leaders. All I could think was "wow!" Priscilla snickered, even more disgusted than she had been. Priscilla was a bit arrogant in her own way, and her way was the right way, of course.

We parted ways at the parking lots and I went home. On a whim, I stopped at the Pizzeria and got lasagna to go for dinner. Living alone, dinner to go was a lot easier than cooking something. And the lasagna from the Pizzeria was better than a frozen meal any day. After letting Charlie out, and feeding her, I turned on the news.

I watched the coverage of the memorial preparations while eating my dinner. It struck me odd, but there was more discussion of who would be at the memorial, the caterer and planning crew, and road closures, than there was of Adam or his family. That saddened me even if I didn't like the man. Between my meeting with Rachel, my run-in with Max, and worry about Kim, I had trouble sitting still. I called and left a message for Kim to call me when she had a chance. I left the television on for background noise, and decided to clean my house, really clean my house.

I had bought this house when I moved to Cold Creek. It was a small house relative to some of the others in Cold Creek, but a three-bedroom was plenty big for Charlie and me. The problem was that I didn't spend much time in the living/dining area or the guest room. I pretty much lived in the master bedroom, the second bedroom I had turned into my office, and the kitchen. As a result, both of the other rooms tended to be neglected.

Often if I couldn't figure out where to put something, like that punch bowl someone gave me, it went into the living room because it was convenient and out of sight. It was always with the idea that I would get around to finding a better place or arranging the various crystal or serving dishes. The last time I had straightened up either room was when my sister visited about a year ago.

With nervous energy, I decided it was time to get everything dusted and rearranged so that it looked a little less scattered. That meant taking everything off the hutch, the coffee table, and end tables. I had about finished dusting and putting everything back onto and into the hutch, when the phone rang. I answered and was glad to hear Kim's voice on the other end.

"Hey, Sheridan. Sorry I missed your call. I finished up the abnormals early and came home to decompress. I turned the phone off so I could be sure I had time to think everything through," Kim explained. "Tomorrow's going to be a zoo, with a lot of people who don't even know Adam speaking and talking about the blow to Cold Creek." I agreed, and she continued, "But, don't worry, Sher, I will be there. The good thing is that because it will be such a farce, I'll probably hold up pretty well," she added with a sneer, obviously trying for a joke.

"Yeah, there probably will be a humorous side of it. You and others who knew and cared for him will have to grieve in your own time and in your own way," I responded, thinking as much of Rachel as Kim.

"I heard Max blew up at you. What was that about?" she asked, moving to a more neutral topic.

"Max accused me of being a spy for McMann. And Priscilla is all out of joint over the memorial," I offered.

"Oh, Sheridan, it's not your fault Jim told

McMann you'd help him. And I don't know if you've noticed, but I think he finds excuses to seek you out, have lunch with you, and such. I saw him bring you coffee the other morning, girlfriend," she teased. I was glad she couldn't see me blushing or smiling.

"Yeah, but maybe he's being nice like that in hopes that I will spill something to nail the murderer. Honest, Kim, I am not 'telling stories' on folks, but I do answer his questions and confirm what he tells me. Including that Max is a jerk, by the way!" We both laughed.

"Smart man! I don't know Sher, he's not my type, but he is good-looking and employed. Have you found out if he's married yet?" she asked.

I sighed and said, "Nope. Don't know if he is married. And I don't know if he is interested. All I know is that he recently was transferred to Appomattox and didn't know Cold Creek existed before Monday." We talked a little more and then. After I hung up, I went back to my hutch and the various odds and ends that seemed to collect over time. By about 9 PM I was getting tired and had identified some of the 'stuff' as needing a new home. I boxed that stuff up and labeled the boxes for the local thrift shop. Someone would have a greater appreciation for them than I did.

I curled up to watch television for a while, checking email and other social network sites. Charlie curled up next to me. I didn't have any new emails of importance. Nothing grabbed me on the social networks. A couple friends had posted the usual humorous posters from various sites. Nothing jumped out at me. Thankfully, no one I was friends with knew Adam. Well, no one that I knew of.

One of those mystery shows was on, and as I watched it I started thinking about Adam's murder. The police on the television show were talking about having to follow the money. I didn't know if Adam had any family, or if he had insurance. He did drive a fancy car, and his clothes cost a lot more than mine. He was a member of the country club. All in all, I assumed he'd come from money. He would have to in order to pay spousal support to four ex-wives.

I kind of doubted that Kim or Rachel, or even Katie or Ali, were named as beneficiaries. Besides, in Adam's case, it seemed to me it was more likely that this was a crime of passion. With that in mind, there was almost an unlimited list and that list seemed to be growing every day. The phone ringing interrupted my reverie.

"Hello, Sheridan? Brett McMann here." I felt my blood pressure shoot up a few points and smiled.

"Oh, detective, hello," I said, surprised by the call.

"Please, call me Brett. I got your email, and wanted to follow up. Do you have time to talk? Do you have any more information about the Memorial?" he asked.

"Sure, and no more details than what was in the email. The campus grounds were a zoo when I left. They have tents, chairs, tables, and a podium set up. It looked like they were setting up a sound system, and the media was setting up as well. Oh, wait, can you pull up KCCX? They are talking about it right now and showing the extensive preparations," I said, sitting up and paying attention to the newscaster.

"Okay, I'm trying to pull it up online. KCCX isn't broadcast up here. Got it and I have to say it looks impressive. I wasn't getting the impression that Adam was that well-liked. His death is certainly getting a lot of attention. You're the psychologist, what do you make of it?" he asked.

"My take? I think all the donors who support the College and the trustees want to get the attention off the violence of his death and re-direct it to a sense of community, everyone coming together at a time of crisis. That was what I got from Cramer's announcement. It was all about the College, not Adam. It makes sense at some level, if you think about it. I doubt there will be any mention of how he died tomorrow. Maybe a mention of his death being 'untimely'. I also think they want to bring this to closure before classes start on Monday," I offered.

"Makes sense to me. I'm going to try to get down there by 10 or so. If you don't mind, I'd appreciate it if you could help me identify some of the players tomorrow, and share your insight on peoples' behavior. That sound okay to you?" he asked. He sighed and I pictured him pulling his free hand through his hair.

"No problem, but I guess that if you aren't on campus long before 10, even with a badge, you won't find any place to park within 6 blocks. I suspect the whole board of trustees for the college, the development foundation members, administrators, some faculty, staff, and students, will make an appearance," I warned.

"Okay, and you said something came up with regard to a student. Something I should know?" he asked, shifting gears.

"Uh huh! Mitch and I were put on "crisis response" and students started seeking us out today as they got back and heard the news. Some are obviously more upset than others. One of them indicated that Adam engaged in, uh, inappropriate behavior with her," I said with some hesitation. It was pretty inevitable that he would ask for the student's name. It was also inevitable that I was not going to give it to him. It would be a standoff.

"Let me get this straight. A female student told you – or did she just give you the impression – that Adam and she were sexually involved? So he wasn't just hitting on faculty and staff, but students as well?" he asked sounding a little put off. I didn't blame him. It put me off, too.

"You've got the picture, I'm afraid. She said they were involved," I answered, sighing again. We talked a little more about how inappropriate Adam's behavior was and I assured him that there was a policy against this kind of behavior. After a few more exchanges on the case, we said good night. The news was over. After I let Charlie out again, I lay down to go to sleep. I still wasn't convinced of Brett's ulterior motives, and I didn't know if he was married, but I was flattered he wanted my opinions. On top of that, his not asking me for the name of the student won him more points in my book.

CHAPTER 6

It was a beautiful morning, not too hot, with a light breeze. This was fairly typical weather for Virginia in late August. I managed to get to campus by 8 AM, and the parking was already pretty horrendous. People were pretty much ignoring the 'reserved' sign in the faculty lot. Either that or a lot of faculty beat me, and I doubted that was the case. I found a space between a Prius and a BMW, another sign that these probably weren't all faculty cars in the parking lot. As I came around to the west side of the Humanities building, I could see a lot of activity, but not much more than when I left the day before. I knew this was only the beginning.

I went up the stairs and surprisingly our floor seemed pretty quiet. I settled down at my computer, and checked my email. Some of the usual announcements, but nothing interesting. Figuring I might have about two hours to get some work done, I quickly pulled up the course notes to see where I left off. I obviously overestimated my time for work though. Within an hour, Kim came by, looking like she hadn't slept and hadn't used a mirror to put her makeup on.

"Kim, are you alright? Come in and sit down," I said, concerned with her appearance and lack of energy. Her usually vibrant and well-coiffed hair seemed to be lackluster and unkempt. She looked even worse than she did earlier in the week. She sat down, but didn't say anything. To say she looked awful would be an understatement.

"Kim, talk to me. Did you take any meds? You seem out of it," I prodded her.

"No, I didn't take anything. I'm not big on meds so I've never taken any. I'm just numb," she answered. She sat there for a few more minutes not saying anything before she continued. "I got a call this morning from the police. Not your detective, but the Chief of the Cold Creek police, Chief Pfeiffe. I have an appointment to see him later today. Sher, they think I killed Adam and I don't have much faith in our local police department to clear me."

"Do you have an attorney?" I asked. At the

same time, I realized I wasn't even sure there was a law firm in Cold Creek, certainly not one that handled criminal cases. I guessed that was a good thing.

She shrugged before saying, "Nope. I called the lawyer I used in my divorce, and she is checking to see if she can find a criminal lawyer for me. She'll call when she locates someone. I don't know what else to do. You have to believe me, I didn't kill him."

I went over and gave her a hug, and tried to be reassuring. I suggested that maybe some cold water on her face would help, and we went down the hall to the ladies room. I helped her splash the cold water on her face and then repair her makeup and fix her hair. I also encouraged her to do some of her favorite yoga moves, and get herself focused. We fixed her clothes so she looked a little less disheveled and then I walked her back to her office. I sat with her for a few more minutes. Then I prompted her to close her door and do some more yoga as that seemed to help. I told her I would stop by on my way out to the memorial or she should come get me when she was ready.

Back in my office, I took a deep breath and tried to figure out what I could do to help Kim. About then Brett showed up. He smiled and noted that I had been right about the parking, the fanfare, and the crowd. He asked if anything was going on other than the memorial. I shrugged and told him about the police wanting to talk to Kim later on. He sighed and muttered "stupid." I asked him to explain.

"Lots of different levels are involved here. We have the State and local police, college security. As usual, no one is talking to anyone else. To bring in anyone at this point is premature. There are still a lot of questions to be answered. The Chief here, he thinks he has the answer and is going to get a confession, close the case, and emerge the hero." He sighed again and added, "This kind of thing happens all the time, when the local powerhouses put pressure on the local police force to close a case."

I nodded and wanted to ask if he had any advice for Kim, but I suspected he'd say "tell the truth", so I didn't bother. Shaking his head, he asked, "Ready? I would like to get down there and somehow figure out where to stand so you can help me identify some of the people, if you don't mind."

"That's okay, but I did tell Kim I'd go with her. Is that going to be a problem?" I asked.

"Not a problem. Let's go," he said with a shrug. I wasn't so sure Kim was going to feel that way, but as soon as she opened the door, he put up his hands. He assured her he wasn't there to talk to her, but to get a feel for the crowd in general, and possibly some individuals depending on what he saw. She seemed to relax and we made our way to the memorial.

If we hadn't been with him, we probably wouldn't have been able to get anywhere near where the action was. It was definitely standing room only, but Brett managed to make his way through, with us both in tow, to the side of where the makeshift stage had been set up. We could see the dignitaries.

The college President, Provost, and Chancellor, at least two of them with their wives, and the mayor and his wife, Chief Pfeiffe, and the congressional representative for this district were all there. Notably, the Chancellor's wife was the only one who evidenced any emotion. She kept dabbing at her rather puffy eyes with a lace hankie. I didn't know anyone had lace hankies anymore.

There also were the husbands and wives of the old money that established Cold Creek College and served as its trustees. Jim Grant was also on the stage, as was Dean Kahuna, the dean of Humanities. There had to be about 30 people on the staging itself. It was a good thing Kim was with us. I only knew the names of about half the people on the staging. Between us, we missed a few trustees, but Brett got the rest. Kim seemed to be feeling a little more human. Either yoga worked miracles or it helped that Brett was obviously looking at other people as possible suspects.

At promptly 11 AM, chimes came over the loudspeakers, and the crowd hushed. Cold Creek College's President, Harrison Cramer welcomed everyone to the memorial and celebration of life for Dr. Adam Millberg. He asked all to bow heads for a moment of silence. As I bowed my head, I noticed that Brett didn't bow his, but seemed to scan the crowd of over 100 people. After the moment of silence, Dr. Cramer introduced the other dignitaries on the stage. It struck me odd that no one on stage was identified as a member of Adam's family.

After the introductions, Jim Grant and Dean Kahuna spoke about Adam and his dedication to his students, to Cold Creek College, and to greater knowledge. When they mentioned students, Brett nudged me and indicated with a questioning glance a couple of students, one of whom was visibly upset. I reminded him that he had met Janet and Wesley. I provided the names of the other three – Courtney, MaryKate, and Raya. Courtney was the one who was so upset. When Brett raised his eyebrows about Courtney, I sighed and indicated that no, she was not the one I had talked to. His facial expression reflected his contempt. I knew Courtney to be a bit on the emotional side, but she did seem more upset than I would have expected. It was hard to tell if this was the way she reacted to a memorial or if she's also been involved with Adam. She didn't quite seem his type, but then he may not have had a type.

The eulogy of sorts officially over, each of the dignitaries had to take their turn, each ending with how they were sure this would not affect the fine reputation of the College. The Chief altered his a little by assuring those gathered that this matter would likely be resolved before classes began on Monday. At that, Brett hissed, "Jesus!" and looked fit to be tied. Dr. Cramer closed the official portion by again thanking everyone for coming. He then invited all to partake of the refreshments provided courtesy of the trustees as the College community came together to heal. It was pretty corny, but it seemed to be well received.

As the crowds thinned out a little, and the media made a bee-line for Chief Pfeiffe, Brett started asking more questions about the people in the crowd. It took us a few minutes to find Katie, who at least had a tissue in her hand and looked to be grieving. We were also able to identify Misty, wife number four, for him. I'd never met wives number one or three, so I wasn't much help there. Kim didn't think she'd recognize number three, but she kept looking. Brett provided us the names for them. Number one wife was Heather McDaniels and number three was Leanna Jones.

The names meant nothing to me. Kim pointed out that Leanna had remarried so her name wasn't Jones anymore, but she didn't remember what it was. In all likelihood, wife number one had remarried as well. Brett didn't offer any more information. He just nodded. I suspected that he already knew at least some of the information we were providing.

Brett asked if either of us knew the Chancellor's wife, the one who had been crying, but neither of us did. He nodded toward the buffet tables. We walked in that direction, got a plate of food, and then walked to the other side. We spotted getting food and she gave us a dirty look before sporting the obligatory smile. Mitch came over briefly, said hello, and then went into our building to escape the crowd.

We finished eating and the crowd was thinning. I could tell Kim was getting restless. I wasn't sure what time her appointment with the Chief was and I didn't want to bring it up. The three of us apparently all reached the same conclusion. The memorial was over and it was time to move on. Brett was thanking us for our help, when Max showed up.

"Oh my gosh, Sheridan, Kim, did you know that Katie was once married to Adam? And he was involved with one of the staff over at the rec center? And I heard that he was – you know – with one of the students? Can you believe it? I bet that was what got him killed – all that tom-catting around," he rattled, shaking his head. Several people nearby turned toward him with obvious disgust.

"Hello Max. Lower your voice, you're creating a scene," I hissed, embarrassed to be associated with his comments, even if they were correct. I hadn't known about the staff person at the rec center, but she certainly would have had opportunity, and the same perceived motive as Kim. Reasonable doubt, perhaps.

"Dr. Bentler, I think we need to chat again," suggested Brett as he physically started to take Max aside.

Max looked at us imploringly, saying, "But, but..."

As the two of them walked away, Kim looked at me, and asked, "What did you make of that?"

I wasn't quite sure which part she was asking about but went with the most obvious and answered, "I'm guessing that Max said something the detective didn't know about. Not to mention, I don't think he is particularly fond of Max."

I couldn't help but chuckle at the grilling Max was likely to be getting. Kim and I went back to our offices. She said she needed to gather her stuff and head down to the police station. I asked her if she wanted me to go with her, but she shook her head. I gave her a hug and went to my office to get some work done. So far, I was not doing too well at accomplishing all that I planned.

I was no sooner in my office, and Wayne called, again concerned about how I was holding up. I again declined his dinner invitation. I managed to at least get a minimal amount done for Monday's and Tuesday's classes, but not without interruption. A few more students stopped by. Rachel wasn't one of them. Neither was Courtney. Thankfully, none of the ones I saw had a story similar to Rachel's.

I wasn't sure what to think about Rachel not being at the memorial, so I went to see Terra and had her pull up Rachel's student record. I asked Terra for Rachel's home number. Terra looked at me funny when she realized Rachel was one of Adam's, but all I told her was that I needed her home number. I wasn't sure what I was going to say to whomever answered the phone, but I had to at least try.

Back in my office, I dialed the number. When a man answered, I said, "This is Dr. Hendley from Cold Creek College, may I speak with Rachel please?"

"Dr. Hendley? What kind of Doctor are you? Why do you want to talk to my daughter?" he asked, a bit agitated to be sure.

I about hit myself in the head, realizing what he might be thinking, and explained myself a little better. "I'm one of the faculty in the psychology department at Cold Creek. I assume you know that Rachel's advisor, Dr. Millberg, died suddenly on Monday. I was calling to see how she was taking it, sir."

"Oh, yes, terrible situation. Rachel isn't here right now. She's been upset enough. No one she knew has ever died before. Her mother and I didn't think that whole memorial thing would be helpful, so they went shopping and to lunch. I can tell her you called though," he responded, sounding a lot less agitated or suspicious.

"That would be good. I will probably see her on Monday anyway," I answered, preparing to say good bye, and feeling relieved. He thanked me for calling, I said good bye, hung up and sighed. Brett showed up just in time for the sigh.

"That bad, huh?" he asked with a smile, leaning against the door jam and looking good enough to eat.

I sighed again, and answered, "Been a busy week and the semester hasn't even started. I checked up on that student I told you about. I was worried about her when she didn't come today, but apparently her parents decided she shouldn't come. I at least feel better about that." He nodded and I asked with a chuckle, "So how did it go with Max?'

It was his turn to sigh and shake his head. "He is a complete … he exaggerated all his so-called information, and wasn't very willing to reveal his sources. He finally admitted that it was Wesley who made a comment about Adam and a student. He didn't know which staff person at the rec center, but they are all students except for the trainers." He sighed again before continuing, "I don't know if it is the same student who is the staff person or two different students. Since the student who was so upset isn't the same student who talked to you, I am leaning toward two students. I will have to interview both Wesley and Courtney." He sighed yet again and asked, "Any word from Kim?"

I sighed again, and shook my head. He put out his hand, and said, "Come on, we both need a break. Show me that arboretum?" He smiled, and I took his hand. His hand was very warm and mine felt pretty small in his.

As we left my office to go downstairs, he

released my hand. We left the building and made our way past the caterers cleaning up, past the first stands of azaleas and rhododendrons, and entered the arboretum. It was a beautiful setting with various spots of color seemingly randomly placed. I explained that there were different paths and they were color coded and different distances.

We took the shorter blue path and started walking. This path would be about one-quarter mile in each direction. There were multiple varieties of trees, and at various points there were flowers and bushes that were indigenous to Virginia, like trailing arbutus, mountain laurel, more azaleas, and more rhododendrons. We came up on some benches nestled amid black-eyed Susan, Queen Anne's lace, asters, and evening primrose, still in bloom, and sat down. It was nice to sit in silence and take in the calm. The folks in horticulture had done a great job of landscaping.

"I know why you would prefer walking here rather than in the rec center. It's very quiet and peaceful," Brett commented as he took it all in and seemed to relax. The trees in some places formed a canopy and offered some shade. An occasional breeze moved the leaves opening the canopy to let sun in much like a skylight.

"Yup, no real 'noise' other than the breeze

through the trees and the warblers and other birds. And it changes with seasons. Spring brings the periwinkle, dogwood and columbine, followed by violets and marigolds. There are some other flowers too, but those are the ones I can identify," I added as I enjoyed the natural beauty. "The horticulture club made sure to mix colors and heights to show off the flora, and they keep it well tended, with some help from a local company."

He nodded and then asked, "So how did you come by the Irish, Sheridan?" I was a little surprised at the sudden change in the conversation, and pleased at how attentive he had been to our various conversations.

"Both my mother's and father's families were Irish stock. My mother's family – the line was originally O'Schaughnessey, but then they dropped the "O" part. My father didn't know of any changes to the Hendley, but who knows. My sister and I tried to do a family tree, but the different variations of the Irish names and combinations became a little too confusing." I shrugged and then asked, "And what about the McMann? Is that Irish or Scotch?"

"Ah, McMann? Irish, but I suspect it changed over time as well. I never looked into it. My mother's parents were O'Brien and Hennessey, definitely Irish. I guess none of us ever were very interested in tracing the family tree," he answered, a somewhat puzzled expression crossing his face momentarily.

"'None of us'?" I asked, curious at his phrasing.

He chuckled and added, "Not that many, though I think my ma felt like there were. Three boys and we are close in age, so we were a triple threat. I look back and wonder how she managed." He shook his head as if remembering some of the trouble they had gotten into.

"So are you the oldest, youngest, what?"

He answered, smiling, "I'm the middle one. Terry, the oldest, is the CEO of Westward Inc. and Patrick, the youngest is still trying to find himself, I think. He has been in finance and marketing, and is currently working at a public relations firm. Pat is by far the most social of the three of us."

He put his hand on mine, and asked, "So Sheridan, tell me about yourself – not just your prior job. No wedding band and you live alone. Ever married?" His voice was relaxed and he was smiling. His eyes seemed softer than they had before. And he certainly had cut to the chase.

"I'm divorced. No children, sheltie named Charlie. One sister, Kaylie, and one brother, Kevin. I'm also a middle child. Originally from Delaware," I answered. "And what about you?" I wasn't sure what else to say, and that seemed to cover the basics. I didn't want to go into the whole divorce thing.

"Divorced as well. I have one daughter, 12 years old going on 30," he said wistfully. "She and her mother live in Richmond. Madison comes to stay with me most school vacations or long weekends, and I try to get over there one weekend a month. Other than that, we talk on the phone a lot."

"I'm sorry. That must be hard," I offered quietly.

"It is, but nothing to be done about it," he said with a shrug. "We married young. We grew apart, wanted different things."

"So how long have you been in law enforcement?" I asked, trying to move away from what seemed like a touchy subject for both of us and back to more neutral ground.

"Oh, I did four years in the Army as an MP, and looked into law enforcement when I got out. I worked for the Bedford police force for about 10 years, and then moved to the State police. I gradually moved up the ranks to Detective. I was at the Roanoke field office, but when the position came up in Appomattox, I requested the transfer. It's closer to Richmond," he explained.

"What do you like most about your job?" I asked, more than a little curious about what made him tick.

"I have to say, I prefer the detective part much more than I ever did patrol. There are some additional pressures, but I like trying to figure things out. Kind of like putting a puzzle together and figuring out how all the pieces of information fit together to tell a story." He smiled and I smiled back. "So what drew you to psychology?"

I laughed and said, "The puzzles I put together relate to trying to explain why people behave the way they do." A little more serious, I added, "Children sometimes have problems, but they aren't always the only ones contributing to those problems. I like trying to figure out the why of the behavior, and the how of changing it. Sometimes it's more challenging, and sometimes there is nothing I can do to change the behavior. Then they end up on your desk. But I like the challenge of trying to figure it out."

"But now you're here?"

"Yeah, well, like I told you, I decided I needed a change, at least in part due to my failing marriage. My husband also worked at the residential school, and so did his girlfriend," I explained. Brett's eyebrows arched, and I continued, "I also was getting a bit burned out like I said before. Now I teach about the ways and why of human behavior. I also have the challenge of figuring out young adults as they try to discover who they are. Initially, I wasn't sure I would like teaching, but I do."

Squeezing my hand, he chuckled and teased, "And somewhere along the way, you get to try to figure out your colleagues, some of whom...." And he shook his head rather than finishing his sentence. Looking at his watch, he sighed, and suggested we finish our walk and head back to the Humanities building. He put his arm around me as we walked and the temperature seemed to go up a few degrees. He dropped it only as we came out of the arboretum and back onto the quad.

Back in the building, the warm feeling that had started to permeate my thoughts seemed to fall away. Brett was back in professional mode and Kim wasn't back in her office. In my office I tried to focus on my course prep again and checked my email. Nothing of note in the email, but I made some progress on the research design class. As I had done the rest of the week, I decided to call it quits around 4, and almost like clockwork, Brett was leaning against the door jamb looking very tempting.

"You are a creature of habit, aren't you?" he asked with a grin. "Just wanted to stop by and let you know that I called the Chief to check on the progress of the case. He confided that he called in your friend Kim, but didn't have enough to hold her, so he had to cut her loose."

I smiled and relaxed a little. "Thanks for letting me know. I was getting worried. She probably went home."

"Probably. So do you have plans for dinner? I'm starving," he added.

"No plans," I answered, not quite sure how I was supposed to be feeling, and feeling a little nervous.

"Care to join me, then?" he asked and then added, "You can pick the restaurant." He smiled and looked so earnest, I had to smile back.

"Sure, but the restaurant choices in Cold Creek are pretty limited. Have you tried the Grill?" I suggested. Other than the pizzeria, a Chinese restaurant, a Starbucks, and a few other fast food chains, there weren't too many restaurants in Cold Creek.

"No, but I'm game. Let's go. I'm parked about four blocks down Main Street, heading east – your guess last night wasn't too far off," he said, still smiling.

"We can walk to the Grill, then. It's not too far from your car!" I explained, grabbing my bag. He nodded and moved out of the doorway. We left and we made small talk as we walked to the restaurant. There were no remnants of the memorial and the campus was fairly empty, as would be expected for the week before classes. Brett asked about the fountains, and I explained that they usually get turned on when classes started and were turned off when classes were not in session. As we walked, I pointed out the driveway that led to the dorms on the eastern side, behind the Student Union. There was considerably more activity now than earlier in the week with students moving in.

It was still early, so the Grill was fairly quiet and we got a booth toward the back. The waitress, Zoe, was the same one who had waited on Kim and me the night before. She gave me a questioning look and a wink. I shrugged and smiled. Of course, that triggered a similar questioning look from Brett.

I explained that she waited on me a lot and probably wondered who he was. He sighed and shook his head, and we discussed the problems of small towns. The thing was though, somehow Adam had managed to be involved with multiple women, one after the other, or it seemed, several at once. Somehow he had managed to do that and stay under the radar. That was not an easy feat in a small town.

Zoe came and took our order after she made a comment about the steak sauce. That meant I had to explain what happened with Kim the night before. I tried to describe the steak sauce exploding from the jar but somehow ended up laughing all over again. Zoe joined me in the laughter and Brett chuckled. I wasn't quite sure if he was chuckling at the picture we'd painted or at us.

Order place, there was silence for a bit, and then conversation. The same occurred once our food arrived. Sometimes the silence was comfortable, sometimes awkward. I wasn't sure if this was a date or not, but it sure felt reminiscent of a first date. The consolation was that he looked to be as uncomfortable as me.

We'd about finished eating when I noticed Zoe gesturing to me about something, but I didn't quite understand. And then I did, as Wayne walked in our direction.

"Sheridan, how are you holding up?" he asked, very solicitous and proper and directing his question to me. He obviously avoided looking at Brett.

"I'm doing well. Wayne Cantor, Brett McMann. Wayne is a dentist here in Cold Creek," I added as I made introductions. The two men shook hands but both seemed to be focused on me.

"I've been worried about you Sheridan," Wayne explained. "I had hoped you would accept my invitation for dinner if you needed company or solace with all this mess about Dr. Millberg."

He continued to ignore Brett as he spoke.

"Thank you for your concern, but I'm okay," I responded. I blatantly ignored his comment about his invitation. Brett watched this interaction with interest. Although he had initially seemed put off when Wayne came over, now he seemed to be suppressing a smirk. Wayne and I went back and forth a couple more times. Wayne again suggested we go out and ignored Brett, and I declined as tactfully as I could. In the meantime, thankfully Zoe brought us our check and Brett paid. I was too busy volleying and dodging with Wayne to argue about the check. Zoe shrugged, winked, and took the money.

I was about to lose my patience, when at an opportune pause, Brett said, "Wayne, nice to meet you." He stood up and extended his hand to me. "Sheridan, you about ready to go?"

In his own way, Brett gave a clear message to Wayne that this was a date, even if wasn't. Just as plainly, he communicated that the interaction with Wayne was at a close. Wayne's mouth dropped and he didn't respond. As they stood together, I noted that Brett had a couple of inches on Wayne. Brett also had a more rugged and strong look to him. Wayne was just Wayne.

I said good night to Wayne as I slipped out of the booth. As we exited the restaurant,

Brett put his arm around me. I didn't look back at Wayne as we left. I also didn't have a clue what to say to Brett. I was a bit embarrassed by the whole scene. Brett broke the silence first. He suggested I find a new dentist and I started laughing. We laughed almost all the way to his car, marked as State police, and then he drove me to my car.

As I unlocked my car, he said, "Well, Wayne aside, I enjoyed dinner tonight." He leaned down and kissed me, first a barely kiss, and then a more definite kiss when I responded. "That was pretty good, too," he added.

"It was, and thank you for dinner, too," I answered smiling, and feeling tingles throughout my body. We stood in the parking lot with both our car doors open for what seemed like a long time, even if it was probably only a few minutes. Brett finally sighed, and broke the silence.

"I'm heading back to the field office, but I'll be back on Monday. Maybe we can do this again then?" he asked, almost a bit tentative.

I answered, "That sounds good. I'd like that." He leaned down and kissed me again with meaning, and tipped his non-existent hat, with a "be sure to lock your doors now". The good night ritual left me tingling and smiling from ear to ear. Someone once told me that when something bad happens, to look for the silver lining. Brett seemed like my silver lining to Adam's murder. I'd have to thank whoever it was who had called the State Police in on the case.

I held that thought all the way home. Once there, I took care of Charlie who acted like I had neglected her for days, instead of only being a couple of hours later than usual. As I fed her, I realized I still had to somehow help remove Ali and Kim from the "persons of interest" list. I wasn't sure if Ali was still on the list, but it seemed Kim surely was. I wanted to give Kim a call and find out what the Chief had wanted. I wondered if she had found an attorney, but it had been a very long and stressful day. I knew I was tired, and I didn't want to wake her if she had turned in early. She'd looked like she needed sleep.

CHAPTER 7

I woke up Friday morning with mixed feelings. On the plus side, I had managed to get at least the first weeks' worth of classes set up. I'd have to tweak a bit once I gauged the students in the classes, but I didn't feel panicked about classes starting on Monday. I needed to make copies of syllabi, and I still needed to physically check out the bookstore and make sure my books were in. I was going through all of this in my head as I showered, dressed, let Charlie out, and drove to work. I smiled and almost giggled at the thought that I might even have a new man in my life.

On the other hand, thinking of Brett reminded me we had a murder to deal with and that my friend was somehow caught in the middle of the whole thing. I suspected Jim would be letting us know what was to happen with Adam's classes and advisees today. He had run out of time. I still had to figure out some way to clear Kim and I was liable to be even busier today with students.

I parked and went to my office. Heading to the main office to make my copies before everyone else lined up to do the same, I checked in on Ali and Terra. Ali smiled and said 'good morning' and Terra shrugged her shoulders. I asked if Joe knew anything, but she shook her head. She mentioned that Officer Hirsch from the Cold Creek police would probably be looking for me. I shrugged.

Copies made and back in my office, I worked on putting all the articles and other papers I had used to set up the classes back in folders so I could feel organized and find my desk. I also checked my email. There was the email from Jim I had been expecting. It seemed he had arranged to hire someone to fill Adam's teaching responsibilities temporarily, someone named Todd Flats. Unfortunately he would not be able to start until October 1.

Jim's email went on to say that until then, Kim would cover the section of abnormal, which I already knew. Doug would have to cover the sensation and perception course, and Max was to cover the learning and memory class.

I sighed with relief, and reflected that the assignments made sense, given Kim, Doug and Max. I suspected Max would be in to complain about the overload though. Jim also announced that he would be assigning Adam's advisees to the remaining faculty. Each of us would get one or two. He told us to see Terra for the list of Adam's students and to let him know if there was a student or students we would like to take on. The rest would be randomly assigned. That was also going to frost Max big time.

As I contemplated the changes, I googled Todd Flats. He was another young psychologist. Looking at his CV, it looked like he would not actually graduate until December. That might explain why he was available for the temporary position. I realized that on top of everything else we would also have to have a faculty search.

I suspected Jim would dump the task of writing up the job description and chairing the search on me. He had done that for the previous search, so at least I had one I could resurrect. I was still reading through Todd's information when Mitch showed up.

"Morning. Anything new?" he asked as he moved my bag and made himself comfortable. Mitch was still in summer attire – shorts and polo shirt.

"I guess you saw the email from Jim?" I asked. He nodded and I continued. "I was wondering if I should volunteer to advise the student who came to see me. What do you think?" On the one hand, it made sense because I at least knew she would be dealing with issues with Adam, and possibly with his advising style. On the other hand, it might be awkward for all the same reasons. And there was a fine line between advising and providing therapy that shouldn't be crossed.

"You're not responsible for everyone, you know," he answered, knowing me too well and knowing I was seriously thinking about it. He continued, "Why don't you wait and see. It's not like you have been involved with her academically. Didn't you say she never even took one of your classes?"

I sighed, and responded, "You're right, I know you're right." Changing the subject, I asked, "Know anything else about the investigation?" Mitch had his own in-roads into the local politics and often was in the know before announcements were official.

"Not really. For whatever reason, there is no longer any real interest in Ali. I heard about Chief Pfeiffe having Kim come in to the station, though. Officer Hirsch stopped by to see me, but he's not as thorough as your detective. He seemed like a good man, but he's still feeling his way. But then, it's not like we often have murders in Cold Creek. He's had no occasion to sharpen his skills." He shook his head before continuing, "I think it is possible Adam made as many people mad as he made women fall for him. And what I don't get is how they each thought it would be different for them. It's not like his affairs were a big secret or that these were stupid women." He shook his head again.

"Yeah, you would think intelligent women could figure out that a man who strays will continue to stray. Speaking of which, did I tell you my old neighbor said that Janie caught Derek with the woman who took my job and there was a big blow up? Obviously, she hadn't figured he would do the same to her." Derek was my ex, and Janie was the psychology intern he was fooling around with and eventually married. I shook my head and shrugged.

"Yeah, well, it seems like you and the detective are getting along pretty well," Mitch teased. He winked and added, "I saw the two of you disappearing into the arboretum yesterday. Judging from the blush, I bet there's a story there." He winked and smiled while I felt the color rising in my face.

"Just a nice walk is all," I countered trying to maintain perspective and somehow control my blushing.

"Oh, and you both happened to be hungry, so dinner was convenient, right? Or were you trying to appease the staff at the Grill for the mess you and Kim made the night before?" he teased again.

"My gosh, Mitch, how did you hear about it so fast? With the gossip mill around here working that fast, why can't we figure out who killed Adam? And how could he be seeing multiple people without everyone knowing it?" I was too surprised he knew about the two incidents to even be embarrassed.

He laughed and said, "I had my teeth cleaned this morning! Wayne was beside himself over seeing you and some man at the Grill. He described the detective and asked me who he was, and how long you had been seeing him. I told him it sounded like the detective, but then he of course put a different twist on the dinner. In the long run, I'm afraid you're not off the hook. Sorry."

I sighed and must have looked horrified. Mitch continued, "No worry, I tried to put him straight, and pointed out that detectives don't usually have dinner with suspects. It's considered bad form. I told him I thought the two of you were becoming friends." He smiled and gave me a questioning look.

"I like him, Mitch. I don't know where it will go, if anywhere. But I like him." Not exactly a rave review, but an honest response. Well, except for the warm feeling and tingles, and the kisses last night, it was an honest response.

"Hey, that's what counts. Enjoy it. If it doesn't work out, there's always Wayne!" Mitch chuckled as he said the last part. He was well aware of the number of times Wayne had asked me out and I had declined. More than once he had suggested I find another dentist, even if it meant going to North Shore or AltaVista. It would only be about 30 minutes away. I began to think it might be a good idea.

"So where is our good detective this morning?" he asked, pretending to look under my desk or behind the door.

"He said he was going back to the field office and would be back on Monday. At some point, Mitch, he is probably going to talk to students. Courtney was visibly upset yesterday, and then there's the student I saw, and Max said something about a staff person at the rec center, also a student," I said, feeling a bit deflated at the potential backlash it could cause.

"He has to do his job, and it's certainly beginning to look like Adam was a very busy man. That said, I am not sure students being upset is the same as his being involved with them." Mitch shook his head and added, "Hopefully, he used something or we could be looking at a rash of STDs or pregnancies." He shook his head again.

I shook my head as well. We chatted a little more about the students and letting students know to come see us if they wanted to talk about Adam's death or safety concerns. Between us, we probably had most of the psychology students and hopefully, they would also share the information. I offered to contact the dorms and let the staff there know as well. We had moved on to sports and baseball in particular when Max showed up.

"I can't believe Jim did this to me! Doesn't he know how valuable my time is? He expects me to teach a class for a month until this other guy comes in. And then I'll probably have to help this Flatts guy! What about my research? I need to get some publications out and work on writing a grant. I hear there may be a position at Commonwealth or UVA. This is important. Doesn't Jim know I am the only one here who can actually do research and write grants?"

Mitch interrupted his tirade and said, "Max, we all have to work together here. You are the best person to cover the Learning and Memory class. Maybe you can find some students in there to help you with your research." This seemed to appease Max and appealed to his ego. He stood straighter and seemed to smile at the compliment.

"Well, of course I am the best person to teach the course! And you're right, maybe I can use this opportunity to get some free labor. But I am not taking any of those advisees. I have enough. Besides whatever the students do, I have to rewrite. Only Wesley seems to get it." Max shook his head.

"I don't think you're giving these kids their due. They are undergraduates, you know, not graduate students," I suggested. The over-the-top expectations were a frequent theme with Max.

"Well, I need them to be better students. If I'm going to advise them, they need to be doing a related to my research. They need to help me get to a Research university, or at least one with a graduate program. This place is pitiful," Max lamented.

"Actually as an undergraduate college, Cold Creek is well respected. Across the college, our graduates get into pretty good graduate programs when they leave here. You may not be aware of this, but about 80% of the Cold Creek grads go on for an advanced degree," Mitch offered. I hadn't realized it was so high, but Mitch had, in the course of his long career, held a number of administrative roles at the College.

"Well... I still can't handle any more students and get my work done. And I am not going to babysit this graduate student, Flatts. Do you realize he hasn't even graduated yet?" Max's voice was getting louder again. His face was getting red and his fists were clenched by his sides. I was afraid for his health.

"Max, calm down. Nobody has asked you to babysit anyone. As for his not graduating yet, he does have his Master of Science, and probably didn't get his dissertation done in time to graduate yet. You never can tell, he might be a fellow researcher," I offered. Most of us at Cold Creek were not into research. Most of the time, we only engaged in research if a student initiated it as part of an honors thesis. Most of those students, though, were more likely to seek out Doug or Max, or until now Adam. Kim, Mitch, and I were more likely to be sought out if they wanted to do a field-based experience or two.

I realized I had no idea which camp the other faculty fell in. Priscilla and Mandy were still too new, so their advising load was light. Certainly neither had mentioned research interests, but then I was discovering I didn't know the people I worked with all that well. I wasn't aware if Jack had any active research, but he tended not to blow his own horn. He was involved with the county Head Start. Students might seek him out if they were interested in that as a field experience. It was possible he also did research. Once again, I realized my interactions were pretty restricted, and mostly limited to Kim. Well, and then Max when he needed to vent and impress on others how much smarter and better he was.

To change the subject, Mitch asked, "So, Max, who do you think killed Adam?"

"I can't believe what people are saying about him! He was apparently having affairs with several women, not to mention Kim Pennzel! And Katie was married to him! I think they all found out about him, and they banded together and beat him to death. Then they arranged for alibis, using each other. That's probably why they still haven't released the body. They're trying to figure out how many people were involved. Do you think they castrated him?" he asked, very serious and wincing a bit at his last thought.

Mitch did his best not to laugh. "That is a theory I hadn't heard. You don't think one of those women could have killed him? I mean, how would this whole band of women not be noticed by anyone else at the rec center?"

Max continued, "Because one of the staff at the rec center was the inside person, and let them all in ahead of time, and then snuck them out. And there wouldn't be any blood evidence on any of them because they could shower. Yup, that's what I think happened. And if he was diddling all these women, well, he deserved it." Max nodded his head emphatically as he explained his theory.

Mitch was too busy trying not to burst out laughing, so I asked, "Max, did you share this theory with Detective McMann or Officer Hirsch?"

"That detective – I don't know what you keep telling him, Sheridan. He keeps coming after me. I don't care if Adam was whoring around. I think it's downright gross. And I didn't tell Officer Hirsch anything," Max responded emphatically.

Recovered somewhat, Mitch suggested, "But Max, the detective may not have come up with your theory. Don't you think you should share your theory with him, you know, help the investigation?" Mitch's eyes were twinkling and he was still having a hard time not laughing outright, but Max was oblivious.

"Hmm. No, I want to stay far away from him. Sheridan can tell him. He gets information from her you know. He can take it from there if he wants to solve this murder. I already shared it with the police chief. That's why I couldn't be bothered talking to Hirsch," he answered and walked away.

Mitch signaled to close the door. Once it was closed, we both had a good laugh. It was kind of scary that Max had already shared his conspiracy theory with the police chief. Scarier still was that Chief Pfeiffe might believe it. We got more serious and pondered Max's complete lack of feeling or empathy for anyone else. Being a psychologist, it was always tempting to assign diagnoses to people we met or worked with, at least amongst friends. After a while, we ran out of profound thoughts on Max's behavior and Mitch went back to his office. I went back to work.

As I had volunteered to do, I called each of the dorms and gave them my office location and phone number, as well as Mitch's. I went down to Kim's office and chatted with her a bit about her ordeal with the Chief. She looked better than she had yesterday. Her hair was combed, makeup in place. She seemed none the worse for wear, but not her old self.

She asked about 'my detective', teased me a bit, and I related the incident with Wayne at the Grill. The story generated a good laugh. At my suggestion, and since it was approaching lunch time, we decided to walk over to the Student Union to grab a bite and check in at the bookstore.

The Student Union was swarming with students. In itself, with the renovations to the original building, it sprawled out in multiple directions. The cafeteria was on the second floor. We got into line, and talked about weekend plans, possibly catching a movie, or going into North Shore for some shopping. The line moved quickly and we got a table without any trouble.

While we were eating, Misty joined us, with Kim making the introductions. We talked about the memorial and how shocking it was to have a murder on campus. Misty shared that things were pretty tense among the upper administration and the trustees. Her boss, the Provost Dr. Banks, had been in meetings almost constantly since Monday afternoon and lots of voices were raised. Apparently the trustees seemed to think the Provost, the Chancellor and the President should have been able to prevent the murder. Given everyone knew at least part of Adam's history, they might have had a point.

We visited for a while. All three of us avoided talking about Adam and focused instead on the fallout from his death. I mentioned that the Chancellor's wife seemed upset at the memorial, and Misty shrugged her shoulders. We all agreed the three of us didn't exactly travel in the same social circle as the administrators and trustees. We talked about the movies playing and the proposed theatre group schedule, and then ran out of small talk.

My first impression of Misty in person didn't jive with the mental picture I had of someone who had been Adam's wife. She was blonde and attractive for sure, but she didn't seem flirty or shallow. She seemed fairly down to earth and likeable in fact. It still surprised me he had fooled so many women who were fairly stable and smart in other areas of their lives.

We finished eating and Kim and I weaved our way to the bookstore. We needed to find out how badly they had messed up the book orders. Kim also had to check on the books Adam had ordered. Not surprisingly, he hadn't done a syllabus, and she had created one similar to hers, but would have to adjust it to match the book he ordered. The bookstore was busy, with students in lines buying books and a few faculty members, like us, checking to be sure the books were in.

I got lucky and at least the intro text was there, a pile that included some used and some new. The textbook for the seminar was there as well. It was actually a collection of readings of important studies in psychology. I wasn't so lucky on the text for research design. It was on backorder according to the card on the empty shelf. Kim was in good shape and all her books were in. Nothing was listed for Adam's class and when we went to ask about it, we were told they never received an order from him. Usually it would have been a problem, but instead it simply meant Kim could use her syllabus for all three sections. She asked the bookstore manager to please order additional copies of her books on a rush order. I asked him to check on my backorder at the same time.

That settled we walked back to our building and offices. I worked some more, adjusting the week's assignments for the research design class as the students likely wouldn't have books until at least mid-week. I took care of that and made sure I had everything copied for the intro class on Monday. I was ready to head out, when a young man in uniform knocked on my door.

He introduced himself as Officer Hirsch. Not quite 6 foot and looking like he worked out, the most surprising thing was how young he looked. I am not particularly fond of moustaches, but some facial hair would have added a few years. Officer Hirsch and I chatted briefly and scheduled an appointment for Monday. Then I was ready to leave. On my way, I stopped at Kim's office and she was just finishing up as well. We walked to our cars together and made tentative plans to take in a chic flick Saturday night.

Heading home, I realized it had been a very stressful week. All I wanted to do was sit with Charlie and watch some television, or do anything else that wouldn't require a whole lot of thought. I stopped and got some groceries without event, and was home by 5. I took care of feeding and walking Charlie and fixed myself a low fat frozen entrée. Then I settled down for the night.

CHAPTER 8

I woke up early the next morning. I followed my usual routine, let Charlie out and fixed a cup of coffee and some cereal. Then I cleaned out my gardens and got the beds ready for fall planting for about an hour or so. It wasn't quite September but the air was crisp and cooler than it had been. Gardening to me is therapeutic and calming and I felt better getting my hands in the dirt. I noticed a few of my neighbors were doing the same thing. I waved to Julie, the neighbor on my right, and she stopped her gardening to come over. She asked about the murder and how I was doing. We chatted a bit about increased violence and then we both got back to gardening.

I kept track of time because I had to be at the beauty salon by 11. An old habit from childhood, I always took the extra effort to look good for the first day of school. In this case, because I would see different students on Monday-Wednesday-Friday than on Tuesday-Thursday, I actually had two first days. I stopped gardening, took a shower and was right on time to the salon.

The plan was to get my hair cut and, of course after the gardening, my nails were in bad shape, so a manicure and pedicure made perfect sense. All in all, about two hours of spoiling myself. The salon was in the center of town, and I had a short wait. I didn't know any of the other customers by name. I pulled out my eBook reader to catch up on some leisure reading while I waited, but I couldn't help but hear some bits and pieces of comments as I waited.

"It's just awful you know, the murder of that teacher at the college. My granddaughter is a student there and often works out at the rec center. My daughter was thinking about getting a membership somewhere else, but there's no other club here. That college has a monopoly on being healthy and fit," one older woman ranted. She had a point. A town as small as Cold Creek couldn't support two fitness centers. Besides, the cost for community members to use the rec center was more reasonable than the fitness center in North Shore or AltaVista.

"Did you know the teacher who was killed? I saw his picture and I think I've seen him around town," Chloe commented to the woman whose hair she cutting. I was waiting for Chloe, so I was sitting close by and couldn't help but hold my breath as I waited for the customer to answer.

"Oh, yes. I knew him and I knew about him. He had quite a way with the ladies, if you get my drift," the woman answered. She looked to be my age or maybe a few years older. I had to wonder if she was another of his many conquests. She was a brunette though, like me, and Adam had seemed to focus on the blondes.

"I didn't know. What was he like?" Chloe asked. Chloe, like most hairdressers, tried to hold a conversation while she cut hair. Her part of the conversation was generally asking questions, and it occurred to me she probably was a fountain of information as a result.

"A charmer that man was. He could walk into the country club and every woman in the room noticed him. I remember when he came to Cold Creek. He was married to some other teacher, I think. He was like a bee pollinating though, and the flowers never seemed to care," she continued. The way she talked about it in the third person suggested that she, like me, was not one of his 'flowers'.

"I had no idea," Chloe answered.

"Oh, yes, he was quite the social one, and I understand he was also quite the cook. Apparently he at one time thought about being a chef," she added. "Many of my acquaintances raved about his cooking. Well, his cooking and other attributes." This was news to me. That might explain why no one seemed to be able to say who exactly he was seeing. He entertained in his home and he even cooked the meal.

"Did you go to the memorial?" Chloe asked next.

"Oh, no, a bunch of us who knew him went out and had our own memorial service. We shared a few stories. Honestly, I think some of them were pure fantasy. We had a few drinks in his honor. He was too much of a 'good times' guy to want anyone to mourn him. The only bad thing was he refused to share his recipes." She looked in the mirror and then added, "You did a good job, Chloe, thanks."

The woman got up from the chair, and giving Chloe a tip, went to pay her bill. I didn't recognize her, but then I didn't often find myself at the country club. I did find it mind boggling to imagine this group sharing stories, related to his dinners or whatever other attributes. It made me wonder if Adam was the only one putting notches on his bed post. I guessed if you don't work, you can get pretty bored. Or maybe the woman was right, and parts of the stories were embellished.

It was my turn, and Chloe asked the same questions of me. I acknowledged I worked with him, and she mentioned his avocation as a chef, almost baiting me. I told her honestly I hadn't known that. I turned the tables a bit, and asked her if she had heard anything interesting. After stating she certainly wasn't one to gossip, she repeated the comment about the rec center and some customers not wanting to go back or have their kids go back there. She also shared that there seemed to be a lot of talk about his being a ladies man, and not always in a positive light. Some of the customers seemed to think he was immoral and deserved to be killed.

Chloe said she heard talk from some students who had been, too. At least one had idolized the man and got all choked up when his name was mentioned. Other students talked about how nice he was, and how nice looking he was. She stopped and caught my eyes in the mirror and asked, "Was he that hot, Sheridan?"

I chuckled and commented, "I guess if you like the beach boy type." I asked if she had heard anything else.

As she finished my hair, she said other customers had talked about how it couldn't possibly be a murder. They said Chief Pfeiffe was making a mountain out of a mole hill. At least one customer commented on a nice looking State detective, and no one seemed to know why the State Police were involved. After she finished my hair, I tipped her, thanked her for the cut and information, and asked if she would tell me the name of the lady before me.

She shrugged and said something about hair dressers not exactly promising confidentiality. She said the woman was Julia Cramer. I tried not to hide my surprise though I was quite sure my mouth dropped to my feet. The wife of the President of Cold Creek College involved at least on the periphery with Adam? If that was the case, then in all likelihood it was one of those women who specifically called and asked for State Police involvement. Maybe it was even her.

Still in shock, I made my way to the other end of the salon to get my nails done. Seated in the last of the massage chairs, I tried to get my head around what I had just heard. I looked around to the others in the chairs and nodded and smiled to the one person I recognized from Cold Creek College. I couldn't remember her name. I remembered she was in Sociology though, and had to wonder if she had been involved with Adam. Of course, at this point, I found myself wondering about anyone who was female and breathing. And even more so if they happened to be blonde and breathing.

"You're in Psychology aren't you?" she asked. When I nodded, she continued, "I see you all the time, you and the red head that is. How are you all holding up?" The last part she asked quietly.

"I'm Sheridan, by the way. We are all pretty shook but holding up pretty well considering the circumstances. Aside from the interruptions of the investigation, we obviously are dealing with students and shifted course responsibilities," I answered trying to avoid any further discussion of Adam. At the very least, I didn't want to be the one to direct the conversation to Adam.

"I'm Yolanda. The State guy was hot, but he hasn't bothered any of us since Monday. Your group must be keeping him busy," she commented, possibly looking for information.

"Understandable, I guess, since we worked with Adam," I answered and shrugged my shoulders. Trying to be nonchalant, I asked, "So did you even know him?"

"Not me, not my type. But he apparently dated one of my colleagues. That was all that the detective asked about," she answered.

"Stressful situation for everyone I guess," was my noncommittal answer. The girl doing my nails, Lily, interrupted to ask me about color and I gave her the polish.

"Well, I think I'm dry and have errands to run. Hard to believe we start the rat race on Monday," Yolanda said as she left. I sighed in relief as I didn't want to answer questions about Adam, though I would happily take in information. After she left, a few of the other ladies getting their nails done commented on how sad it was, who they knew at Cold Creek, and how they hoped the killer would be identified soon.

Once my nails were done, I went back home. I called Kim and we agreed to go the matinee and see the chick flick people were raving about, and then go to dinner. The movie wasn't very crowded that early, but the movie might not have been a great choice. As is the case with most chick flicks, there was of course a romance. In this case the woman chose the gigolo over the accountant. In the end, the gigolo was just that, and the accountant rescues her. Unfortunately, the gigolo part hit a little too close for Kim.

We went to dinner and, trying to cheer her up, I likened the accountant to Wayne. Little did we know he would be at the Grill. It was awkward as usual with Wayne, but it did take Kim's mind off Adam. Wayne, of course, was all concerned. He worried the detective had overstepped his limits, given that I could be a possible suspect. Amazingly, he was trying to be protective, but it didn't quite come out that way. It came out as very possessive when he had no reins on me. Not to mention, he more than implied I was a possible suspect. What did that say about his opinion of me?

Kim and I had a few good laughs at Wayne's expense after he left. Zoe was our waitress again. After a teasing dig at Kim about steak sauce, she wanted to know who the good looking man was. She also made it real clear that if I wasn't interested, she sure was. Kim and I talked about Brett and where we might have dinner on Monday. She did her best to allay my concerns about a relationship with someone who lived about an hour or so away. That of course led to the continuing problem of not many choices other than Wayne for single men in Cold Creek.

We walked around Cold Creek center for a bit after dinner, and then we parted ways. I went home to take care of Charlie and get some sleep. On the way home, I thought again about the country club ladies and their private celebration of Adam's life. I still found it hard to believe he was involved with those women. On the other hand, I didn't know if their relationships with him were limited to recipes and dinners. It was going to be bad enough if Adam's inappropriate behavior with even one student got out. It would rock the community and the administration if his involvement with these wives was more than culinary.

I watched some television and the news. Chief Pfeiffe was still hoping to solve the case, but no details were being shared. Chief Pfeiffe was dreaming. There still had been no indication of a murder weapon or actual time of death or assault. I still didn't understand the reason for withholding information. I redrew my relationship map, this time with many more circles. I started to put in negatives on all the women I now knew Adam was involved with, but something about the way Mrs. Cramer portrayed their party made me wonder if those women considered it a negative relationship. After all, unlike Ali, Kim, or even Rachel, they were not interested in a long term commitment. This seemed like a diversion to them. Hmmm. I decided I was getting more and more confused and called it a night.

CHAPTER 9

I slept late Sunday morning, and Charlie was a bit impatient as a result. I decided to take her for a run at the park. Fall was definitely in the air and it felt good to be running. I realized with all of the hubbub the past week, I never did get any exercise. Even the walk in the arboretum with Brett was only a quarter-mile. I smiled to myself when I thought about our walk. Charlie and I were not the only ones taking advantage of the weather. There were some others running, jogging, or walking as well.

After about a mile, I spotted a bench and sat down. I also hydrated both of us. I was sitting there when a woman sat next to me. She had on sweats like me except hers were a designer brand. She had a bandana on her head so it took me a while to recognize her. In fact I didn't recognize her until she looked directly at me. She was the wife of the Chancellor, the only person who had been on the stage who responded emotionally at the memorial. I didn't remember ever seeing her at the park before.

Charlie sat and looked at her. That prompted a discussion of Shelties and Charlie in particular. When she looked at me, my gut tensed though I couldn't think why it would. I had an uncomfortable feeling about her and her sitting down with me. I wondered if she was another of the country club ladies. Either way, it had to be coincidence tat she had chosen to sit on the same bench as me. After all, my runs in the park tended to be when I could get them, not planned or regular.

After we talked about Charlie and the weather, I decided to heed my gut, and finish my run. With a "have a good day", Charlie and I jogged away. I didn't look back, but it felt like I was being watched, the hair on the back of neck standing up. I kept talking to Charlie and did not dally all the way to the house. Only when I got home, did I dare to look behind me. Then I felt silly. Of course there was no one there.

After a shower, I fixed myself something that resembled a combination of lunch and breakfast as it was now approaching noon. I went into the living room and finished the task I had started earlier in the week. It felt good to get more closure on the life I'd left behind four years ago. I boxed up all the rest of the stuff I didn't need or want and I put it all in the garage. In the process, I realized I did need a new chair or two if I ever was to have company and perhaps a new coffee table as well. That would mean a visit to furniture stores, and particularly Ikea.

Deciding furniture was not an immediate need, I moved on to the guest bedroom. The only times anyone had stayed in the guest bedroom was when my sister, Kayla, came to visit. The last time had been last December. I dusted the tops of the dresser and the night stands, and I checked to make sure I had changed the sheets after she left. I had.

The easy part done, I opened the door to the closet. The boxes I had never unpacked were still stacked there. When I moved in, still hurt from my failed marriage, I had only unpacked the boxes . contained 'my' stuff as opposed to 'our' stuff. There had been joint things I'd opted to keep. There was a part of me that realized that if I hadn't used the stuff in these boxes for four years, I probably could toss the boxes without opening them. The sentimental side of me, however, knew there were some things in these boxes, photographs in particular, I might want to keep.

I was resigned to my task. I knew I needed to clear this out before I started a new relationship. I pulled down the first box. I pawed through the figurines, a quilt Devon's mother had made us, and found some photo CDs. I put the quilt aside to get it cleaned. It was a star quilt in shades of blue and I'd always liked it. It would look nice in the living room or even on this bed. The figurines I put back in the box. The photo CDs I put aside to look at and then decide to keep or discard.

I went through the same process for the next two boxes, with one or two things I had picked out for the house salvaged. I trashed the rest. I now had two more boxes of stuff that needed a new home and three less boxes in the closet. After coming across my wedding album in the third box, I decided I had done enough for one day. I couldn't even decide what to do with the album to tell the truth. Lots of my friends and family were in those photos. I had fond memories of the wedding. I truly had fond memories of the marriage, right up to the time I caught him in bed with the intern. Our bed, no less.

I went and sat in my now clean and organized living room and contemplated for about the hundredth time what had gone wrong with my marriage. This was not a new exercise, and each time, I usually concluded we probably both were at fault. This time, with knowledge that the intern he married after our divorce had found herself in my shoes, I decided perhaps more of the fault was his. Thinking about my ex's wanderings, I realized I only knew about the intern. Maybe like Adam, he had diddled more than once in our 10 years of marriage.

Initially, I had assumed maybe it was because I hadn't been able to conceive. But he and the intern hadn't had children either. I also blamed myself for not being more adventurous in the bedroom, but I don't know if the intern was any more so. No, in hindsight, it was probably neither of those reasons. He was who he was. Just like Adam was who he was. I wondered if any of these women actually 'knew' Adam. I wondered if there was anything below the surface. Even Kim had never shared any insights about him.

Around 5, it was time to call my parents. I think my mother loved my ex more than I did. Our conversations usually turned to why couldn't I work things out. This time when she brought him up, I shared with her that he was getting divorced again. He planned to marry a still younger woman. She didn't have much to say after that. Mostly she talked about her aches and pains and my father's health issues. In their

60s, they were both retired and were pretty healthy. Somehow as they had aged, their health took on more importance even if it wasn't poor. We chatted for about 10 minutes, and predictably, when I asked about what she was doing with her time, my mother decided it was time to hang up. I smiled at the phone knowingly. My mother didn't go out much and didn't have a wide circle of friends. Her life was my father and it worried me that when he passed, she would be completely lost.

Charlie nudged my leg. I let her out and got her food out. I fixed myself a salad, and watched television for a while. Sunday was family phone call night, and the only way that worked was to call each other at the same time each week. Promptly at 7, Kaylie called. She shared the ups and downs of her job. She was in charge of public relations at a major conglomerate in New Jersey. Her job always sounded stressful, and usually the majority of our call was her venting, while I listened.

Eventually, she asked if anything was new at Cold Creek. I am sure she expected my usual negative response. This was the usual segue to her criticizing my choice of jobs and living in a small town. She often commented on how boring Cold Creek was, but she liked it fine when she needed to escape big business. I visualized her sitting upright in surprise when I told her one of my colleagues had been murdered in the rec center. She was all excited, and wanted all the details. I told her what I knew and she teased that she hoped the police appreciated my insights. That started another whole discussion.

Kaylie is about four years younger, and also divorced. In her case, her ex contended she was unfaithful in the worst way. She cared more about her job than him. He was probably right. Her marriage lasted less time than mine, but a frequent complaint of us both was the lack of decent men who weren't married or gay. She groaned when I shared with her the results of a study that indicated the likelihood of a woman in her 40s finding a soul mate was lower than the likelihood of the same woman being run over by a train. Not optimistic odds.

So I told her about Brett and our one dinner and plans for the second one. She wanted all the details. She wanted to know how tall was he, how old was he, and so on. Her questions made me realize I didn't know much about this man other than that he had a good job. By his report he had a stable work history. He was divorced without much hostility or blaming. He had a 12-year-old daughter. Oh, and I knew he was one good kisser, but I didn't share that part with Kaylie. A girl has to keep some things private.

I pointed out to her, and reminded myself, this might not go any further than a second dinner. As she pointed out, that would put me back with Wayne as the only option. In her own way, that was Kaylie telling me not to blow it. She asked what I was going to wear and suggested I try for something at least a little on the sexy side. I assured her I wasn't going to end up with Wayne, I was saving him for her. We ended the conversation teasing each other and laughing. Always a good way to end a conversation.

I headed to the kitchen for a snack, and found some Girl Scout cookies. I was pouring myself a glass of milk to go with them, and the phone rang.

"Hey Kim, how are you doing?" I asked noting the caller ID.

"Doing good Sheridan, but I am starting to panic about tomorrow. I realized I will be teaching two to three sections every day! And that means so many more students to deal with!" she said. After a slight pause but before I could respond, she asked, "Sorry to rant, Sheridan. How are you?"

I chuckled and offered, "I'm okay. I felt like I got as much done as I could before I left on Friday. I teach the same classes every day, and I never remember which class is which or what I said when. You need to do what you can, and hey, you can decide which section to give to the new guy!" She laughed and then asked how my sister and parents were. I relayed the highlights of both conversations, and asked how her mother was. Again telling her not to worry, I hung up.

As I got ready for bed, I realized I needed to figure out what I was going to wear for the first day, and for dinner. Kaylie's comments aside, I couldn't dress too sexy since I would likely be going from work to dinner. I went with a dress instead of the slacks and top I had been wearing all last week.

It wasn't quite a sundress, but more casual than dressy. It was not too low cut, but not exactly Victorian either. The dress was a medium blue and often when I wore it I was complimented on how it brought out the blue in my eyes. Being a brunette, the blue eyes were somewhat unusual. I had a light cardigan in case the AC in the building or restaurant was too high. Looking at my pedicure, I decided I would definitely go with sandals. Everything settled, I set the alarm and went to sleep.

CHAPTER 10

I fussed with my hair for what seemed like forever, and redid my makeup twice. Finally satisfied, I made it to campus at 7:45, and was ready to teach my 8:00 class. Most of the faculty avoided the early classes as much as the students. I liked to get it over with and this section would be small due to the early hour. For this section, I would have the more serious students or the ones who waited until the last minute to register. Both sections would be large, about 30- 40 students each, typical for an introductory course. I think every student took either intro or human sexuality their first year. It would take me most of the semester to learn the names of even half the students in the classes. Inevitably, if they didn't take another class with me in the spring, I would likely forget their names by the time they showed up in research design.

On the way to my classroom, I grabbed a coffee at Georg's as was my habit. Balancing all I now had to carry, I made it to the room without dropping anything. I arranged everything at the front of the classroom, got the computer and projector turned on, and pulled up my course online. I passed out the syllabus and the pre-test and looked for those eager faces Mandy had talked about. Okay, there were a few of the coeds who were dressed to the nines and looked eager, but my guess was it wasn't necessarily for my class.

Students continued to wander in and take seats. The last few to arrive ended up in the front row, a fitting natural consequence. An hour after I started, I was done. That was the way of Monday-Wednesday-Friday classes. I gathered everything up and went back to my office. Yes, it was only an hour, but my adrenalin rush about wiped me out. Dropping everything else on the desk, I took the roster and went to see Terra to find out about the students who weren't on it. She and Ali were both in Terra's office area talking. Not wanting to barge in, I hesitated before walking in.

"Hi Dr. Hendley. How was your first class?" Ali asked. Both she and Terra looked at me expectantly.

"Good, but about five students who were there weren't on the roster. Can you check on them please?" I asked and handed Terra the roster.

While she was looking up the names I'd written down, I asked, "Did either of you do anything exciting over the weekend?"

Both shook their head, and Ali asked, "What about you?"

"Kim and I went to the movies and saw the chick flick, but wouldn't recommend it. And dinner at the usual," I answered.

Terra's fingers had been flying and her printer beeped, and she handed me the printout. "Here you go. Four of them are showing up now. Not quite sure where the fifth came from. Sorry, he still isn't showing for this section," she explained. This was not unusual. He was probably on the roster for the Tuesday-Thursday section, but came to this one with his friends. I'd have to address that with him on Wednesday.

I thanked Terra and smiled at both of them. I realized they kept looking at each other. "Is there something I should know, ladies?"

"Yeah, well, Officer Hirsch is looking for you. He says you put him off on Friday, and now he thinks you are avoiding him," Ali offered with a smirk. "He was hanging around here for a while this morning."

"We explained you were teaching from 8-9 today, so don't be surprised if he is lying in wait for you at your office," Terra added with a sigh.

I returned the sigh, shrugged my shoulders and went back to my office. Our appointment had been for 9:30 so why he looked for me earlier was beyond me. Sure enough there was the officer, still looking like he was about 15 years old, standing at my door.

"Good morning, Officer. What can I do for you?" I asked, taking the offensive, and walking past him and into my office.

Somewhat nervously, he responded, "I need to ask you some questions about the incident with Dr. Millberg. May I come in?" I nodded, and he came in and sat down. I gathered from his statement 'incident' was being used as a euphemism for 'murder' and found it a bit amusing.

After a minute or so of silence, and no direction from him, I asked, "So what were those questions, Officer?"

"Where were you Sunday night and early Monday morning?" he asked. He took out a pen and a notebook from his shirt pocket ready to record my responses.

"I was home, alone, until I came here. I

was on campus about 7:45 AM on Monday. The ambulance and police were here when I arrived."

He looked a bit disappointed with my response, and asked, "Can anyone vouch for where you were?"

"No."

"How well did you know Dr. Millberg?" he asked next.

"He was a colleague. I did not socialize with the man." I figured I would state that outright. Hopefully it would shorten the number of questions, but no such luck.

"Um, were you romantically involved with Dr. Millberg?" he asked, his face showing increasing hues of red.

"No, I was not."

"Are you sure?" he asked, seemingly surprised at my answer. Maybe I was the only one who hadn't been involved with Adam so far.

"I think I would know if I was romantically or sexually involved with someone, don't you?" I responded, getting a little impatient. Unfortunately, that usually translated to a bit of sarcasm.

He stammered and answered, "Yes, ma'am, but I have to ask these questions. The Chief said so. One more question here. Do you know of anyone who would want to see Dr. Millberg dead?"

"No. And Officer Hirsch, it is the first day of class, and I have work to do here," I hinted not so subtly.

"Yes, ma'am. What about Ali Bough? Was she seeing Dr. Millberg recently?" he asked.

I wasn't sure where that came from, but answered, "Not since I've been here and that's four years."

"Is she seeing anyone that you know of?" he asked looking a bit more interested on a personal level. I suspected this was not one of the questions for the investigation.

Smiling, and noting he was putting his notebook and pen away, I said, "No, I don't believe she is."

"Thank you for your time," he answered with a sigh and left.

I was working on grading the pre-tests when Kim came in. She had already taught her first section of abnormal and was due to teach a section of diversity at 11. I didn't envy her at all. I at least had until after lunch before my section of research design.

She sighed, looked at me, and teased, "So is this the usual Sheridan dressing up for the first days or dressing for dinner, huh? Oh, my, you're blushing." She chuckled and I smiled, trying not to blush. She seemed to be holding up and that was a good thing. She sighed again and walked back to her office to get ready. She no sooner left and Rachel was at my door.

"Dr. Hendley, my father said you called last week," she said, almost making the statement a question.

"Yes, Rachel, I wanted to check in and see how you were holding up. You were pretty upset earlier in the week," I explained. "How are you holding up?"

"I'm okay, I guess. I've been trying to keep busy," she said, her tear-filled eyes belying her words. "Uh, Dr. Hendley, my parents don't know about you-know. They think I'm upset because I never knew anyone who died. You aren't going to tell them are you?"

"No, Rachel, I'm not. That's not what I do," I explained.

"Good." She hesitated and then asked if I knew who would be teaching the Learning and Memory class and the Physiological Psychology class. I told her. She thanked me and then she left. As I watched her go, I wondered who would be advising her. I also wondered how she would do with Max instead of Adam for the learning class, not to mention Doug for physio. Doug might actually expect her to have learned more about sensation and perception than she had described. I was still pondering the conversation when Brett came by.

"Morning, Sheridan. You look very nice this morning. I like the dress. It highlights your eyes," he said as he appraised me, smiling. He also looked a little less like work, with a light blue shirt with yellow pinstripes and navy dress pants.

"Thank you, and good morning to you," I answered, smiling back at him. "Did you have a good weekend?"

"More or less. It was mostly work, getting paperwork caught up, reports and such. And you?" he countered.

"It was good. I got stuff done around the house, got a run in, and went to a movie," I told him. "I also had a very interesting conversation at the hair salon," I added.

"Must have been interesting for sure. Your expression just went from friendly to confused. You have a very expressive face you know." Brett continued, "Is this a conversation I should be privy to?"

"Hmmm, probably," I answered. He looked at the door and I nodded. He sat down and I shared what Julia Cramer had said, or at least the part I remembered. Brett didn't look too surprised at the thought of these high society women involved with Adam, but he raised his eyebrows at the chef part. "Anyway, I figure it was one of those powerhouse women who decided the State police should be involved."

He put his hands up indicating he was not going to confirm or deny, and I continued, "I know you can't tell me, but that's my conclusion." He smiled. "And based on your expression, I guess you didn't know about the chef role or dinners at his place. I'm not the only one with an expressive face."

He smiled again and then more seriously noted, "That probably explains why waiters and waitresses aren't able to identify many of his partners. They didn't eat out."

Realizing Kim and Adam did eat out, I clarified, "Well, it wouldn't do to eat out with someone who was respected in the community and married, would it? And we are assuming there was more to the relationship than trying out recipes, you realize." I wondered if Adam not only was using Kim sexually, but also to keep people focused on his relationship with her so they wouldn't notice or look for other relationships. Unfortunately, the fact that she didn't get the chef's treatment could be seen as motive.

"Touché. But it may also be how he managed to have a relationship with at least one or more students, playing house at his house," he added. I nodded in agreement. I couldn't hardly imagine them having sex in his office, and it would be difficult for him to get a hotel room without somebody noticing. On the other hand, the fact that someone was affected by this death didn't necessarily mean Adam was having sex with them.

"So did you figure out anything you can share?" I asked. I hoped he had found something that would clear Ali and Kim both.

"Not much, I'm afraid. I do want to talk in general to students. Mostly to ask them to come forward if they have any information that could help in the investigation," he said.

"That could probably be arranged. I have some of the upperclassmen. Doug and Max do as well. I guess you will be looking to see their reactions, huh?" I asked.

He nodded, and shifting gears asked, "So did you think about where we should go for dinner? Preferably some place your dentist friend won't find us."

I smiled and suggested the Steak House or Perky's. Both are about the same distance. Deciding on the Steak House, we discussed what time and there was a knock at the door. Brett stood up, planted a kiss on my forehead, and with minimal hesitation opened the door saying, "Thank you Dr. Hendley. We appreciate your help with this investigation." It was a good thing he was once again formal since it was Max knocking, but his easy shift in demeanor did give me pause.

Max was beside himself about the unexpected class and complained about the students. I told him the detective wanted to speak to all the classes with psychology majors. Max went off on how that would definitely not help matters. He related how one student burst into tears halfway through the class and he told her to come to see me. I asked who it was, but of course, Max hadn't gotten her name. Granted, I often don't know all my students' names in the intro sections, but I have 30 or more students. He had 10-15 in his classes, and somehow he couldn't catch the name of one student so upset. I reminded myself that was probably a difference between researchers and practitioners.

Although ready for crisis, and students advised or sent to see me, few were seeking out services. I managed to get the pretests scored before my afternoon research design class. Mitch stopped by briefly to tell me about a student who stopped by his office. He said she was upset and although she didn't acknowledge a relationship, he was suspicious.

Unfortunately, because of confidentiality issues we had no way to determine if Rachel, the girl who sought out Mitch, and the girl in Max's class were the same girl, two girls, or even three girls. We also didn't know if the girl or girls were distressed in general or distressed because of some perceived or real relationship beyond that of student and faculty. Mitch and I discussed the possible backlash of allowing Brett to speak briefly with classes, but couldn't see any way to refuse. All we were able to offer was that we would be available if students needed to talk to anyone.

After grabbing a quick sandwich at Georg's, I was off to my next class. As with the morning class, there were a few stragglers, but these were seniors mostly, with some juniors. I recognized most of them, including Janet and Wesley. Altogether, 15 students, not exactly dismayed their books weren't in. I passed out and collected the pretests for this class, same as for the intro class.

Then I went over the syllabus, and told them, no books or not, they were to write up a possible study they would want to conduct. At the groans, I reminded them the library or online databases had lots of research studies. They needed to look up some, and use them as a guide, follow the script, and add in their own ideas. This was received with more groans. I also pointed out I had posted some sample formats on the online set up for the course.

I was explaining that one component of their grade would be to 'polish' their initial proposal as we covered the principles of research design, when I noticed Brett outside the door. I motioned to him to wait a minute. I finished describing how their grade would be determined, when the papers were due, and the nature of the exams. While I did that, several of them were looking at the door. I leaned back against the desk behind me and motioned Brett inside.

"Class, this is Detective McMann with the State Police. He asked if he could speak with you for a few minutes," I announced as he entered.

"Thank you, Dr. Hendley." He turned to the students after the greeting. "I know it may be difficult for you to talk about, but I am investigating the death of Dr. Millberg," he explained. I noticed a few of the students sat up straighter, one of the girls, Jodi, looked about to cry, and Janet and Wesley both nodded.

He continued, "Were any of you here on campus the Sunday before last? Or last Monday?"

Janet and Wesley raised their hands, and then a few others did the same. Only a few of them didn't raise their hands after a few minutes, including Jodi.

"Okay," he said, nodding, "Did any of you happen to be at the rec center last Sunday? Not yesterday, but the previous Sunday?"

One of the seniors, Jimmy, raised his hand a little tentatively. "I was there early Sunday though, and it was fairly empty at the pool. Only my girlfriend and I swimming laps, sir."

"Thank you," Brett answered. He looked around some more, but nobody else volunteered any information.

"Okay, next question, did any of you ever see or hear Dr. Millberg have an argument with anyone? Hear anyone threaten him?" His questions now focused on Adam, Jodi began crying and Janet moved over to comfort her. Courtney started to tear up as well, and I remembered she had been upset at the memorial. With Jodi's crying, everyone was becoming anxious. Brett was making notes, and probably coming up with a lot of questions as he watched them. I cleared my throat, and looked at him. I sure hoped he was through.

"Sorry, folks. If anyone thinks of anything that might be helpful to the investigation, please contact me. My email is bmcmann at vasp dot net." He turned and left. The class was silent and no one even moved for what seemed like a long time, likely about a minute.

"Okay, before you all leave, please remember that Dr. Pilsner and I are available if you need to talk about this situation. It is a very disturbing situation for us all. Hopefully, Detective McMann and the Cold Creek police will wrap this up very soon, and everything can get back to normal," I offered. The students filed out, still pretty quiet, and I finally exhaled.

Brett was waiting at my office and shook his head. "Sorry, Sheridan. I don't take pleasure in intimidating or upsetting your students." He sighed and as I entered my office, I motioned him inside and he closed the door.

Sighing again, he asked, "So what is the female student count up to now?" He shook his head and looked toward the window.

"Judging from their reactions, at least three are upset by this, but only one has actually reported any kind of sexual behavior," I answered. Sighing, I added, "No telling how many more may have been involved. Mitch had one student come see him too. To keep confidentiality, we aren't using names so…" I shrugged my shoulders to make my point.

"He may only have been inappropriate with one student, after all. Many of the female students get crushes on faculty, and he was definitely a prime candidate. Honestly, as much as I think of Adam as a scumbag, I would have trouble thinking he was simultaneously seeing multiple students, faculty, staff, and high society."

I had to get some perspective and yes, Adam could have been involved with any number of people over the past 10 or so years. He certainly had enough ex-wives, but it was unlikely that he was in that many relationships over the past three months. At least that was my conclusion, and I was not going to let my imagination get the better of my good sense. There were, after all, only so many hours in a day and he did manage to hold down a job.

Brett left with the promise to come by between 4 and 5 to go for dinner, and I went back over everything I needed for the seminar at 3 and for Tuesday's classes. The problem with Tuesday-Thursday sections was that the class time was longer to make up for only meeting twice instead of three times per week. Ultimately, I would have to cover what I covered today, plus half of what I would cover on Wednesday. I pushed the limit, and ran for my 3 o'clock class in the smallest classroom downstairs.

Rushing to not be late, I almost tripped over the seven students listed on the roster. They were all sitting on the floor outside the room. I looked through the window in the door, and Jack was still leading his seminar. I stood and waited patiently for about five minutes, and then asked Wesley to see if any of the other classrooms were open. It took about five minutes for Wesley to return, shaking his head. I looked in the window again, and it didn't look like Jack was in any hurry to wrap up. This tended to be a pattern with Jack.

Getting aggravated, but trying not to show it, I handed the students the syllabus so they could at least start reading. They finished reading, and I started a discussion of the topics we would be discussing. I explained that each of them would be expected to lead two of the discussions. That started some panic and conversation, and I noticed Jack turn his head toward the door. I made efforts to maintain the hallway conversation to give him a hint. As the students talked and volume increased, the door opened.

"I am teaching in here. Can you please keep your voices down!" Jack demanded.

"Afraid not, Dr. Halloway. You see, my class is scheduled in this room at 3:00 and it is now 3:30," I responded as politely as I could muster. This was not the first time Jack had done this. I continued, "I hope no one in your class had a 3:00 class."

Jack turned various shades of red, and stormed back into the classroom and promptly dismissed the class. His students filed out, and my students filed in, a bit flustered and not sure what emotion to be showing at our altercation. I could tell a few were suppressing smiles, and others looked surprised. As I walked in after the students, Jack grabbed his books, gave me a dirty look, and exited.

The room the seminar was in was a small room, with chairs arranged like a parlor. I wasn't sure, but I suspected it had been a parlor way back when. The seven students sat in the cushiony chairs and made themselves comfortable. I sat down as well. The idea of the seminar was that everyone took a turn at being the 'teacher' so there was no front of the room.

My job was to moderate and guide the discussions around contemporary topics in psychology with the seminal studies a backdrop. In the last 20 minutes I now had left, I randomly drew names and asked the person what topic they wanted. I continued this until all the names were gone and so were all the topics. Obviously the last name didn't get a choice. But it was random. I then tried to lay down a few rules. The first student, Janet, would have two weeks to get ready. Next week I was still on.

Class dismissed, I asked Janet to hang back, and asked her if Jodi was okay. She nodded and shrugged her shoulders. I also asked about Courtney and she indicated she thought Courtney's upset was because her brother had died this summer. The memorial had brought all that back. I reminded Janet that Mitch and I were available, as was the staff at the Student Counseling Center. She nodded and we walked out together. She turned toward the door and I went back to my office. Janet was pretty responsible. I was sure she would talk to Jodi and Courtney about getting some support. And at least there was some reason other than a relationship with Adam behind Courtney's upset.

First thing back in my office, Terra called and asked when she could schedule an appointment for me to meet with Jim. She said she had no idea what it was about, and I groaned. Whenever Jim wanted a meeting with me, it usually meant I was going to have something new to do. Groaning, I told her to schedule it between my Tuesday classes. That ended up being 11:30 to fit his schedule. I hung up, knowing I was not the only one shaking my head. Terra would be shaking hers, too. Hopefully, she would get a hint of what was up before then so I could try to head him off at the pass.

I put away the stuff from today, finished putting together the materials for both classes tomorrow, and checked my email. I had multiple listserv emails and emails from all levels of administration on the first day of classes. These I could delete easily. I had an email from my sister asking me what I knew about the murder and 'my detective' as of today. That one would wait. One from Wayne, asking how I was doing, quickly deleted.

One from my ex which I read. He wanted to know which month I would stop receiving spousal support. I advised him he stopped paying me support in June. It had been paid through an automated system, and apparently he didn't realize it ended. Money management was not his strength. I suspected the new ex was hitting him up for spousal support now. That thought made me smile. I also had lots of emails from book publishers, journal publishers, and various department stores. Sad to have junk mail on the internet. Deleted.

I must have been very engrossed, because I didn't realize Brett was standing there until he said, "Are you ready to take off or do you need more time?"

"I am very ready to go," I answered with a smile as I stood up and grabbed my bag.

"Okay, then let's go. My car is in the faculty lot where you park. Do you think they ticketed me?" he asked with a smile.

"Uh, is there any way they would know it was the car of a Statey?" I asked, teasing him.

"Well, it is my personal vehicle because otherwise it would be inappropriate for me to drive you to dinner, but I did leave a VERY large placard stating who it belonged to and why it was there, so I can hope. Of course, the College security could have decided a ticket was their way of making me feel welcome," he suggested with a smile and shrug as we walked down the stairs.

"How about if I follow you to your house, so your car isn't sitting here? Or would you be more comfortable leaving your car here?" he asked. I appreciated the reasoning behind both choices and hadn't thought about it.

"You might as well follow me. I live close to the highway leading to AltaVista. No point in driving back onto campus or leaving my car here," I answered. I wasn't sure it mattered, but at some level, it would seem more like a date if he drove me home instead of back to campus. Effectively, it would help keep the campus and work separate from our dinner. I don't know if he felt the same way, but he seemed to relax with my answer.

At the parking lot, he walked me to my car and I gave him basic directions and made sure he had my cell number and the street address in case we got separated in traffic. It was approaching the five o'clock hour and the campus was emptying out. He cheered when he got to his car with no ticket. Like me, he drove a

Honda, though his was a newer model.

Once at my house, I asked if he'd mind if I let Charlie out, and he indicated that was fine. I invited him in, and introduced him to Charlie. Charlie seemed to like him but wanted to get to the backyard or go for walk. She got the backyard. I fed her when she came in, and we were off to AltaVista.

AltaVista was about 25 miles from Cold Creek, and we made relatively good time despite increased traffic. On the way, Brett commented on the older neighborhood I lived in and the vast difference in the houses from one neighborhood to the next in Cold Creek. That led to a discussion of the old money and southern society component in Cold Creek as compared to the rest of us. I pointed out it had been the old money who initiated the boarding school. It also was that group or their descendants who made up the country club crowd. The same group made endowments that kept Cold Creek College able to maintain state-of-the-art educational services.

We covered the basics of how my day went including my short conversation with Officer Hirsch and my getting aggravated at Jack. I commented that if Hirsch's interview with me was any indication, the Chief was not exactly getting a wealth of information. Brett shook his head. I also mentioned my meeting with Jim the next morning. I shared my dread that he was going to give me something else to do. He teased me, pointing out that he was the last 'something else to do' Jim gave me. I smiled, feeling warm inside. Obviously, not everything Jim dumped on me turned out onerous.

The Steak House was just past the center of town. It was one of the few nicer restaurants, with ambience that could be professional or romantic. Not small, and not large, it had several sections, as well as a bar. Once we got there and parked, Brett walked around to get my door, and he put his arm around me as we walked in. Thankfully we were seated right away, and at a corner table for two away from most of the traffic, in one of the smaller, cozier sections. The hostess seated us and gave us menus, and the waitress came by with the wine list and lit the candle on the table. This time there was no doubt we were on a date.

"So, Sheridan, are you a wine drinker or would you prefer something else?" Brett asked. As with any first date, neither of us had a clue what the other preferred.

"Wine is good, but I have to tell you I'm not a big drinker, so unless you're going to drink a lot, we'd probably do better ordering by the glass," I responded. "Basically, I'm a one glass drinker."

He smiled, and suggested, "Do you have a preference?" Given that we were at a steak house, we discussed the cabernets and the merlots. Then we went on to discuss the various other wines on the list. I decided on a cab and he did as well. He studied the menu and asked what I recommended. I shared with him what my favorite was, and then told him what other dishes I had heard were good. The Steak House was obviously best known for its steaks, but they did a great job on the pork loin as well.

Salads and entrees ordered, Brett asked, "So do you eat here very often?"

I couldn't tell if he was making conversation or trying to figure out how often I dated and came here, but I answered as honestly as I could. "This is one of the restaurants of choice whenever there is someone here for an interview, or we have a guest speaker, or someone is celebrating some special occasion. Kim and I usually treat each other to dinner here on our birthdays. In all, I probably eat here about once a month or every other month. So, yeah, I eat here often, but not often enough to know the wait staff, like at the Grill."

He smiled and nodded. "Seems like a nice place and the reviews are good. I checked."

I laughed and commented, "Well, I hope it lives up to those reviews!"

Our salads arrived and gave us an excuse not to make conversation. When we both had finished, I asked, "So, you mentioned you had only been in Appomattox for about a month. I think I may have driven through when I moved here but I didn't pay much attention. Have you gotten settled in?"

"More or less. I have a small condo in a settled neighborhood that is pretty much all families. It isn't located in the historical section or anywhere near the various attractions that draw tourism to the area. It's in the more newly developed area and much quieter. The neighbors are pretty friendly, but seem to keep their distance." He laughed and then added, "I guess it's because I sometimes bring the State vehicle home, and they are afraid I somehow know about the stop sign they ran or the speed limit they exceeded." He smiled and shook his head.

"Well, maybe it will take some time. Eventually they'll figure out you're not psychic after all," I replied. "So where do you stay when you are down here in Cold Creek or wherever you end up going?"

"This trip, I'm staying at a hotel in North Shore. Last week, I stayed at the hotel in Cold Creek. It was a little small and, I don't know, too close. I think the manager kept track of my every move." He sighed and continued, "I wanted a little distance and the opportunity to check out North Shore this visit," he explained.

"So is this the norm for a Detective? Spending a lot of time in hotels?" I asked, wondering if that may have contributed to his divorce. He certainly seemed like an attentive person.

"Unfortunately, it happens. Most times, I could probably drive back and forth, but that gets tiring, and makes for long days. And with an otherwise empty condo to go home to, the hotel thing works for now. I'll stay over tonight, and unless something breaks and requires me to stay longer, I will head back to finish up some other cases. I'll come back down when I need to." Speaking a little softer, he added, "But it's only an hour from Appomattox to Cold Creek, so it's not a daunting distance."

I smiled, the warm feeling back again, and wasn't quite sure of a good response to his comment. I was saved by the arrival of our food. Conversation waned while we ate. As I finished eating, I sighed and smiled as I watched him finish his steak. He smiled and leaned back, watching me. Instead of making me nervous or self-conscious, it felt good. Despite the occasional first date awkwardness, he was easy to be with, comfortable.

I raised what little was left in my wine

glass and held it toward him. He raised his to mine and they clinked. "To great beginnings!" I offered. He smiled and took my other hand in his. We looked at each other, smiling.

Eventually, he asked, "So how will you spend the long weekend coming up?"

"I haven't given it any thought, actually. With the first week of school, I am going from day to day here. I may sleep the whole weekend, but hopefully I will get to at least go for a run in the park," I answered. "I remember you said you spend long weekends with Madison. This weekend one of those?"

He looked pleased I had remembered and answered, "Yup. I will head over to Richmond Friday afternoon, and then we'll head to Appomattox. It will be her first visit to my condo, and we'll spend part of the weekend getting stuff for her room. We'll find some other things to do, too. I'll try to get a history lesson in with all the historical homes and Courthouse Square. Madison likes the outdoors, so we'll take rides and go running. I'm sure she will discover other things she wants to do. She might like some of the quaint shops. And then on Monday, I'll drive her back to Richmond." He sighed as he finished, obviously wishing he could spend more time with her.

"Well, I bet she'll enjoy fixing up her

room. She's at the age where that is kind of important." I didn't want to think about what was going to happen when she got a few years older and weekends were for friends, not for dads.

"I hope so." He laughed and then added, "'Course I also hope she doesn't want something too trendy or out there that has to get redone in just a few months." Shaking his head, he continued, "Sometimes she has some crazy ideas. She mentioned wanting a 42" flat screen television so she could watch her favorite reality show and wanting to paint the room black. I already set some limits. I wonder if she is testing me to see how far she can push or if she thinks those are reasonable requests."

I laughed and told him I tended toward her pushing limits. We chatted a bit about teen age girls and kids in divorce situations. I was impressed as he seemed very grounded.

"It's still early. So, is there anything interesting here in AltaVista to do?" he asked when we'd finished dinner.

"Uh, not really, but it is a nice night if you feel like walking around. Some of the stores may still be open and some of them are interesting. They try for quaint in case there's any tourist traffic. There's a pretty good ice cream and frozen yogurt shop around here somewhere.

Maybe by the time we find it, it will look good," I suggested.

"Sounds good," he responded, squeezing my hand. He paid the check and we went for a walk. Brett's arm around me felt good, and as we walked we were in sync. We each pointed out different things on the storefronts and started getting silly.

At one point as we looked in a store window and tried to guess who would buy pots with flowers on them, or pots that glowed in the dark. We laughed at the odd combinations one could come up and Brett leaned over and kissed me lightly. Then he kissed me again, not as lightly. His eyes looked heavy when we parted.

We looked at each other for a few minutes, and then Brett turned me around and we walked back toward where we parked the car. At the car, as he opened my door, faced me and rubbing both my arms, he kissed me again. I put my arms around his neck, responding to his movement, and we moved a little closer. Then he stepped back, and finished opening the door. I was definitely feeling warm, and the outside temperature was dropping to the 60's so I knew it wasn't the weather.

He got in, started the car, and asked what kind of music I liked. I was trying to think of which groups to suggest, and he commented,

"Don't think so hard Sheridan, I see the steam." He chuckled and directed me to the CD case in the console. There were a number of them I had, and I picked a few and fed them into the CD player. He looked at me and smiled as my choice of a country singer who tended on the easy listening side registered. I smiled back.

Before long we were almost back at my house, and I started to panic. I wasn't sure if I should invite him in or not. Being honest with myself, I wasn't sure I could handle too many more of his kisses. I was still trying to decide what to do when we pulled in the driveway. He came around and walked me to the door. I started to ask if he wanted to come in, with a lot of trepidation. I hadn't gotten beyond the "Do you.." and he leaned over and kissed me again. Then, he put his finger on my lips, and said with what seemed like great effort and a thick voice, "I don't think that's a good idea. Let's not rush things."

I nodded, feeling both relieved and disappointed. I think I sighed and he chuckled. I smiled, and said, "Thanks for a great night. I enjoyed it." He nodded, kissed me one more time. He let go of my hand and he walked toward his car.

I unlocked the door, but watched him drive away before I went inside. I closed the door and leaned back against the door. Charlie looked up at me with her head cocked to one side. Letting her out, I noticed it was getting late and went for bed. As I got into bed and looked around the bedroom, it occurred to me I might need to be a little neater in the future. I was kind of glad I hadn't had to make a decision about inviting Brett in tonight.

CHAPTER 11

I slept well and was on campus early. I even had a few minutes to appreciate the fountains before I went in. I was certainly back in my office in plenty of time for my Tuesday morning class. Starting a little later, this section of intro was a little larger. I was re-checking to make sure I had everything and printing out the roster when Kim stopped by. She looked like she was bouncing back from Adam's death and the extra work load, but still a little haggard.

"Morning! How'd your day go yesterday?" I asked her, remembering her panic.

"Morning yourself. Wasn't as bad as I expected, but it was late by the time I went home. After I ate, I soaked in the tub for about an hour. I needed that," she answered. "How did your first day go with all three classes?"

"Oh, it was hectic for sure, and Jack was his usual self, extending his seminar half-way through mine," I answered. I didn't mention the evening or Brett on purpose.

"And last night was your dinner!!! I completely forgot! Did he like your dress? Did you have a good time?" She suddenly was full of energy and fired off questions.

Trying for some composure, I answered, "It was good. We ate dinner and walked around for a while."

"Do you realize you are blushing, Sher?" she teased with a smirk and we both started laughing. I didn't have an answer for her. Worse, each time she looked at me, I could tell I was blushing again.

Looking at her watch, she commented, "Time to rock and roll. I'll catch up with you later for more details!" I blushed again and she turned away, still laughing. I grabbed all my materials and went to class as well.

This section had 35 students. I looked at the roster I noted that the student who wasn't on the roster yesterday, was in fact on this one. That would have to get fixed if he was going to stay in the Monday-Wednesday-Friday section. Although later in the morning, students continued to straggle in as I passed out the syllabus and the pre-tests. I introduced myself and gave them the directions for the pre-test. A few more came in late, but eventually I got all the pre-tests back, and went through the syllabus.

I covered all the material I had covered yesterday, and then started what would be a series of activities that would run throughout the course. I showed a video clip of a robbery, and then asked them to write down what they thought they had seen. Following on the video still, I asked for a show of hands for who thought the victim was a blonde, the robber wearing blue, and so on through a number of details.

Then I showed the clip again, and they saw how far off they each had been, and how easily their memories had been swayed by my leading questions. We ended with a discussion of why some aspects of a scene are more salient to some than others. I'd start the other section with the same activity, but a different clip the next day.

Class over, I grabbed a cup of coffee and walked back to my office. I gulped some of the coffee, and headed to Jim's office. I was right on time, but his door was closed. Checking with Terra, she said he had gotten a phone call, and he'd told her to have me wait. She shrugged and said she still didn't have a clue. I looked over to Ali's desk, and she wasn't there.

Terra explained that she had a bookkeeper training meeting. We chatted a little bit, and I tried to find out if Joe had any new information and if Officer Hirsch was as brief with everyone as he had been with me. Other than with Ali, it seemed we all got the same few questions. I wondered if his extra time with Ali was less related to the case and more related to his interest in her. I was about to tell Terra to call me when Jim was ready and head back to my office, when his door opened.

"Come on in, Sheridan. Sorry to keep you waiting. This whole thing is just playing havoc with my schedule," he explained as I entered his office. He closed the door and took a seat on the other side of his conference table. He looked tired and more stressed than usual. I nodded, but didn't say anything. This was his show.

"So, how are you holding up? A lot of students coming to see you and Mitch?" he asked. He had a pad of paper in front of him, and was fiddling with it. I couldn't tell if this was why he asked for the meeting – to get an update – or if he was just stalling. I was betting on the stalling part.

"I'm doing okay. As for students, some of the juniors and seniors are a little upset, but that is understandable," I answered. I didn't want to get into Adam's inappropriate behavior, since it was no longer an issue with him dead.

"Sheridan, there are some rumors floating around, and we need to talk about them," he said, not quite making eye contact.

Not being prone to volunteer information, I simply responded "Okay" and waited for him to continue.

"Max apparently told some people Adam was involved – inappropriately involved – with students. Is that correct?" he asked, still avoiding eye contact.

"It does appear he was involved with at least one female student, yes. She believed their relationship was serious." I hesitated, and added, "It isn't possible to know if there were others. It's not exactly good form to ask the students en masse."

"Sheridan, people are upset that this may have happened. I am not going to confirm it did happen. Students have had crushes on him and on Jack for years. I've even reviewed the sexual harassment policy with both of them before. But, with all the talk and his murder, I am being asked to explain how this could possibly have happened in my department on my watch," he said, his voice getting a little louder.

There wasn't much I could say, so I just waited for the other shoe to drop. It certainly sounded like he had some sense this was going on not only with Adam, but also with Jack. I would have to pay more attention to my colleagues. Issues with Jack over classroom space I was familiar with, not inappropriate behavior.

"I am getting pressure from above to do something to make sure this type of faculty student relationship doesn't happen in the future, just in case it ever did happen, you understand," he continued. I nodded, but still didn't say anything. I still couldn't tell where he was going or what the 'something' was about to be dumped on me.

"So, Sheridan, why didn't anyone report this? Are any of the other faculty being inappropriate? The college could be sued you know," he ranted. I shrugged and didn't have any answers for him.

"I'm sure you appreciate my position. This whole thing is making me look bad. So, I am making you the sexual harassment officer for the department. Your first task will be to identify some training program – or create one – for the faculty and for the students," he said, and then sat back as if he had done his job and no longer had responsibility for the problem.

"Sir, I understand your position. I am not an 'officer' and have no desire to be designated as such. All of us should be aware of the potential harm and issues surrounding sexual harassment, or any other form of harassment. I will be glad to identify some programs and to oversee the dissemination of the information. And I do agree it might be appropriate for one faculty member to be identified as a 'mediator' for students if they have a problem with a faculty member." I spoke very slowly and very carefully. I could tell he was listening by the rising color in his face.

"Sheridan, I need someone – I need you – to take control of this. If you would rather be called a mediator, so be it. Give me a plan for training. The plan will be to implement it once things calm down. After they figure out who killed the idiot!" With that, he got up from the table and moved to his desk. I was obviously dismissed, but as I got up to leave, he added, "I told the Chancellor I was putting you on this, so don't be surprised if he calls you."

I was dismissed. And dismayed. And a bit angry. I was angry at Max for shooting off his mouth, and then at Jim for saddling this on me, instead of taking responsibility to begin with. Not to mention at the male faculty who couldn't seem to keep it in their pants. And the last thing I wanted to do was hear from the Chancellor. I shook my head at Terra but did not answer her raised brows. I was still befuddled, about to blow, and definitely not quite grounded when I ran into Brett outside my office.

"You okay? Lunch?" he asked, his smile fading as he caught my expression.

"No, I don't think I'm okay. Lunch would

be good. I'm hungry," I answered in clipped speech, trying to maintain control. Part of me wanted to scream and the other part wanted to cry.

"Okay. I have an idea. How about if we grab sandwiches and go eat at the arboretum, and you can tell me what has you all out of sorts, and your face all scrunched up," he suggested gently.

I nodded, and we went and got our sandwiches. As we walked toward the arboretum, Brett commented on the fountains. I didn't say another word. We found the same bench we had sat on last week. I was working on getting myself under control. Eating my sandwich, I regained at least some of my manners, and offered, "I'm sorry. I never asked how you were."

He put his hand on my shoulder, and smiled. "Not a problem, I am going to make a wild guess I had a better morning than you did."

That seemed to be my opening, and I related my conversation with Jim. I also related my frustration and anger at Jim's unwillingness to deal with this himself or with any other conflict. I vented for a few minutes and then sighed.

"Okay, I feel a little better now," I said with a smile.

Brett gave me a squeeze, and then said, "Okay, can you explain what the jobs are of all these officials – the Chancellor, the President, the Provost, and the Board of Trustees? Seems like a lot of "chiefs" for a small private college." I wasn't sure if he was interested for some reason, just curious, or trying to redirect my focus.

I sighed, and then explained, "In most cases a Chancellor would be the financial CEO for several campuses, say for a university system. We're only one campus, but we have a Chancellor and he is still the financial CEO who answers to the Board of Trustees, which in turn provides the financial backing for the college. Basically, he is appointed by the trustees to keep an eye on the monies they invest. Keep in mind that because we are private, we are not funded by tax dollars." I paused and he nodded.

I continued, "The President answers to the Chancellor, but retains some of the financial decision-making and is also involved in fund raising, public relations, and such. He may have pet projects that are not under the purview of the Chancellor if he brings in the money for them. If there weren't trustees, he would be the CEO. The Provost is the easiest one. He is in charge of the academic side of the college and has nothing to do with finance."

"So, Sheridan, why would the Chancellor

and not the President want to talk to you about sexual harassment? Seems like it would be a public relations issue or a legal issue, not a financial issue," Brett suggested.

"I don't know. Unless somehow the trustees got wind of the issues with Adam and students, and they are putting pressure on the Chancellor," I countered. "The Chancellor is more or less their eyes and ears on the campus. And the pressure is getting passed right on down to me."

"Which one would deal with complaints of sexual harassment, aside from a murder?" he asked.

"Hmmm.   actually would be the Dean of Faculties in most institutions. Our Dean of Faculties is also the Provost, so I would think it would be the Provost's office, not the Chancellor. I just hope I don't hear from any of them. I certainly don't want to hear from all of them!" I answered.

"One more question. How often does a faculty member interact professionally with any of these administrators other than your Dean or Department, now?" he asked. His questions were making me uncomfortable. Well, actually it was my answer.

"We sit on the stage with them at graduation. We get policy updates once in a while. A meeting with one of them? Not unless you are in deep trouble, like you are being fired. And even then I suspect they still have a Dean or Head deal with a single faculty member," I answered and sighed.

"Well, don't go borrowing trouble, and think positive. You haven't heard from anyone yet other than Jim. You are not in any trouble, so if you do, maybe it is to commend you and Mitch for your efforts?" he offered and then sighed. He pulled me close and that helped. A lot. "I had a good time last night, you know, so I am not letting anything bad happen to you," he added softly.

"I had a good time too," I answered. I leaned in and kissed him. I had intended it to be 'just a kiss', but he had other ideas. The kiss certainly put me in a better mood.

As we walked back to the building, he told me he had a meeting with the Chief Pfeiffe, and then he was going to stop by the Rec center. He said he would check back before he before he left for home. I went back to my office and before I had a chance to even think about checking my email, Mitch came in and shut the door.

"So, I heard through the grapevine Jim dumped sexual harassment issues on you. Sorry," he said shaking his head. In response to my puzzled expression, he explained, "Max was telling Jack and me about all the students he thinks Adam was messing around with. He said he was the only one to have the balls to let Jim know about it. Jim assured him he was going to put you to work on it right away. Thankfully, this was in the men's room and not the hallway." Mitch sighed and rolled his eyes.

"Trust Max to blow everything out of proportion. But, it's true. I am supposed to identify or create training materials for students and for faculty, and provide Jim with a plan of action. But I shouldn't plan on doing anything until this whole thing has gone away," I explained with a shrug.

"That's crap and he knows it. The policy is in the faculty handbook. This isn't exactly the first time a faculty member has been involved with a student. Not even the first time for this faculty member if the truth be known. Hell, in a few other cases over the years, the faculty member married the student," was his response, along with more head shakes. He leaned back and asked, "So what are you going to do?"

"I haven't figured it out yet. For now I will at least look and see if there is some modular training online he can require everyone to do. You know like the other useless ones on safety, security, and not using college vehicles or property for personal use," I answered with a smirk. "The ones we all page through and then take the quiz to find out the answers and then take it again."

He chuckled and asked, "So how was your dinner last night?"

I hadn't told him about dinner, so I was a bit surprised at the question. I also could feel my face getting hot. I hesitated a nanosecond, and countered with, "Who was there and saw us? I know it wasn't Wayne this time."

"No, it was Katie. She was almost as paranoid as Max this morning with thinking you were in bed with the enemy," he answered. At my expression, he added, chuckling again, "Not literally, figuratively."

I sighed, realizing once again, the downside to a small town. "Yeah, well, Max seems to be the one talking to everyone and anyone. Jim basically told me to expect a call from the Chancellor on the sexual harassment stuff." Seeing Mitch's facial expression made me add, "I guess that doesn't make any more sense to you than it did to me."

"That is odd. To say the least." He shook his head. "So have you heard from him?"

"Not by phone, for sure. But I haven't checked my email since I spoke with Jim," I answered. Mitch looked from me to the computer, and taking the hint, I brought up my email and scanned the list. There was one email from a name I didn't recognize. An email from a Janice Wickson with a college email tag. I clicked on it and sighed in dismay, moving to the side so Mitch could read it.

'Dr. Hendley, Chancellor Oakland asked me to contact you to arrange for a meeting with him. Can you be available at 10:30 on Wednesday? His office is on the third floor of the Administration building. Please advise if there is a conflict. Thank you. Janice Wickson, Administrative Assistant'

That made it official. I had been summoned, with no apparent reason for the meeting. Mitch looked at me and shrugged. We spent some time discussing whether I should have someone go with me. In the long run, we decided that unless it looked like I was about to be fired, I probably should go to the meeting, and just not offer any information. We also discussed if it would be a good idea to suggest his Admin Assistant sit in to take notes.

We decided that might be tacky. Mitch shook his head and then he left. I stared at the screen, and took the message to mean I didn't need to respond unless I couldn't make the appointment. The Chancellor, or Janice most likely, had access to my teaching schedule.

With the new section of research design, I

went through the same back up plan since the books weren't in yet. I went through the syllabi, passed out and collected pretests, and was caught up with the Monday class. Because of the longer class, I pulled up some of the articles in the online format, and walked them through the various sections of a research paper.

Finished, I went back to my office. I worked on scoring the pretests and sighed in relief that it looked like entry knowledge for both sections was the same. Notably, for intro, they seemed to know what the average person would know about psychology from the media. A lot of half-truths and not much fact. The upper-class students seemed to have some basic knowledge of research design and at least most had taken a statistics class.

In between her classes, Kim came in to vent. She seemed like she was getting a better handle on the temporary overload. When I told her about my meeting with Jim and my summons from the Chancellor's office, she was sympathetic. I worked on getting everything ready for both classes on Wednesday, and got started on Thursday. At least today, there was no seminar.

A little before 4, Brett came by. "It's almost 4 and you're not ready to go yet. What's happening?" he teased.

I sighed, and answered, "Oh, I am ready, just haven't closed down the computer yet. Come on in, if you have a few minutes."

He did and as he shut the door, I asked, "Did I ever tell you I ran into the Chancellor's wife when I went running with Charlie on Sunday?"

"No, you didn't mention it. Tell me about it," he asked, looking a little concerned.

"It was probably just coincidence, but I took Charlie for a run in the park. We usually run about a mile and stop at the benches near the playground and people watch. Then we run the mile back to the car. On Sunday, when I sat down on a bench, this woman came and sat down as well. I recognized her from the memorial. She was the one crying a bit." I paused and Brett nodded and motioned with his hand for me to continue.

"I didn't say anything to her at all until she asked what kind of dog Charlie was. We exchanged a few words about Charlie. Something seemed off, and so I cut our rest stop short and we left. It may just have been a coincidence..." I added.

"But something didn't hit you right or you wouldn't be mentioning it now. Can you identify anything? Had you ever seen her at the park before? Is there any way she would have known you ran in the park? Or you would rest right about there?" he asked.

"I am a creature of habit and always stop at the same place and turn around. But no, I don't think there's any way she would know or know that I would be at the park at all. And no, I don't ever remember seeing her at the park. I might not have placed who she was before, but someone in a designer jogging suit would stand out. I think her clothes were what seemed out of place. Most of us in the park either are in sweats, shorts, or jeans and a t-shirt." I answered him as best I could.

"Sheridan, is there anyone who knows your routine there? Or when you go?" he asked more directly.

I shook my head and answered, "Maybe. Maybe if Kim was looking for me, stopped at the house, and noticed that Charlie wasn't there. Then maybe it would occur to her to head over to the park. She went with us a couple times last spring when the rec center was closed for renovations. But, I don't go every weekend on the same day, or even every weekend, or at the same time. That's why I decided it was a coincidence."

"And you're bringing it up now because?" he asked, his brows knitting and set of his chin firm.

"Because I got this email from the Chancellor's Admin Assistant to meet with him tomorrow morning, and I'm not real big on coincidences?" I offered with a shrug.

Brett shrugged back, and suggested, "It doesn't seem likely his wife followed you to the park or even knew you would be there. It is certainly possible that without Millberg's murder none of this would have come out, or only the sexual harassment issues would have surfaced."

He paused and looking at my dismayed expression, he added, "For the record, I don't believe in coincidence either, and I think you have good sense. If your gut says something is funky, it probably is. Maybe it will come together after the meeting with him, maybe not. Do me a favor, though, Sheridan? No more running unless Kim or someone else is with you? There is still a killer out there." He ran his fingers through his hair, looking tired all of a sudden.

I nodded and he stood, pulling me up and into his arms. He held me and kissed me. Then he just held me for a few minutes.

"If you're ready to go, I'll walk you out," he said as he looked down into my eyes.

I nodded, turned off the computer, and grabbed my bag. We walked out of the office, and about ran into Kim. She seemed all flustered, but smiled, winked and said she'd call me later. As we walked to the parking lot, Brett asked, "So just how small a town is this anyway?"

I laughed, guessing he'd seen Kim's wink, and answered, "Very small. In fact, Katie apparently also had dinner at the Steak House last night. I didn't see her, did you?"

He laughed, and commented, "I didn't see anyone but you." He paused while he gave my shoulder a squeeze, and added, "I gather she saw us, though?" I nodded and smiled. I decided not to share the rest of her concerns.

At my car, he said he would call me the next night to see how my meeting went, and he figured he would be back on Thursday. He suggested maybe we could catch dinner then, and I nodded. He kissed me, and then prompted me to lock my doors.

I stopped at the grocery store on my home and got a pre-cooked chicken and salad makings for dinner. I realized I was much more vigilant of my surroundings and told myself to relax. I was halfway home before it dawned on me that Brett's suggestion I go running with Kim suggested she was no longer a suspect. At least she wasn't in his book. Yippee! Once home, I took care of Charlie, ate my dinner, and turned on the television. Later on, on a whim, I went into my office. I hadn't ever put away the papers or articles from teaching summer school, and it was a mess. That wasn't my focus though.

I turned on the computer and googled Kenneth Oakland. I didn't remember when he had become Chancellor or his background and figured it might be helpful to be in the know before I met with him. I pulled up the articles on when he was vetted for the position and was hired. He had been the CEO for Primrose Manufacturing, a company that produced garden and landscaping products. He was probably about my age, had a Master's degree in Business Administration, and had been hired as Chancellor shortly before I came to Cold Creek.

The major reason for his support was his business acumen and his prior experience as President of a small agricultural college in Indiana. The newspaper articles talked about how he was able to increase the financial backing of the college and improve their rankings as an agricultural college. He had cited the reason for his move as needing a new challenge, one that Cold Creek could provide. It sounded like political double speak.

I stared at the screen thinking it made sense for someone who specialized in gardening and landscaping to head up an Ag college. I wasn't sure that our horticulture program, though well known, was in the same league. I wondered if its current rising status was a reflection of his influence.

I googled some more and from what I could tell, he had apparently continued on with Primrose while being the President of the other college. So, in effect, he had semi-retired when he came here. He might still be connected to Primrose, but certainly wasn't still functioning as CEO from Virginia. I tried to find some more information, but nothing new came up.

Charlie had been lying at my feet, but she suddenly started to growl. Now, Charlie is not the greatest watch dog, so this was not usual. I got up and walked toward the living room, and she started barking. My living room is next to the kitchen, so I walked into the kitchen.

The lights were out, and I looked out the kitchen window to see if I could see anyone. Charlie was still barking at the front door, but I couldn't see anything, and, of course, hadn't turned the outside light on. I checked the back door. It was locked and deadbolted.

I decided there was nothing else to do, but to go turn on the outside light. Charlie was lying in front of the door growling. That about creeped me out. Avoiding any of the windows in the living room, I got to the switch and flipped it. I also checked to make sure the front door was locked and deadbolted. Then I sat on the floor and held Charlie. After a few minutes, she stopped barking and growling and lay down next to me. I sat there until the phone rang.

"Hi, Kim," I said as I answered my cell. I moved back into the kitchen as I answered and Charlie followed me.

"Hi, Sheridan. You okay? You sound funny," she said.

"Charlie just got spooked and that kind of spooked me. No big deal. Some animal must have been in the yard is all," I answered. Still in the dark, I looked out the window toward the now lit front porch, but couldn't see anything. Most of the drive was also lit up, and my car was still there.

"Charlie spooked? That is odd. Did you see what it was?" she asked.

"Nope, but she's settled down now. So it must be gone, whatever it was. How'd the rest of your day go?" I asked, trying for a change of subject.

"It went well. I feel better now I have at least had all the classes once," she answered. She continued, "I came by this afternoon for a couple of reasons. First, I heard Max made a big stink and now Jim has dumped responsibility for sexual harassment on your lap. That's crappy. If there's anything I can do to help, let me know."

"Yup, Max opened his mouth and now I

get to do more work. Funny, he never seemed concerned before, but now he is going to save the students and the College in one fell swoop," I answered in disgust. I wasn't sure I wanted to get into the real reasons behind the sudden interest with Kim given her relationship with Adam.

"Yeah, well, there have always been stories about Adam and students. I wouldn't doubt he stepped over the line, but I doubt it was as often as Max makes it out to be," she said with some resignation. Obviously, this was not news to her.

"Agreed. I think Max has blown it way out of proportion. And to make it worse, he apparently managed to get the message to upper administration. Now I get to meet with the Chancellor tomorrow," I added with a sigh.

"What? That is crazy Sher!" she replied.

I agreed, and asked, "So what was the second reason?" I suspected it was about Brett, but figured I'd let her lead into it.

"I just wanted to let you know Katie was at the Steak House last night. She saw you and the detective. She came to tell me because we were friends. She thought you might be telling him all sorts of things about me. Right. When I said I doubted it, Sher, she actually told me she was pretty sure you were a lesbian. So in her mind, what other reason would there be for you to be dining with him. Can you believe that?" she said, now quite excited and speaking quickly.

"What?!" was all I could say.

"I asked her what gave her that idea, and she basically said that for you not to be taken in by Adam, you had to be a lesbian. I set her straight, and told her, no, you were just smarter than the rest of us," she continued. Kim chuckled.

"That is just plain craziness," I responded. Even though I'm a psychologist the explanations people come up with to explain the behaviors of others still surprise me.

Kim and I talked for a few more minutes, and we made plans to have dinner on Wednesday. I told her I would probably need therapy after the Chancellor and any run-ins I had with Katie or Max. I went back to the computer and did a cursory search for training modules on sexual harassment and bookmarked them. That way if the Chancellor asked me what I had gotten done since talking to Jim, I could say I had at least identified some possible modules.

Past my earlier paranoia, Charlie and I watched the news in the living room. Before heading for bed, I let her out the back with some apprehension, but no problems. I checked the door several times, and shut off the light out of habit. Then I decided to leave it on.

I re-checked the front door and left that light on as well. Thankfully, neither light shone into my bedroom.

CHAPTER 12

The next morning went downhill fast when I went to leave for work and had four flat tires. I called for a tow, the police, and Kim in rapid succession. The police arrived first. They introduced themselves and shook their head. The two of them determined all four tires had been slashed, and wrote up the report. Officer Joseph shrugged and said it was probably some kids. Officer Ramiro nodded and just shook his head some more. I told them I thought someone or something had been out in the yard or drive last night. He agreed it was probably the person or persons who did this. His partner nodded again. I asked if they had any other reports in the neighborhood. If it was done by kids and my car was random, there would have been other reports. They said no other reports. They didn't seem concerned, but I certainly was.

As they were getting back in their car, Kim pulled up. Behind her was the tow truck. I signed for the car, the tow, and four new tires, and Kim and I were on our way. With luck, we'd get to Cold Creek in time for my 8 o'clock class. I told Kim what the police said about kids, and she asked me the same question I asked the police about other complaints. I could tell from her expression she wasn't too sure she bought their explanation any more than I did.

She no sooner had the car in park and I ran to my office, grabbed a coffee, and then ran to my class. I went through the video clip activity and then the discussion. Then I asked questions about the first chapter they were supposed to have read. It was the opening chapter and the authors of the text did a pretty good job of linking psychology with everyday occurrences, including eye witness testimony and advertising. Before I knew it the hour was up, and I definitely needed another cup of coffee.

When I got back to my office, there was a note on my door that John's Tire Service had called. I quickly called them back and approved the tires they recommended and provided my credit card information. I turned on my computer and checked email. Unfortunately, the first thing I saw was a reminder. My calendar showed the appointment with the Chancellor and I groaned. I drank my coffee, read my email, and got everything set for research design in the afternoon. Before I knew it, it was time to head over to the Administration building.

It was a nice enough day, not too hot and not too cold. The fountains were flowing and gave a picturesque quality to the quad. The arboretum and its quiet and calm called to me, but would probably have to wait until afternoon. I made my way across the walk and into the administration building. Right inside was the rotunda. Like many old buildings, the rotunda had a high domed ceiling with winding stairs on either side.

There were several bronzed busts of men I assumed had something to do with the history of Cold Creek, the founding fathers, or the trustees. There were also some portraits. I recognized the picture of the Chancellor, and assumed the others on the wall were prior Chancellors. With a sigh and filled with dread, I took the closest set of stairs and on the first landing, ran into Misty.

"Hi, how are you? What brings you over here?" she asked.

"Oh, got a summons from Chancellor Oakland," I said, trying to sound like this was a common place occurrence. Unfortunately, her face indicated this was definitely not usual. She raised her eyebrows and her smile disappeared pretty quickly.

"Uh, that's ... umm. His office is on the third floor. Take a left at the top of the stairs," she faltered as she tried for a response.

"Thanks, Misty," I said, still trying for nonchalance, and I trudged up the stairs. When the stairs curved, I could see her still standing there and looking in my direction. Her reaction did nothing for my sense of well-being. I took a deep breath and turned to the left. Up ahead were glass double doors, and a lavish reception area. It occurred to me the leather sofas in this reception area were probably much more expensive and comfortable than the sofa in my living room.

Entering through the doors, I addressed the woman sitting at the desk, "Hi, I'm Sheridan Hendley. I believe the Chancellor is expecting me."

"Yes, Dr. Hendley. Please be seated," she answered without so much as looking at me. She continued to focus on her computer screen, though she didn't appear to be typing. She definitely was not going to get the Miss Congeniality award. She was older, probably in her 60s, and judging from her expression, she enjoyed sucking lots of lemons.

I took a seat and waited. I imagined this was probably a ploy on the Chancellor's part to assert his position of power. I likened it to the stories of police leaving suspects in a room for a while twiddling their thumbs to increase their anxiety. About 10 minutes later, the woman stood, and said, "Dr. Hendley, please follow me." I hadn't heard a phone or even the chime from a text, but I followed. We went to the door, she knocked and opened the door, then signaled for me to enter. She then asked the Chancellor if he needed anything, and he asked her to bring us each a cold bottle of water. I guessed I looked thirsty. She left.

"Dr. Hendley, welcome. I'm Kenneth Oakland. Please have a seat." He indicated the seat in front of his desk, and I sat. He was a large man and reminded me of a football linebacker. He wore his public relations smile. His mouth was curved upward, but the emotion didn't quite reach his eyes or the rest of his face. He was nice looking, but in a rough sort of way. He still had his suit jacket on which ensured a formal presentation.

I am not a short person, nor am I a very tall person. At about 5 foot 9, I can generally sit comfortably in a chair without having to fold my legs under the chair. The chair I sat in was lower than usual and a bit uncomfortably so. I also noted the Chancellor sat higher than me. It occurred to me his furniture was intended to be a show of power.

"Nice to meet you, sir," I said. I tried to keep my facial expression neutral. As I surmised what the chair situation was, I smirked.

"So I see from your personnel file you have been here at Cold Creek for four years now. Looks like you received a teaching award your second year. And you're involved with a fair number of service activities." He paused while the woman from the reception handed us each a bottle of water. "That will be all, Janice. Thank you, and hold my calls, please," were his directions to her.

I opened my bottle and took a sip, just to do something. He did likewise, before continuing, "It's not in the file here, but I understand you often are the go-to person for Jim Grant." It was a statement but sounded like a question. I shrugged, not sure how to respond.

He continued, "I spoke with Jim about the investigation of Dr. Millberg's murder, and some rumors that have come to our attention. Did he mention this to you yet?"

"Yes, he did, sir," I replied. Now we were getting to the meat of this, the sexual harassment. Or was he looking for dirt on Jim, I wondered. That had been a pretty pointed statement about his passing off things to me.

"Good. I'm glad to hear that. I understand he also assigned you to … I have it here… Detective McMann of the State Police. Is that correct?"

"Yes, sir, that is correct," I answered struggling to keep my face as blank as possible. This was something I had learned to do at the treatment center. I hadn't needed to do it for a few years. The last thing I needed to do was to start blushing here.

"Did he ever tell you how the State police became involved in local matter?" he asked. "I've just been curious," he added and shrugged.

"No, sir. I asked him, as I was curious as well. He declined to answer," I said.

"Oh, okay. Has he indicated who he suspects or discussed the case with you at all?" he asked, leaning forward a bit in his chair. With him sitting a bit above me, his leaning forward seemed almost threatening instead of just interested.

"No, sir, he hasn't. He asked who people were, and I took him around to the departmental faculty members and staff. I have tried to be helpful in putting him in contact with the people he needed to talk to. That is what Jim asked me to do," I answered.

"So, no pillow talk about the case, huh?" he asked looking like the cat who ate the canary. I wasn't sure if I became flushed from embarrassment or anger, but I suspect that was the reaction he was looking for. He appeared quite satisfied.

"There has been no 'pillow talk', SIR, and I resent the implication," I just about spit out.

"Oh, hit a nerve did I? I heard the two of you were an 'item'. I was hoping he had confided in you. Guess I have to look further," he sneered. He cased me over, and then added, "Maybe you're right, no pillow talk. I'll have to check with some of the other female faculty." He smiled and waited for a reaction.

"I guess you do, sir," I answered and shrugged. He looked a bit deflated, and just stared at me. I stared right back and he broke eye contact first. I sensed another murder at Cold Creek in the future. I was going to kill Max or the Chancellor. And if I didn't I suspected Brett would.

"That's all Dr. Hendley. Please tell Grant to keep me posted on the sexual harassment issue," he said, and turned his chair so his back was to me.

I got up, placed my water bottle on his desk and left. I didn't say a word to Janice, I just walked out. I about ran down the stairs and the stress of it all hit me. I could feel my eyes tearing up and stumbled on a step. I saw a ladies room and decided to duck in there to get myself together. I was getting cold water on my face when Misty walked in.

"Are you alright?" she asked, sounding genuinely concerned. I wondered if she had kept an eye out for my retreat.

"Yeah, I'm okay," I answered, not sure I was particularly convincing. Taking a deep breath, I asked her, "What do you think of the Chancellor?"

"For real? I think he's scary. He's on a big power trip and everything is a control issue. I don't know what you did to get in his sights, but I'd be real careful if I were you." She looked outright serious and patted my arm. It made me wonder about his character and just how far up sexual harassment went. Or at least just plain harassment.

"Thanks, Misty. I'll keep that in mind. In the meantime, I have to go teach a class," I smiled, gave her a quick hug, and left. I walked back to the building and reminded myself to stand up straight and walk purposefully so as not to look as vulnerable as I truly felt.

I stopped at Georg's and got another coffee and then went to my office. I made it a point to give a pleasant 'hello' and smile to everyone I saw. It was particularly hard to maintain a friendly demeanor when I tried to pass Max, murderous thoughts on my mind.

"Sheridan, this schedule is making me crazy! I can't get my research done!" was Max's rant.

"Max, I am sure you will get it done, and I don't want to take up any of your time talking. Besides, I have to teach in just a bit," I said as I continued on my way. His mouth dropped at my brush off, but there was no way I could hold a civil conversation with him right then. I had about an hour, but I was going to need that to regroup.

I thought about stopping by Mitch's office to see if he was in, but I couldn't quite wrap my head around the meeting enough to discuss it with anyone. I was pretty sure it wasn't the sexual harassment issue. That had been a ruse. I wondered if the pressure on Jim had also been a ruse. From what Mitch said, inappropriate student-faculty involvement had happened before. Back in the day, it had been fairly common and that was actually the impetus to sexual harassment policies. The one comment about Jim had been pretty pointed, but it seemed like a set up. He put out the bait, but I didn't bite.

The more I thought about it, the conversation got more intense when it came to the investigation. It seemed to me that if he wanted to pressure someone for information, he should be talking to Chief Pfeiffe not me. Now Chief Pfeiffe hadn't impressed me as being particularly on top of things, and if the meager information Hirsch was collecting was all he had, well, that wouldn't be much.

But the demeaning digs about 'pillow talk' and the implication Brett probably was having that 'pillow talk' with someone else if not me were just as insidious and blatantly sexist as Adam's womanizing. If this was all about concern for Cold Creek and the trustees, they needed to get a more tactful person in the Chancellor's office. I wondered to whom I could complain. Then realized that would likely mean I'd need to find another job.

Before heading to class, I checked with the bookstore by phone about the text for the research design class, and the manager confirmed they had arrived. Coffee finished, I chalked my interaction with the Chancellor up to a domineering and overbearing personality, and vowed to avoid him at all costs or have someone there as a witness. I walked to class with a sense of purpose and tried to think positive thoughts. They weren't too thrilled when the first thing I did was collect homework. I was definitely short a few. They also weren't too thrilled when I told them the text was in.

I asked them what they thought the purpose of research was. Having established that the purpose was to answer a question, we discussed how the questions came about. The rest of the class was spent on this last part, and they were given the assignment to come up with some questions for the next class. I sat in the classroom for a few minutes after they left. Then I went and got a sandwich since I hadn't eaten yet. I hoped eating would help to restore my energy.

Back in my office, I ate my sandwich while I checked email, and looked over what I needed for the Thursday classes. Having figured that out, I put together the stuff for Friday, and started working on Monday. It was a never ending process, and I needed to get a few days ahead. My only interruption was the tire place to tell me my car was ready. I assured them I would be there before they closed.

Around 5, Kim came by and we drove over to the Grill. She talked about her classes. She already had a sense the section that should have been Adam's was going to be the most difficult. She commented that it was mostly female students, while her other two sections were more evenly males and females. I joked with her it was her being female that was the difference. We both suspected Adam had been the draw for the coeds who signed up for his section. Maybe they would be happy with Flatts, once he arrived. Once at the Grill, Zoe seated us, and took our orders.

"So, Sheridan, tell me about the other night? How did it go?" Kim wanted to know.

I felt the heat rising to my face, and knew Kim noticed it by her chuckle. I smiled and answered, "It was great. We're going out again tomorrow night I think. By then the gossips will have us married for sure."

Kim looked at me half amused, half questioning, and I continued, "Katie may have made remarks about 'sleeping with the enemy', but the Chancellor actually asked about 'pillow talk'!" I then related my appointment with the Chancellor and his intimidation tactics.

"Sher, that is awful. He should be more professional. I don't know much about him, but someone in his position… That's just not right." She continued, "Do you know much about him or what brought him to Cold Creek?"

I shared with her what I had learned on the internet, and then added, "But I don't know if he has been involved in the horticulture program. That certainly would be his area of expertise. Do you know anyone over there, Kim?"

"Not really. One of the profs over there

asked me out, but it was right after the fallout with Adam and I had sworn off dating. I don't even know if he is still there. I could check though," she added.

"I just hope that if and when I get this sexual harassment training up and running, the first complaints aren't against our Chancellor." I shook my head, and continued, "Misty certainly was scared of him. I wouldn't want to run into him in dark alley." I shook my head again.

"So, anything new on Max?" Kim asked, I think just to change the subject. We often got a laugh out of his antics.

"Nope, not that I know of. I considered killing him, but decided he wasn't worth the trouble. I have to say Priscilla is being more abrasive and terse than usual. Either that or it's just I've seen more of her in the past week than usual," was my response.

"She's always pretty abrasive, and generally communicates in her own way how the rest of us are incompetent or at least not as knowledgeable as she is." Sighing, Kim continued, "Max at least does it in a way – his frenzied need to get to a better university to do his great research – that's a little less personal or judgmental. Just today, one of the students asked me why Priscilla told him to go talk to Jack about doing a thesis on abnormal psychology and what makes it 'abnormal'. The student wanted to know why she didn't send him to me since I'm the one teaching the class." She shrugged. At some level the politics of the academy were often frustrating.

I chuckled and offered, "At least the student was smart enough to figure it out. Speaking of students, did you offer to pick up any of Adam's students?"

"No. Don't get me wrong. Unlike Max, I am more than happy to take on a few students. When I looked at the list though, none of them jumped out at me. I'll just let Jim assign me some and do my best to help them finish," she explained.

"That's my attitude as well," I said. "So how are you feeling about the investigation? Are you still concerned you're a suspect?" I asked. She hadn't mentioned anything since her meeting with the Chief.

"I go up and down. Worried Chief Pfeiffe'll arrest me one minute, pretty sure the he has given up on me the other. I do have an attorney, Martin Cohn, but I actually haven't met him. I talked to him on the phone and explained the situation. He said to call if the Chief pulls me in again and told me to send him a check of $10 as retainer. Knowing I have someone to call at least makes me feel a little better."

"How'd you find him? Did your divorce attorney recommend him?" I asked.

"Yeah, seems she was his divorce attorney as well and knows him from some professional group lawyers belong to. Guess they have conferences and meetings just like psychologists," she added with a smile.

As we finished eating, we talked about our plans or non-plans for the upcoming long weekend. There was to be a carnival of sorts in town, and we made plans to check it out. I looked at my watch and prompted Kim that we needed to go get my car. I picked up the check and we drove to the tire place. For just under $400 I was on my way home to Charlie.

Arriving home, I parked as close to the front door as I could. I wished I had a garage I could pull into, instead of one that was used for storing stuff I didn't know what else to do with. I had left all the lights on and tried to be sure to park so my car would be somewhat in the lighted area. I hoped the lighting would dissuade whoever had vandalized the car, kids or not.

Charlie and I took a quick walk along the street, staying under the street lights and not venturing too far. Then we settled down for the night. I still thought about the tires and felt like a victim. I couldn't imagine what I had done to have brought this on. I wondered if it had anything to do with Adam's murder.

I decided to approach this whole thing like a research study. I put down three headings on a piece of paper – what did I know, what questions did I have, and what were my hypotheses. I then filled in under the 'what I did know' all the facts I had. Adam was murdered, blunt force trauma, weapon of force not identified, time of death sometime between Sunday night and Monday morning.

Under the questions, I started with the State police involvement, the Chancellor's agenda, and who of the various people he had been involved with Adam had pissed off the most. My major hypothesis was that it was either a woman he scorned, or the father or husband of a woman he was involved with. Still too many to even test my theory. On the plus side though, it looked like Ali and Kim were in the clear. I sighed and the phone rang. Remembering Brett was going to call, I smiled as I reached for the phone.

I answered, somewhat disappointed as I looked at caller ID, "Hello Kevin. What's up?" My brother usually only calls on holidays and birthdays, so his call was unusual. Like Kaylie, he was involved in business and always at meetings. I was surprised his relationships lasted as long as they did. I personally thought his girlfriend was a saint for putting up with him.

"Kaylie called and said there was a murder at your college. Are you ok?" he asked, sounding genuinely concerned as only big brothers can.

"Yeah, I'm fine. It just made the beginning of the semester even more disruptive than usual is all. Adds to the excitement a bit," I replied. I didn't elaborate anymore and hoped the conversation would shift.

"Uh huh, so what's this I hear about there may be a new man in your life?" he teased.

"Ahhh, Kaylie spilled the beans huh? Well, it isn't anything yet. I mean we had dinner twice. Don't go renting your tux yet," I teased back. "Speaking of which, how is Meredith?"

He laughed and answered, "Probably a bit impatient with me right now. She wants to set a date, and I just don't see the rush." He and Meredith had been living together for about four years, so I had to agree with her. But he didn't seem to be in any hurry to tie this knot. I was surprised Meredith had hung on this long. My phone buzzed, and I told him I had another call. We disconnected quickly so I could answer Brett's call.

"Hi, Brett. How did your day go?" I asked, smiling.

"Hi, Sheridan. It went well. It's sometimes hard to believe just how much paperwork is involved, but my paperwork is done and I had several meetings. How about you?" he asked.

"Well, not one of my better days, I have to say," I answered. I then related the issues with my slashed tires and all that entailed. He asked the same question about whether tires of neighbors had been slashed Kim and I had asked. He also insisted I check both doors and make sure all the windows were locked while I had him on the phone.

"Brett, is there any reason I would be in danger? I don't know anything more than anyone else living in this town about Adam's murder!" I asked, concerned at his obvious concern.

"I don't think so, but better safe than sorry. For sure, if Charlie starts growling again, do not hesitate to call 9-1-1. Better to be safe. Hopefully, we will have this all settled by the weekend, but not all the pieces have come into place yet," he added. That definitely piqued my interest.

"Like what?" I asked innocently or at least I tried to sound innocent.

He chuckled and ignored my question. He then asked, "How about the rest of the day?" Well, that led to my telling him about my meeting with Oakland. I explained to him the point of the meeting had little to do with sexual harassment and more about trying to find out about the investigation.

"See? That's one of the reasons I can't share some of this information. Better to be able to honestly say you don't know. Especially with that expressive, and quite appealing, face of yours," he said.

"Yeah, well for the record, I didn't like him at all. He was rude, crude, and intimidating, and not a gentleman!" I said, and then was a little sorry I had said it.

After a second, Brett prompted, "Uh, just what did he do or say to warrant that description?" His voice was a little more serious.

"Um, he just was demanding. He tried to intimidate me by having my file there. He even has his chair at a different height than the chair on the other side of his desk so he is effectively looking down on you. Oh, and he implied I would know what was going on because of what he heard about our relationship." To try to move on from that one, I added, "Misty says he scares her too. And I think it's more than his size."

"Let's back up to before Misty. What exactly did he say about 'us'? I can tell that frosted you from the change in your tone of voice, Sher. It isn't only your face that is expressive," he said.

"He just made a snide remark about 'pillow talk' is all. No big deal," I answered. And in all seriousness, it was just one comment. I wasn't exactly going to share his implication that Brett must be having said 'pillow talk' with someone else if not me.

"You're right. That is crude and rude. Even if it were true, it would be none of his business. I'm sorry I put you in that position, Sheridan." He sounded both angry and apologetic.

"Hey, no need to apologize. If anyone needs to apologize it's Max for shooting off his mouth and possibly Katie for shooting off hers about our having dinner," I answered.

"Well, I am sorry you had a bad day, and I wish I could have been there," he said softly.

"Just talking to you has improved my day," I answered equally as softly.

We talked for a few more minutes, and then hung up. He was going to be back in Cold Creek, hopefully by late morning for another meeting with Chief Pfeiffe. At least it looked like they might be working together finally and he had hinted they almost had all the pieces of the puzzle. I went back to my research questions, and underlined the statement about the Chancellor. I wished I had a better feel for who he was and his motives, not only in relation to Adam's murder investigation, but in coming to Cold Creek. Adam's murder aside, I didn't like the man and didn't want any further contact with him. No answers in sight, I let Charlie out somewhat nervously. After I checked all the locks, I went to sleep.

CHAPTER 13

I approached my car with trepidation after yesterday's fiasco, but my car was intact. Breathing a sigh of relief, I drove to campus. I stopped at Georg's to grab my usual coffee, I ran into Wesley, and cornered him for a few minutes to get his take on how students were doing. I also again put out the word for students to come see Mitch or me if they needed to talk. He hedged a bit and indicated he wished he had never said anything to Dr. Bentler. I knew exactly how he felt.

Reminding myself I never had talked to Mitch yesterday, I walked in the direction of his office, but he wasn't there. Mitch liked to have all his classes in the afternoon, and often didn't come in until mid-morning as a result. I stopped in the main office on my way to my office. Both Terra and Ali were there. Jim was among the missing.

"Hi, Terra, Ali. How is everything going?" I asked.

"It would be so much better if the police would make an arrest or something. No offense, Terra, but between the press and the police, it is hard to get work done," Ali offered.

I suspected it wasn't just the work that was the problem. Jim certainly had been out of sorts the last couple of times I interacted with him, and Ali and Terra had to deal with him more often than I did. Officer Hirsch was still hung around, probably making people nervous. Then there was Joe who likely lurked around and hoped to pick up some bit of news.

Terra sighed before answering. "I know what you mean. By way of warning, Joe is coming back today. He was told to get a follow-up, human interest story on how students and faculty are dealing in the aftermath. I already warned him some people may not be willing to talk to him."

"That is probably a good bet. Is Officer Hirsch through with everyone, do you know? I didn't find him to be particularly thorough or effective, but that would be one less person to dodge." I was beginning to think the additional questioning was not particularly fruitful, but for some, like Ali and Kim, was more like rubbing salt into a wound.

Terra looked at Ali and chuckled, and Ali blushed. I looked from one to the other, and then

Terra finally explained, "Officer Hirsch was very thorough with Ali here. He even asked her out!" Ahh, so that explained his frequent visits and his questions about her dating status.

With that, I looked at Ali. She shrugged and commented, "I know, I know, he looks like he's 12. I tried to tell him I was too old for him. He got all upset and insisted he was only 'a year or 2 younger' and that age shouldn't matter."

I chuckled and asked, "Uh, did you ask to his driver's license? I don't mean you're old, but he sure looks young."

"No, and pay no attention to Terra, I declined his invitation. I told him I was flattered and thanked him for the invitation," Ali explained. She was still smiling, and even if she wasn't interested in Hirsch, she had been flattered by his interest.

Times like these, it was good to be able to kid around and break the stress with a little laughter. They bantered back and forth, and then I asked, "So where's Jim? He said anything about the investigation?"

They looked at each other, exchanged looks and rolled their eyes. Finally, Terra answered, "I think this has put him over the top. He gets more phone calls from the Chancellor, President Cramer, the Provost, Dean, and, yeah, the press, including Joe. If he wasn't bald before, he sure is now. I won't be surprised if he announces his retirement this year, retirement package or not. He seems to think someone's going to have to take the fall here, not just for the murder, but for tarnishing the reputation of the College. I think he's afraid the trustees may set it up to be him."

"Yeah, he is pretty stressed out. When he comes in, he just goes in his office and closes the door. We can hear his voice raised once in a while, and sometimes he comes out and barks for something, but that's it," Ali added with a shrug.

We chatted for a while about who the most likely faculty member would be to replace Jim if he did retire. Mitch had already held the job and there had been some issues with his not following rules. He tended to see rules and policies as suggestions. If the rule or policy didn't make sense, and most don't, he'd ignored it. That only left Doug or Jack as the most senior faculty. Neither seemed likely to volunteer, but then they might be appointed. If Jim retired, it would be one more change to deal with. I made my excuses to get back to work, a bit discouraged.

"Oh, and you're probably going to win another job – he mentioned as he was leaving yesterday somebody was going to have to pack up Adam's office. I'm betting you'll get an email, if you haven't already," Terra said with a sigh. "One of these days Dr. Hendley, you're going to have to start saying no."

I groaned, ignored her advice, and went to my office. I figured I better check my email before class. No telling what else Jim had decided I was the best person to do. Initially, being told I was the 'best person' had been flattering. The flattery had worn off some time ago. Sure enough, I had an email from Jim, and also another one from Janice Wickson. I decided to just jump in and read the one from her first. It might make the one from Jim seem less objectionable. It was rather direct, but puzzling:

'Dr. Hendley, Chancellor Oakland asked me to remind you that you should keep him posted on any new developments re the investigation of Dr. Millberg's demise. He will be expecting updates daily beginning today via my email. Thank you.'

That seemed a bit strange. First, there was no reason I would have any updates, and second, we certainly hadn't discussed this in our strained conversation. I half wondered if it was Oakland who wanted the updates or Janice. I decided this was likely one task I could ignore to some extent, but added a reminder to send her an email before I left each day that simply said 'nothing to report'. That way, if it was from

Oakland, he couldn't get me on insubordination. I was thinking I might need a lawyer. Maybe it was me, and not Jim they were targeting as the fall guy, or in this case, gal.

I sighed and then opened Jim's email. Sure enough, he directed me to box up and clean out Adam's office. He indicated Ali would help me with inventory. She would be the one to determine what should remain in the office for its new resident, Todd Flatts. I sighed again, and figured I could work on Adam's office between my classes, and possibly enlist Mitch to help.

Visions of 'gentleman' magazines flashed through my mind. On the other hand, I assumed the police had already been through his office and removed anything that might incriminate someone in his death. In the meantime, I had to go teach Intro. I forwarded Jim's message to Mitch and asked him to meet me at Adam's office at 11:30. I also forwarded it to Ali, with the same message plus a request she bring boxes with her.

Class went well until the end. As we were discussing some of the studies on eye witness testimony, someone in the class raised their hand and asked if that was why the police were questioning so many students about Adam's death. I realized that with energies focused first on Adam's students, and then on the psychology majors, I hadn't given much thought to the general student population. Certainly, not beyond passing on our availability to provide support to the RAs at the dorms.

"That's correct. If you think back to Tuesday and the clip we watched, and on the differences in what each of you paid attention to and recalled, police collect information from multiple people and then focus on the similarities in the information they obtained. They also interview multiple people to see if they can catch someone in an obvious mistruth or to get some information that may turn into a lead." I paused, and then asked the class in general, "So what are your impressions or thoughts on the investigation?"

I didn't expect any of them to answer, but the one who asked the question, Jeff, offered, "I found it interesting to see the local police here, the State police here, and the press, all talking to many of our teachers. Does that mean you are all suspects?"

"That's a good question, Jeff. Whenever there is a crime against another individual, I think it is standard practice to talk to all the people the victim socialized with or worked with. So, initially at least, probably everyone who knew Dr. Millberg, including all of us, probably were potential suspects," I explained, purposefully emphasizing the 'potential'. I continued, "At this point, I would imagine the police have eliminated most if not all of us from the initial list. Obviously, they haven't arrested anyone as yet."

Another hand shot up, this time from a freshman whose name I didn't remember. She commented, "I know television shows aren't real, but they always indicate the longer before an arrest the less likely it is they will catch the guy. How accurate is that?"

"I'm afraid I don't know the answer. Television and movies have to tie everything up quickly. I am not sure that is always the case in real life. Even lab results, which are very quick on all the crime related shows, would take much longer," I answered.

"Anyone else?" I asked. No one else raised their hands, so I put in a plug about the availability of faculty for counseling if anyone was distressed. I also added the suggestions to try to travel in pairs or groups. I thought about bringing up sexual harassment, but I changed my mind. I wasn't ready to go there, and I wasn't sure it was a problem. I decided to put in a plug about psychology's involvement in the criminal justice system and forensic psychology instead. It occurred to me perhaps I should try to find a clip on forensic psychology for this class.

"Sometimes psychologists get involved in terms of helping the police by picking up on nonverbal cues. This is often the case in high profile cases with jury selection. Sometimes they are involved in determining the competency of an individual to stand trial, or in evaluating whether there are mitigating circumstances that should be considered in the sentencing phase.

There is an entire subspecialty in psychology called forensic psychology that is focused on the application of psychology to various aspects of the legal system." No one had any questions, though some nodded and looked interested. I dismissed class and was walking back to my office when I collided with Joe on the stairs. My sheaf of papers fell to the floor.

"Hi, Sheridan. I hoped to run into you, but not quite literally," he joked. He had a look of anticipation and determination on his face.

"Sorry, Joe. How's it going? Anything new on the murder?" I asked as he helped me collect all my papers.

"Nope. Nothing. Nada. It is very frustrating. This is the most exciting thing that has ever happened in Cold Creek. I could possibly get a great story out of it, but it seems to have stalled," he answered, obviously dismayed.

"Afraid I can't help much," I said, fully intending to escape without further comment.

"Come on, Sheridan. Can't you tell me anything? How are the students reacting? I covered the memorial a week ago, and some of them seemed pretty upset," he prompted.

I smiled, and said, "Of course students are upset. Faculty members are upset, too. So are administrators. A violent death of someone you know is upsetting. Mitch and I have been available to students. Last week some students came by, but that seems to be tapering off. With the structure of classes, a sense of normalcy is probably helping to alleviate some of the distress." It dawned on me Jim still hadn't told us the advising assignments for Adam's students and I hadn't run into Rachel in a few days.

I must have looked perplexed because Joe asked, "What? Tell me!"

I responded with a laugh, "Sorry, Joe, I just remembered Adam's advisees hadn't been reassigned yet. Nothing to get excited about, honest." Still chuckling, I walked up the stairs and back to my office. I put everything down on the nearest chair. Then I went to the main office to find Ali and attack Adam's office. I saw Max talking to Priscilla in the distance and hoped he didn't come to 'help'. They seemed very involved in discussion and I figured that was a good thing.

I helped Ali carry some of the boxes paper comes in, and she unlocked the door. She had a clipboard and a listing of specific items to remain in the office. When we walked into the office, we looked at each other and gasped. The office was a disaster area. It looked like someone had taken books off the bookcases randomly and thrown them on the floor.

There was trash on the floor, as well as part of what had likely been on or in the desk. It was a mess. A whirlwind or tornado would have created less of a mess than what we found. I wondered if the police had made this mess or someone else. Some of the papers looked to be torn and I couldn't quite see the police destroying papers.

Ali spoke first, her eyes wide. "I'll go get the trash bin from the custodial closet. It looks like we'll need it."

I just stood there and stared, and then pulled out my phone and called Terra's number. "Terra, can you check with Chief Pfeiffe and make sure they are through in here before we start. It looks like someone trashed Adam's office. I don't want to touch anything until we're sure the police are through here," I explained.

She said she would. I hung up and then I used the camera on my phone to take pictures. First of a global view, then the floor at the doorway, the desk from the doorway, the bookcases and piles of books on the floor, the torn papers, and the overturned chair.

Ali came back with the bin. I let her know that we weren't touching anything until the Chief said it was okay. We discussed the possibility that this may be the mess they made searching, but it looked pretty random and almost personal. As we waited to hear from Terra, I scanned the room. Obviously Ali was doing the same thing.

"Eeeeuuuu…" came out of her mouth. She pointed to the floor about 2 feet from us, to a box of condoms. I grimaced and realized that condoms in Adam's office definitely didn't need to be public knowledge. I sure hoped that Joe was long gone. Too bad Mitch hadn't come to help.

Terra came down the hall and looked into the office. Her eyes registered shock. She related, "Officer Hirsch will be here in a minute. The Chief didn't seem to think there was any problem cleaning this out since they know the body wasn't moved. It isn't a crime scene, he said. But he wanted Officer Hirsch to be here to oversee just in case you found something." She turned around and left.

"Dr. Hendley, I think I'm going to go get us some gloves out of the closet. Be right back," Ali commented, looking pretty disgusted. I couldn't blame her. I decided to take a few more pictures, being sure to get the box of condoms while we waited. At least they weren't used.

In short order, Officer Hirsch arrived and Ali came back with gloves. The way he looked at Ali had 'puppy love' written all over his face. I had trouble suppressing a giggle. He was not bad looking at all, just didn't look old enough to shave. That might have to do with his being blonde, but he truly had a baby face. It again occurred to me he would look older if he had a moustache, that is, assuming he could grow one. Ali just rolled her eyes at me, but Officer Hirsch didn't seem to notice.

I suggested we start where we were and work our way in. Most of what was on the floor was going straight into the trash bin, and until we cleared it, the trash bin wouldn't fit in the office. Besides, I wanted to get the box of condoms off the radar in case anyone else stopped by to watch. I hoped Terra didn't encourage Joe to stop by to see the mess.

Gloves on, I picked up papers. As I determined they weren't important or student work, I tossed them. As I got closer to the box of condoms, I signaled Hirsch and he reluctantly left Ali's side. I gave him a questioning look, pointed to the box. He blushed and told me to hold up and not touch it. He asked us if there were any small trash bags, and Ali nodded. She went to get him one. She also got him gloves. He was disgusted and embarrassed as he picked up the box. He opened it, and found it about half empty. He shook his head and put it in the bag. Better him than me.

We went back to work and in short order had most of the floor near the door cleaned up. We found a few photos and they went into the bag Officer Hirsch was holding, just in case. I recognized one as Katie, and one looked familiar, but was obviously of a much younger girl. She looked to be about 18 or 20, but wasn't a student I remembered. I also noticed the style of dress wasn't current. Although fashion was a bit retro these days, plaid and denim hadn't made a comeback recently.

Maybe it was a picture of a sister, if he had one, when she was younger, like 20 years ago. Most of the papers were pages from journal articles that had been scattered and just went into the trash bin. There were also remnants of lunches, almost as disgusting as the box of condoms. Finding the leftover food reminded me I needed to grab lunch before my next class.

Ali and I agreed to meet back there at 3 to see if we could make more progress. Needless to say, Officer Hirsch said he would be there as well. We left the trash bin inside with our gloves on the desk and Ali locked up. Hirsch left with his goody bag and said he was taking the stuff to the station. From there, the Chief would decide if anything else needed to be done with the contents.

I went back to my office, but made a point to swing past Mitch's door on my way. There was a note on his door saying he was out sick, and I made a mental note to call and check on him later. He was not one to call in sick. I checked my office, but no notes or messages. I went to Georg's to get a sandwich though I was getting pretty tired of Georg's fare already. I made a mental note to bring my lunch in the future, at least a couple of days a week. Back in my office I ate while I checked my email. Nothing of interest, I set about making sure I had everything ready for research design, and finished eating.

By the time I had to go teach, I still hadn't seen Brett and wasn't sure if he was back in Cold Creek yet. In class, most of the students in this section had completed the assignment, and I managed to get a few to share their research ideas. At this point, these were ideas or interests, and some were a little less realistic than others. Ultimately, it didn't matter as the ideas would be honed and shaped, sometimes completely altered, by the end of the semester. For many students, just coming up with an idea and writing it down was the hardest part.

I again pulled up some of the articles I had uploaded and we discussed different aspects, including the level of detail needed. For those who were having difficulty with the first step of idea generation, I intentionally pointed out that each article had a few sentences at the end talking about what additional research was needed. Using a mock completed assignment, I had them work in groups on how they could improve it.   Then, with each group providing input, I modeled making the changes to the initial version. Class over, I gathered my papers and realized I would be spending part of my long weekend reading and grading their assignments. Although tedious and sometimes boring, the grading would provide some normal structure to the weekend after the stress of the last week or so.

I went back to my office. Brett was waiting for me, cup of coffee in hand. He looked serious, but his expression softened in response to my smile. After exchanging pleasantries, I told him about Adam's office. He looked fit to be tied that the Chief hadn't interceded. I handed him my phone with the pictures I had taken. Just by his expression, I knew when he hit the package of condoms. He was going back through the pictures when Ali came to the door.

"We still doing this, Dr. Hendley? Officer Hirsch is waiting at Dr. Millberg's office," she said with a sigh. She looked about as enthusiastic about this chore as I did.

I looked to Brett for direction, and he shrugged and said, "Let's go. And let's keep a photo journal on your phone, Sheridan, if you don't mind."

I nodded, and off we went. This time, we focused on getting some of the books off the floor. I tried to decide which ones could just get tossed and which might be useful to someone. They were boxed accordingly, but, at Brett's suggestion, only after we shook each one in case any thing was left inside them. The shaking yielded a few more photos and a rather passionate note from someone named Cara. Brett took pictures of each with my phone before giving them to Hirsch. I mentioned there had been a couple photos earlier that Hirsch had taken to the station. Brett made a note.

We worked for about an hour, and most of the books were off the floor. The trash and papers under the books had been taken care of as well. We weren't done but we had made a dent. We still needed to finish going through the books still on the shelves and the desk. Luckily no more condoms were found in the afternoon. With the boxes and trash bin inside, we called it quits and Ali locked up. She went back to her office and Hirsch followed behind her. Looked like he had it bad.

Brett looked at me with raised eyebrows as they left. I told him about Hirsch's crush and he smiled. I noted he didn't look old enough to shave, vote or drink and asked Brett if he had any idea how old Hirsch was. Brett just laughed and assured me Hirsch was old enough for all three. He didn't answer my question though. Instead he asked, "So how old are you, Sheridan?"

"Old enough to know better, but still young enough not to care?" I answered with a smile. He chuckled and repeated the question. He obviously wanted a specific number.

"Turned 45 last April. And yourself?" I countered. I guessed him to be about the same age, but with a 12-year-old daughter, he could be younger.

"I'll be hitting the big 5-0 comes next July," he answered with a sigh. Once back to my office, he sighed again, and said, "Looks like I am going to have to hunt down Chief Pfeiffe again to get a look at the pictures Hirsch collected. It may be best if I come by your place when I'm done, and then we can go get something to eat."

It wasn't a question really, but I answered, "Sounds good."

"In the meantime, can you send all those photos to my email, please," he asked, eyebrows raised. I nodded, and he was gone.

I thought of Mitch, and concerned, called his house. His wife, Dora, answered and explained he had what seemed to be a 24-hour bug of sorts. He came on the phone, and sounded tired. He began by apologizing. I related my interaction with the Chancellor and he confirmed Oakland was definitely a bit on the sexist side and quite used to using his position and power to get his way. I couldn't tell if that included sexual harassment or just typical politics. I told Mitch he missed helping with cleaning out Adam's office. He chuckled, and commented that maybe he wasn't feeling up to working tomorrow either.

It was a short call, and I moved on to archive the photos from Adam's office. I took care of the photo transfer and walked to the parking lot. As I approached my car, I felt the hair on the back of neck rising, and realized, just a little too late, someone was behind me. He or she grabbed my arms, pulled them behind me, and caused me to drop everything. When the person spoke, I could tell it was a female. I didn't recognize the voice.

"What were you doing in Adam's office? What did you find?" she demanded. She virtually hissed the words. I couldn't tell but it seemed like she was very angry about something, possibly his death.

"I was told to clean out his office. Papers and books, what you'd expect in an office. What should I have found?" I tried to sound calm, wondering at her behavior. I didn't try to resist so I couldn't tell just how strong she was. Since she surprised me, she probably didn't have to be that strong, but at that minute I wasn't feeling threatened. I didn't want to be the one to elevate this situation to a more physical interchange.

"Did you find any pictures or letters or personal papers?" she hissed. I decided then she was obviously worried we had uncovered something.

I didn't want to lie and I didn't want to answer her. I must have hesitated because she jerked her grip on my arms. That was enough to tell me she was strong and I would have very sore shoulders. I answered, "We found some photos, probably of family or friends. The police have them now." I added so she would know I didn't have them and they weren't in the office any more. I tried to figure out how old she was from her voice and she didn't sound young enough to be a student.

"Did you recognize any of the people in the pictures?" she asked. Her tone switched from hissing with anger to anxiety and concern. I still couldn't recognize the voice but I got the feeling she was worried there was something incriminating in Adam's office.

"No, I didn't," I answered with conviction. She must have believed me. The next thing I knew she shoved my back and pushed the back of my knees at the same time and I was on the ground. I turned and saw someone with a hooded jacket running toward the dormitory area. I hadn't had a chance to move, when Kim came running from the other direction.

"Sheridan, are you alright? Who was that? One minute you were standing with someone behind you and then you were gone and they were running away. Did you get mugged? Oh, my god. First, Adam is killed, and now you've been mugged! Are you alright?" she was screaming.

I sighed and tried to right myself, I said, "Kim, chill. I'm okay. A little dirty, and I'll probably be a little sore in spots later. I think my knees are skinned. But I'm okay."

I was trying to be calm, but I was shaking and Kim noticed it. "Sheridan, you have to call the Chief or Brett. Right now! You're shaking and there's blood seeping through your paints at the knees, so don't tell me it's no big deal." She had calmed down a bit and took stock of the situation.

"Okay, okay." I pulled out my phone and called the number I had for Brett from when he had called me.

He answered, "I'm in a meeting, can this wait?"

I answered, "I'm not sure. I was just accosted in the parking lot. I think you better identify the women in those photos."

"What? What do you mean 'accosted'?" he asked, his voice a bit louder this time.

"Some woman. In the parking lot. Wanted to know why I was in Adam's office. Wanted to know if I found any pictures. Then if I recognized any of the people in the pictures. Then she took off," I explained as concisely as I could. "No big deal..." I started to say, but Kim grabbed the phone.

"This is Kim, and yes, big deal. She assaulted Sheridan, whoever she is," she said. She sounded very calm and there was a pause before she continued

"No, I didn't get a good look. I just saw Sheridan standing at her car with someone very close to her. Sheridan looked awkward one minute, then she disappeared. This other woman ran away and I found Sheridan on the ground. The woman had on a hooded jacket and it happened so fast. I couldn't tell if it was a man or woman, but Sheridan said it was a woman." Kim explained.

Brett must have asked her about me, because then Kim said, "She was on the ground. Her knees must be cut or scraped. There's some blood on her pants, but not much. The bimbo knocked her to the ground. Sheridan said she was going to be sore, but I don't know anything else."

Then another pause, and Kim said, "Okay, I'll follow her home and stay with her until you get there. Here's Sheridan." Kim handed me back my phone.

"I'm really okay. A little shook, but okay, honest," I told him. I looked at my pants and there was some blood but not a lot. My knees burned, but what pissed me off was that I liked these pants and now they were ruined.

"Look, go on home. I got the email and we scanned the photos Hirsch collected. I sent them to the field office. The Chief is looking at them now. When you get home, go through the ones on your phone with Kim and see if she can identify any of the women. I'll be there as soon as the Chief and I finish up here," he answered.

"Okay, I'll see you in a while." He said bye and we both clicked off.

I finished putting everything back in my bag, got in my car and drove home. Kim followed me. At the house, Kim let Charlie out in the back yard. I found the photos on my phone and handed it to Kim. I asked her to see if she recognized any and went to change my clothes. The slacks I had worn had a rip in one knee from the gravel and blood on both knees, so I tossed them. I cleaned my knees with some antiseptic where the gravel had resulted in broken skin. My blouse was dirty, but not obviously torn. I put on jeans, but the denim hitting my knees hurt, so I put on shorts instead along with a t-shirt. In the process I realized my shoulders were already getting stiff, probably from when the woman jerked my arms behind my back.

I fed Charlie and then found Kim and Charlie in the living room. Kim stared at one of the pictures on my phone. I hoped it was because she recognized someone, but when I peeked over her shoulder, it was the photo of the condoms.

"He was a scum bag, huh?" she said. She sounded pretty deflated. I could tell she was still grasping just how much of a scum bag he was.

"Afraid so, Kim. I guess from the expression on your face, you weren't the reason for his need to have condoms in his office?" I asked as gently as I could.

"Nope, I always provided the condoms this time around. We always hooked up at my place. It was my own way of feeling like I had some control of the situation and hadn't given it all to him," she answered wistfully.

"Well, I guess the good thing is he seemed to use them. Better than the alternative," I offered.

"Yeah, well maybe I'll give you my supply!" she said with a chuckle. "Looks like you may need them before I do." I was glad she was able to find a way to deflect from her despair, but I wasn't ready to go there yet.

I put my hands up and retorted, "We aren't there yet! Not sure if or when we will be..."

She laughed and teased, "Oh, you are so just not admitting it. I've seen the way you look at each other. Just a matter of time." She picked up one of two glasses of wine, and said, "Here, I think you need this."

We drank our wine and discussed the pictures for a while. She thought one of them might be a younger Katie. And she thought one might have been the third wife. Neither of us could remember her name. We speculated that maybe one of the older pictures might be his first wife. It dawned on me the photo that looked to be from 20 years ago could be her.

We also talked about the mess, and if neither local nor State police was responsible, who had trashed it and when. And how had they gotten in to the office. It could have been the person who accosted me, but obviously from her questions she hadn't found the photos or whatever she was looking for. We were still talking when Brett arrived.

I answered the door, and he immediately took me in his arms and kissed my forehead. Then, noticing the way I was dressed, he pirouetted me around, and commented, "Ah, the casual Sheridan! I like it. But not the knees so much. You cleaned them up good?"

I nodded and then remembered he had said we would go out to eat. My hands flew to my face and I said, "Oh, dinner. I forgot. I'm sorry." I was certainly not dressed for a dinner date.

Tilting my chin and looking into my eyes, he said "You're just fine. We can order dinner in. Not a problem." After a pause he added, "There are places here you can order from and either pick up or get delivery, right?"

We had walked all the way into the living room by then. Kim answered, "Italian or Chinese?"

Brett chuckled, and said, "Hi, Kim. Hope you can join us." Then looking at me and then her, he commented, "How about Chinese?"

Then, prompted by Kim's gestures, he massaged my shoulders, and I winced. He grimaced a bit.

Kim and I both nodded and I went to my study to get the menu. I could hear them talking, but I couldn't make out what they were saying. As I walked back into the living room, they stopped. I looked from one to the other, and Brett said, "Let's order and then we can try and sort some of this out, okay?"

I nodded, and Kim took charge of placing the order and volunteered to go pick it up. She left and Brett took me his arms and kissed me again, a little more intense than his initial kiss now with Kim gone. He asked if I was okay, and I assured him I was. He massaged my shoulders again and shook his head as I winced again.

Charlie decided she needed a little attention too, and he played with her a bit. When I went to get down dishes, he nudged me into a chair and got them down for me. Then he set the table in the kitchen. I offered to make coffee, but Brett said he had had enough all day. He helped himself to a glass of wine from the bottle Kim had opened earlier. Kim got back in no time, and we ate before moving back to the living room.

"Okay, Sheridan, I want you to explain and show me what happened this afternoon. Come over here," he directed. Looking at Kim, he asked, "Can you come over here, Kim, and you will be Sheridan."

"Start from the top," he said to me.

"I walked to my car and was holding all my papers in my left hand and unlocking the door with my right," I explained, gesturing with my right hand. Brett motioned to Kim and she turned her back on us, and pretended to unlock a pretend door.

I continued, "All of a sudden she grabbed me at the elbows and jerked my arms backward." He gestured for me to pretend to do the same to Kim.

"Okay, so it was a sudden jerk, and you dropped everything. Did you offer any resistance?" he asked.

"No, it was too fast. I didn't see it coming," I answered, shaking my head.

"So it wouldn't have taken a lot of strength then. Close your eyes a minute. When she jerked your arms back, was it back and up, back and down, or just back straight?"

"Huh?" was all I could respond, and Kim, turning her head, also looked confused by the question. He moved in and said as he demonstrated on Kim, "If I were to pull her arms back, I would also have to pull them up. I'm much taller so pulling them straight back would be awkward and wasted effort." He released Kim's arms, repeated the question, and both looked at me expectantly.

"Straight back I think. That would make her about my height right?" I asked. He nodded.

"Possibly. Now when she talked to you,

did it seem like she was talking down to you or on level with you?" I must have again look confused so he stood behind me and spoke in a whisper. Being a good six inches taller than me, he was talking over the top of my head. He signaled for Kim to come over and she did the same thing. Kim is about my height, maybe a little shorter.

"More like Kim," I said.

"So what happened next?" he asked. I explained how she asked questions and when she didn't like what I said, she jerked my arms again. Then told him how she'd asked if I recognized anyone in the pictures and then knocked me down.

"One last thing, show me, gently now, how she knocked you down," he directed.

I moved to behind Kim and pulling her arms back at the elbows, said, "She pushed against my back and arms with her arms, and at the same time pushed against the back of my left knee with her knee." I demonstrated without using force. Kim and I both turned around to face him.

"So, we have someone your height, who isn't necessarily strong, but likely has had some self defense or martial arts training. And she's probably right handed," he concluded. "Not much, but we can eliminate anyone much shorter than you or much taller than you. You're about 5'8"?" I nodded.

"Did you recognize the voice at all?" he asked next. I shook my head, and he continued, "Was there anything noticeable when she ran away?"

This was to both of us and we both shook our heads. Kim said, "Not really. She had on a hooded jacket with the hood up so I couldn't even tell you if her hair was long or short, never mind if she was blonde or brunette."

I added, "She was behind me the whole time so I can't tell you anything about what she looked like. I didn't see much except a blur after she knocked me down."

"Either of you ever taken a self-defense class?" he asked. When we both shook our heads, he groaned. "Sheridan, when you're working up those sexual harassment trainings, you might add on self defense!" He sighed and then seemed to get a second wind.

"Okay," he said, and waved us back to the couch. He continued, "Let's take a look at these pictures."

He pulled enlarged copies of all the photos I had taken and the ones Hirsch had bagged earlier out of an envelope. Kim immediately pulled out the one she had indicated on my phone. "I'm pretty sure this is

Katie. I recognize the hair style and the blouse she has on. This is an old picture though, like from when I first started here."

I pulled out the one that seemed so old, and stared at it. "This face is familiar, but I can't place it. It's definitely not anyone in our department. I'm pretty sure I have seen this person somewhere, or at least someone who looks a lot like her." I handed the picture to Kim.

"Yeah, she does look familiar." Putting that picture aside, she pulled out another one, and commented, "This is Misty I think. And this may be the number three wife here. I don't know any of the others. Oh, wait, isn't this woman in Sociology?"

I looked at the picture and said, "Hmm, maybe, I'm not sure." Once again, I kicked myself for paying so little attention to the people I see virtually every day.

Brett sighed and said, "Okay, so he obviously had pictures of his various wives, and perhaps some of the others he was involved in." After a pause, he added with a sigh, "And you've only picked up or gone through the stuff on the floor. We could have a hundred pictures before you're through." He sighed again and leaned against the sofa back.

"Yup, and we haven't even touched his desk yet," I added. I also sighed. We were silent for a few minutes, and then Kim broke the silence.

"Okay, it's getting late, and I hate to bring this up, but I think we all have to work tomorrow. So far this week, Sheridan, you have had your tires slashed and now you have been assaulted. I know I have a reputation for being a bit over-reactive, but I don't want you staying here alone," she said, obviously very serious.

What followed was an awkward silence. I hadn't thought this far ahead. I didn't know if Brett had. When neither of us said a word, Kim chuckled and offered, "We are all adults here. We have options. Granted they are limited by Charlie. I can run to my house, grab what I need and spend the night. Or I can leave and Brett can stay here." She paused and added, "Or both if you two want a chaperone."

Brett looked at me and said, "I agree with Kim. You are not staying here alone. I can crash here on the couch. It's your call, Sheridan."

So now I had both of them looking at me expectantly. This certainly hadn't been something I had considered, but did seem to make the most sense. I took a deep breath, and said, "Kim, thanks for the offer to stay, but I know you are spent from the double duty all week. As long as Brett can stay, you're off the hook."

She smirked and got up to leave. We both walked her to the door and then out to her car. She looked around and then at Brett. At her questioning look, he explained he had parked his car on the next street. He also told the Chief he was doing that so he wouldn't get a ticket. Then he added that he'd requested additional patrols of the neighborhood. Kim gave me a hug, and drove home. Brett asked if we needed to take Charlie for a walk. I nodded and we took her around the neighborhood. I suspected it was as much a chance for him to check out the neighborhood as it was anything else.

As we settled ourselves in the living room, Charlie on the couch with us and enamored of her new friend, I realized I'd never had a man stay over. We watched the news and Brett pulled me onto his lap and held me. It felt good to be held and we both chuckled at Charlie's attempt to also climb onto his lap. As the news ended, we kissed. It was one of the long, lingering kisses that made my toes tingle and my insides melt. We sat there on the couch making out for a while, like a couple of high school kids. When we pulled apart, his hazel eyes were swollen and glistening. I imagined mine were as well.

"Time out," he said very softly, with a sigh. "I think we better ... Sheridan, how about we get me a pillow and blanket, and say our goodnights so we both can get some sleep."

Smiling, I said, "Probably a good idea. The sleep that is, but the couch isn't long enough for your 6 foot frame." Pausing slightly and noting as a range of emotions crossed his face, I added, "I do have a guest room. Let's take a tour of the house so you can get your bearings." I sensed he was trying to be the gentleman, and as warm and tingling as I was feeling, I appreciated it. Add to that I was feeling stiff despite the tingles. I also wasn't sure if either us were prepared. I might have to take Kim up on her offer of condoms.

We checked the back door and he flipped on the outside light. We put the dishes in the dishwasher, and made sure all the leftovers were in the fridge. I showed him the guest bathroom, where the towels were located, and so on. It would have been like having any other guest except each time we brushed against each other, it was like being hit with electricity.

In the guest room, the last box I had filled of stuff to be disposed of was still there and he moved it for me. Then we were in the room and staring at each other. He took me in his arms again. He held me close enough I knew his body was responding as well as mine. Moving to establish at least some distance, he kissed me again.

"Sheridan, go to bed – in your bed, now. I'll see you in the morning," he said emphatically enough so I was sure he meant it on some level. I smiled, sighed, and waited for Charlie to decide who she was going to be sleeping with.

CHAPTER 14

When I finally fell asleep, I slept well and the night was uneventful. I got up earlier than usual, made some coffee, and let Charlie out. I was heading for the shower when Brett came into the kitchen. I was suddenly a little self-conscious of my nightgown. I quickly forgot about it when he took me in his arms. As I fixed him a cup of coffee, I said, "I hope you slept well. Was the bed comfortable?"

He came up behind me and put his arms around my waist and answered, "I slept fine, but it was lonely." He kissed the top of my head and then stepped back. It was looking like it would be a cold shower I'd be taking.

He sat down with his coffee and I joined him. He said he was meeting with the Chief today, and they hoped to have some information by the end of the day. His initial plan had been to leave early for Richmond, but he wasn't sure they would be able to wrap everything up in time. I could tell he would be disappointed if he had to cut any part of his weekend with Madison short.

While we drank our coffee, his phone rang. I could tell from his greeting that it was Madison. I didn't want to eavesdrop so I took Charlie out in the back yard. A few minutes later, Brett came out and put his hands on my shoulders. My wince drew another grimace. Brett asked how I was doing, and I assured him I was okay and he should go on. I figured it was daylight and I would be alright to get to work. He kissed me and left for his hotel to change before his meeting. I headed for the shower, and got dressed.

I was feeling good and about to get in my car when an arm came around my neck, knocking me off balance. My shoulders and neck burned. I gasped, and dropped my bag, and I swore to myself to take a self-defense class sooner rather than later. I tried to talk and managed to gasp "What do you want? Who are you?" Not all the sounds came out, and all I got in return was a grunt.

I could tell this was not the same person. The way his arms came around me, he was taller and had more girth than the woman yesterday. In fact, I figured it was a man from the way he grabbed me. He pulled me backward and toward the street. I hoped that the additional watch on the neighborhood would occur about then, but no such luck. I tried to think of something I could do, but whoever he was, he was stronger and bigger than me. At least part of the time my feet weren't hitting the ground and it was hard to breath. My hands had a death grip on the arm across my neck so that as he dragged me along, I wasn't completely choked.

He dragged me to a car, a shiny new black BMW, at the end of the drive. He opened the driver's door, and shoved me inside, but not quite out of reach. He had to let go of my neck, but he had a vice grip on my left arm. Rubbing my neck with my right, I glanced sideways and realized it was Oakland. I must have gasped again, because he looked at me as he managed to get the car in reverse. I was scared, dumbfounded, and all I could think of was I didn't have my seat belt on.

I tried to pull from all my training and work at the residential center. I tried to speak as calmly as I could so as not to escalate the situation. "Chancellor Oakland, what is it you want from me? I'm sure we can work this out." My voice sounded raspy to me, probably from the pressure he'd had on my throat.

He grunted and said what sounded like, "You bitch, why did you have to keep poking your nose in everything, going through that ass's office?"

"Because Jim Grant told me to?" I offered. I tried not to sound at all aggressive or offensive. Oakland had scared me in his office, but now I was downright terrified. "But whatever it is you think I found... I don't know what it is," I answered, still calm, but realizing it didn't matter anymore. And it probably didn't matter if I didn't understand his motive for murdering Adam either. But I was pretty sure it was Oakland who killed Adam. That didn't bode well for my future.

"You're no dummy, you with your P-H and D. Sooner or later, you and your boyfriend from the State police are going to figure it out. Did you find the pictures in his office? Or the DVDs?" he hissed. Obviously my calm speech wasn't having much of an effect on his hostility.

I began to get a better idea of what might have happened. I figured I had nothing to lose. He was probably going to kill me too. I asked him, "Adam had an affair with your wife, didn't he? And he had a picture maybe?"

He grunted and hissed something about Adam wanting him to pay for the picture or pictures. On a roll, and because it came to mind and just popped out, I asked, "Was he using it to blackmail you?" My opinion of Adam, as low as it had ever been, was taking a quick nosedive.

Pictures, DVDs, blackmail? We hadn't seen any DVDs or flash drives in the mess we had cleaned up. For someone in Oakland's position and obvious chauvinism, having it get out that his wife cheated on him would be a huge blow to his ego and his power. Not to mention his caveman mentality would likely kick in and he'd feel a need to protect his wife's, as well as his own reputation. So much for his need to feel powerful and in control.

His grunt in response to my question was confirmation. That gave me some room for negotiation, maybe. I suggested, "Look, so far I haven't found anything in Adam's office to incriminate your wife. If you get rid of me, someone else will just have to clean out the rest of his office, including his desk. I could finish the job, and give you whatever I find." I wasn't sure he bought it, but his grip on my arm loosened enough that I might get circulation back. If nothing else, I might at least be able to buy myself some time.

We were heading for campus. I prayed someone was going to see us and realize there was something odd about me being in his car. Of course, in his position of power, even if they did think it strange, they might choose to overlook it. He pulled into the gated lot where I assumed he usually parked. Unfortunately, it was early and apparently administrators don't come to work at 8 AM. He looked at me sternly and cautioned, "Do what I say, and don't scream. Understand?"

I nodded. He increased his grip on my arm and pulled me out his door. If he'd had a stick shift, it would have been worse. Once out of the car, he kept hold of my arm and we walked in the back entrance to the administration building. I didn't even know there was a back entrance, or back stairs, but up we went three flights. Once again, my feet didn't always reach the stairs. We finally reached the back door to his office. I guessed back doors were probably a good thing if you needed to avoid somebody. Once in his office, he let go of my arm. He pushed me in the direction of a chair and hissed, "Sit down, and shut up."

I did as I was told and as he pulled his cell phone out, I remembered I had my cell in my pants pocket. I rubbed my arm in an attempt to regain circulation to my fingers. Oakland didn't take his eyes off me as he said into the phone, "Yeah. I got her." Then after a pause, "Just get over here now so we can figure out what to do." He didn't have the speaker on and I couldn't hear the voice of who he was talking to. I concluded from his end of the conversation he had a partner in this mess. As he stood there glaring at me, I tried to guess at who it might be. Janice?

His wife? Coming up empty, I again tried to convince him I could help, rather than being a threat. I somehow didn't see myself as being a threat. I just needed to convince him and his partner.

"Like I said in the car, if there is something in Adam's office, I can look for it for you. I can imagine how embarrassing it might be for you if any photos came out that implicated you or your wife in his murder," I suggested. I still worked at speaking calmly and hopefully being perceived as an ally instead of a threat. I also tried to convince myself all he wanted was any intimate pictures, rather than that he was the murderer. Unfortunately, my first impression of him when he grabbed me from my own driveway was making it difficult to deny he was the murderer I still had to consider I was likely to be the next victim.

While we waited, he opened the cabinet below his book shelves and poured himself a drink. He never stopped looking at me. I had a need to fill the silence, but I knew from my training to keep silent. I waited him out and hoped he would talk. At one point, when he sighed, I offered, "Do you want to tell me about it?" in my best, non-judgmental, therapist voice. He shook his head, but then started talking anyway.

"I should have known there was a reason Heather wanted me to take this job. I had a great job, loved my job. I was happy. I was semi-retired and doing just what I'd always dreamed of doing. Agriculture is my life, but she said she wanted a change of scenery. She said she'd be happier here. She convinced me I could get involved with the horticulture department here and make it a nationally known program. I've done that almost. The horticulture department is ranked in the top 10 nationally." He was speaking quietly and his wistfulness was apparent.

I nodded, and he continued, "Heather is the light of my life. I can't imagine loving anyone the way I love her." I could see the tears in his eyes, and I could almost feel his pain. She had obviously betrayed his love.

"I was ready for retirement, wanted to spend more time with her. I needed to retire to something that wasn't as demanding in order to spend more time with her. She said we could spend more time together. You understand?" he asked. I nodded.

"We came down here to visit, and I was impressed with the horticulture program. Heather talked about the social venues, the country clubs, golf, and the women she met. She said she would be very happy here. I wasn't sure I would be, but Heather was happy and I accepted the position. It didn't dawn on me to check out everyone on the faculty. I only looked at who was in horticulture." He shook his head and was quiet. As he sat there, I could almost palpate his rage building back up. And in that few minutes, his mention of his wife's name, his comment about not checking the rest of the faculty, and her tears on the stage at the memorial came together. Heather was Adam's first wife.

I didn't know what to say, and didn't want to just blurt out my conclusion, so I just sat there, silent. I glanced at his clock when it chimed 8 o'clock. I cleared my throat and said, "Mr. Oakland, you probably remember my schedule. I teach at 8, and someone will be looking for me."

I had hoped that would trigger a need for him to let me go, but instead he handed me his phone, and said, "Call the office. Tell them you are sick. Tell them to cancel class. One wrong word..."

As he loomed over me, I called the office and Terra picked up. "Hi Terra. It's Sheridan," I paused. Terra responded and asked what number was it I was calling from. Oakland motioned with his hand for me to get on with it. "Terra, I woke up feeling badly and I'm not coming in. Can you go let my class out?" I asked. I was careful of what I was saying, but hoped she would pick up that something besides the phone number wasn't right.

When she answered, "Dr. Hendley, are you alright? You never call in sick," I was very glad he again hadn't thought to put the phone on speaker.

I answered, "No." Then after a pause, I said, "Must be the fish I had with Kim last night."

She replied, "Are you telling me to go find Dr. Pennzel, that something is fishy?"

I silently thanked her for catching on and answered, "Yes, thanks. Talk to you later." I hung up as I could see Oakland's impatience rising. Then I handed him back his phone. To him I said, "She'll take care of it." I only hoped that when she found Kim, Kim would grasp the meaning and call in reinforcements. And maybe they could trace the cell phone back to Oakland.

I tried to get him back to telling me his story, but there was a knock on his back door. He didn't take his eyes off of me as he let his wife into the office. I suppose I could have tried to run for the other door and hoped Janice would be there and save me. I had a feeling he would have decked me in a single bound. It's not that I was giving him super powers, but physically he resembled a football player. I could see him tackling me without any problem or hesitation.

As I watched the two of them, it dawned on me that the 20 year old photo was of Heather, probably before or when they were married. I must have made a sound as I came to the realization, because they both directed their attention to me.

"What?" Heather asked.

"I just realized that we did find a photo of you yesterday. An old photo. It looked to be from about 20 years ago. I didn't recognize it then, but I'm sure it was you," I explained as matter of factly as I could muster. I was still trying to maintain calm and diffuse the situation.

"Where... who has it now? Did you find any others, more recent?" she asked. As she asked her eyes darted between her husband and me.

I noted Oakland's face was getting red again, and I chose my words carefully. "Just the one photo of you. There were lots of other photos, but just portrait-type shots. Officer Hirsch took all of them," I explained.

Heather looked at her husband and then at me. I realized she didn't look particularly sorry, just scared. After a few minutes, she asked, "Did you get to his desk or his cabinets?"

"No. I told your husband all of this. All we did yesterday was get the stuff off the floor. Some of the photos were in the books on the floor. We didn't get to the desk, the rest of the books on the shelves or the cabinet beneath the shelves. One way or another, somebody is going to go through all the stuff and find whatever you think is there, you know," I offered. I was still trying to make myself useful as opposed to disposable. Oakland hadn't responded to this bait earlier, but it was worth a try with her. Besides, based on his statements earlier, she had a lot of control over this man.

They moved a little further away, but directly in line with me, and had a hushed conversation. I looked around, trying to see if there was anything I could use as a weapon. Then the phone on the desk rang. I think all three of us jumped, and Oakland moved toward the desk. Heather, she pulled a small pistol out. She aimed it at me with one hand, while she put the index finger of her other hand to her lips. I got the message. I decided it was a good thing she hadn't been here when I'd talked to Terra.

"Yes, Janice. Please confirm with the President and Provost that I am available for the meeting at 2PM today," he said into the phone. I was impressed that he sounded like this was just another day at the office despite the beads of sweat on his face and his obvious anger.

"I am in conference this morning. Janice, why don't you take the day off and start the long weekend early? It's pretty quiet and I don't believe I will need anything else today," he suggested. My heart fell. I thought that at least if she were on the other side of the door, there was a chance she'd walk in and wonder at this 'conference'. Maybe think to bring in cold water. Cold water sounded good right about then.

"You, too," he said and ended the call. Then he looked at Heather and me. "Chief Pfeiffe has called a meeting for this afternoon to review the status of the investigation," he stated and moved toward me. His nonverbal cues and just his size were threatening. I tried to back up in the chair, but that was pretty hopeless.

"What are they going to say? What did your boyfriend tell you? And don't play innocent, I know he never went back to his hotel last night," he snapped.

"He didn't tell me anything." Deciding to go with his insinuations instead of being affronted by them, I added, "Do you think we spend our time talking about Adam and his murder?" I made a valiant effort to smile to support the innuendo.

Heather sniffled, and he looked dismayed. The two of them continued their discussion at a distance. I couldn't make out any of what they said. Then Oakland had another drink. Whenever he was not focused on me, she made

sure I knew she was armed. I had no doubt she
not only had taken self-defense classes but that
she knew how to use the gun.

"Excuse me, but could I use the restroom
please?" I asked. I figured maybe if I got to leave
the office to go to the ladies room, maybe
somebody else would be in there. Maybe Misty.
Or maybe I could use my phone to call for help.

Oakland walked over to a door I hadn't
noticed and opened it. I went in and he locked
the door behind me. Funny, most bathrooms
have a lock on the inside. Why did I get so lucky
as to suggest something that ended with me
being locked in? I pulled out my phone, but I had
no signal. I used the facilities, and then knocked
on the door. I got a resounding, "Make yourself
comfortable" from Oakland, and leaned against
the counter to wait.

I went over the conversation with Terra,
and hoped she had gotten to Kim. I also hoped
Kim would figure out that she needed to call the
Chief or Brett, though I wasn't sure she had
Brett's number. Hopefully, Terra would think to
give someone the phone number from Oakland's
phone and they could trace it. The thing was, I
wasn't too sure how long all that would take, or
if they would think to check the most obvious
place – Oakland's office. He had done a pretty
good job on the phone with Janice so they might

even conclude he wasn't involved. Or maybe the phone was one of those throw-aways. I decided to enter a text to Brett and Kim and anyone else and hope that at some point the messages would get sent. I put my phone on silent to make sure the beep wouldn't alert them I had the phone or a message had been sent.

I used one of the paper cups and helped myself to some water. I shifted to thinking about Adam. I now believed he had taken incriminating photos or recorded his activities, at least with Heather. I sure hoped he hadn't done that with Kim. I was pretty sure that if any recordings were found, they would become evidence. Any good defense attorney could use those DVDs as motive for multiple people to get to reasonable doubt. I hoped Martin Cohn was a good attorney if Kim needed to use him.

They left me in the bathroom for about 30 minutes, and several times I checked my phone for a signal, but nothing. I heard the tumblers and then the door opened. Oakland took my arm and pushed me back to where I'd been sitting before. Then he handed me a bottle of water. I opened it, noting the seal had not been broken, and drank, glad it was at least cold. What I wished for though was a cup of coffee.

Finally, Oakland cleared his throat. He then explained, "Okay, here's the deal. That scumbag had some pictures and a DVD of Heather in a … compromising position, let's say. We think these are in his office. You're going to go to the office and tell them you are feeling better now. You're going to spend the morning searching for those pictures and the video. Heather is going to help you and make sure you do what you are supposed to do and nothing else. Understand?"

I nodded. I looked at Heather. She held the gun by her side, and then slipped it into her pocket. Yup, I did understand. Here, in Oakland's office, I was the only one in danger. Back at the department, with students, staff and other faculty, there would be a lot of people in danger. Even if her gun had only six bullets, that was six too many.

Oakland looked at his watch, and added, "You might as well relax, we need to wait another 20 minutes or so in order for your upset stomach to settle and be believable." Obviously, he had used the comment about the fish in hatching this plan. Guess it was a good thing I hadn't come up with flu as my excuse.

I sat and drank my water and said, "Just curious. How do you know there is a DVD or photo to find? Couldn't he have lied about it?" I wouldn't discount his being a liar given what a scumbag Adam was. I watched the color rise in

Oakland's face and I wished I hadn't been so curious.

"Believe me, it exists or at least it did. He sent me a clip to make sure I believed him," Oakland responded and looked ready to kill. Heather put her hand on his arm, and muttered something that sounded like "I'm sorry". I didn't say it, but I thought it was a bit late for sorry.

Oakland continued, "That man was like an addiction or a cancer. No cure. And he preyed on women. You know he was screwing students too, and not one of them ever came forward to complain." His description of Adam as an addiction certainly jived with Kim's behavior. I wondered if Misty and Katie were similarly prey to relapses. And what about all those women he had over for dinner. Would the DVDs include the entrée that was prepared? Hmmm, maybe the recipes were in the desk too.

There was silence for a while and at about 10, Oakland signaled to Heather. She said, "Let's go, and don't forget I have a gun. Ken made sure I knew how to shoot, and I am rather good. I just wish I'd shot Adam's nuts off."

For some reason I thought of how Max would have winced at that comment and it made me smile inside, but the smile didn't quite make it to the surface. As we walked down the back stairs, I tried to figure out a way to trip her without risking getting shot. Definitely a self-defense class. As we crossed the quad to the Humanities building, I asked her, "So, Heather, how am I supposed to explain your help here?"

She hesitated and then said, "You just introduce me. Just say my name and that I'm the Chancellor's wife. I'll take it from there."

I nodded, not quite sure how to avoid any interactions. I hoped other faculty and staff would be sufficiently intimidated by her position to leave us alone. And, hopefully, at least one person would think to call and ask about the strangeness of it all. As we entered the building, I decided I had nothing to lose and asked, "Do you mind if we get coffee? It will look odd if I don't have coffee."

She nodded, and we entered Georg's. The line was short, and nobody approached us until we were about to leave the crowded café. Max came barreling in, and stopped short. "Sheridan, I thought you were sick? Terra cancelled your class and seemed concerned. I hope you're not contagious and coming in here spreading germs," he rattled. He seemed completely oblivious to the woman by my side.

"No, Max, no germs. Probably some bacteria in the fish I ate last night. You know, food poisoning. But I am feeling better and figured I'd better come in and get some work done," I answered. He didn't ask about Heather and I didn't volunteer. I'm not sure he even noticed her.

"Glad to hear you're better. I have too much to do with the new class and more students. I'll talk to you later Sheridan," he responded and was gone.

My coffee in hand, I started up the stairs. Heather followed, not saying a word. I went directly to the main office to get the keys from Ali. Terra looked surprised to see me. Then registered additional surprise and confusion when she spotted Heather following behind me. I wasn't sure if she knew who Heather was or if it was just that someone was following me.

Taking the offensive, I said, "Hi, Terra. I'm feeling a little better and didn't want to waste any more time getting Adam's office cleaned out. Ali, can I have the key to his office please?" I paused, and then as if an afterthought, I explained to Ali, "This is Heather Oakland, Chancellor Oakland's wife. She volunteered to help, so you don't need to worry. Just keep on with the budget."

Ali and Terra looked at each other in confusion, and I added, sounding as exasperated as I could, "The keys, Ali, and the clipboard so I can check off the inventory, please." This time it was a statement, not a question, and Ali handed me both items. "Shall I call Officer Hirsch?" she asked.

"Mmmm... I don't think so, not unless you want to pursue that romance with him. I suspect he is busy with things other than cleaning out an office. If I find anything I will put it aside for him. I'll bring this back when we're done," I told them as I took the items and turned to go. I hoped they figured something was odd and that yes, they should call Hirsch, and not for dinner. I would have described my manner as out of personality. I only hoped they felt that way too. Heather didn't say a word. She didn't give a greeting or any type of acknowledgement as we left the main office.

Heather followed me to Adam's office. After I unlocked the door and we walked in, I closed the door. It was kind of stuffy, but with the door closed, it was less likely anyone would stop to chat. That at least would limit the possible casualties. Nothing looked any different than when I left yesterday. The trash bin was still there, as were the cartons to put the books in. I waited for direction from Heather. She looked around the office, and from her facial expression it was clear to me she had never been in here. She was looking at each shelf and then the desk with a look of disbelief. So who had trashed the office?

I wasn't sure why she was so sure he would leave his blackmail evidence here and not at home. I asked her. I sure hoped the next stop wouldn't be going through his house.

"He had too many people coming to his house all the time. Somebody might have found them by accident. Or they might have been looking for something else and found them. If he did the same with others, I doubt he told them about the camera until he was through playing with them", she answered. Her bitterness was clearly evident. I reassessed the situation and I wondered if maybe she didn't kill Adam.

"There weren't too many other places. He only went to the country club and here. He always said he didn't do much here. I just don't think students would have been as nosy as some of the women he took home. I suppose he could have a safe deposit box somewhere, but I think this is the best bet." She paused, and then directed, "You take the desk and I'll take the cabinet." That effectively put her between me and the door. I had to think of some way out of this office.

I sat down at the desk and opened the center drawer. The usual pens, pencils, staples, rubber bands, and a pad of paper were there. I pulled out some loose sheets, apparently printouts of excel sheets. Grade sheets was my best guess. I went to throw them in the trash bin, and she stopped me. She looked at them. She apparently agreed they weren't useful and nodded. I assumed that was going to be the way it went. I moved the pad and found another picture, but not of her and not in a compromising position. I put it on the side of the desk. She looked, sighed and went back to the cabinet.

She was pulling everything out. All of the books, DVDs, CDs and checking all the titles. I was tempted to point out that I doubted he labeled the DVD "Heather compromising position" or "Sex with Heather", but I kept my mouth shut. Middle drawer empty, I started on the right hand side drawers. The first one was empty. Its contents had most likely been on the floor. The second one hadn't been emptied, and right on top was another box of condoms. At least, he was always prepared. I sighed as I went to toss them. She looked over and nodded.

There were some tickets from various theatre productions and with her nod, these were trashed as well. A few dried flowers and some birthday cards. I asked her if she wanted to check to see if any were from her or if I could just toss them. She took them from me. She withdrew one and put it in her pocket, tears in her eyes. She tossed the rest. I found it strange that this man, who certainly was not a romantic in the classic sense, would keep so many mementos of his various relationships. I guess maybe they were like the souvenirs of serial murderers. Or maybe part of the blackmail evidence.

Underneath the cards, there was an envelope and it was filled with photos. I cleared my throat and she looked my way. I handed her the envelope. She leaned against the desk and dropped the photos on the floor one by one. I could tell these were not the portrait-type that had been loose in his desk or in his books. You certainly couldn't date the pictures by the clothes the women weren't wearing. Somebody would need to gather and destroy these or they would destroy the women pictured in them. And Adam had definitely been busy.

There was another envelope still in the drawer, and I pulled it out. Instead of pictures, it held several more excel sheets and these had initials, dates, and numbers I guessed were amounts. I easily found the initials HO. I looked for AB and KP but they were not there. Adam apparently only blackmailed the ones who could pay. This, in itself, was probably enough to eliminate Kim and Ali as suspects if the Chief still had them in his sights.

On the other hand, the 15 or so names on here gave a lot of powerful people motives. I couldn't immediately attach names to the initials, but I bet the country club roster would make it fairly easy. Trying to think positive, it occurred to me that maybe neither Oakland killed Adam. Maybe the Chancellor just wanted to save his and his wife's reputation. That should have made me feel better, but somehow I wasn't convinced.

Heather gasped, and a photo went into her pocket. There were pictures all over the floor and she looked at the ledger I was holding and asked, "What's that?"

I thought about playing dumb, but I never could carry that off. I sighed, and answered, "I think it is a record of who he was involved with, when, and how much he was blackmailing them for. You can probably tell if it's accurate." I pointed to the line with her initials. Tears fell off her cheeks as she took in the largess of the ledger. I found myself feeling sorry for her. At some level she was a victim.

Wiping the tears from her face, she said, "Keep looking, there is a DVD here somewhere. Probably more than one."

I sighed. I finished with the drawers on the right and moved to the ones on the left. The top drawer had pads of paper. I took each one out, shook it, and stacked them on the desk. The third one down, a DVD or CD fell out. It wasn't titled, but had a number. We both looked at it, and she pointed to the computer. I powered it up, but pointed out I didn't have Adam's password.

"You probably do think I am that stupid. I don't blame you. But I know you can sign in as yourself and not Adam and still play the DVD. So do it," she demanded, her hand going to her pants pocket.

She was right. I had been hoping she was that stupid. Computer powered up, I selected the "other user" option, and signed in. This would leave a record, but it wasn't exactly going to help me now. She handed me the DVD and I popped it in. We both waited. I noted the date stamp on the DVD and asked her if it matched one of her dates. She consulted the sheet and shook her head. Within seconds, we established the woman sitting on the bed wasn't her. It was Katie.

While I ejected the DVD and looked for something to destroy it with, she pulled out more of the pads of paper. Holding scissors in one hand and the DVD in the other I gave her a questioning look and she nodded. I cut the DVD in half and let the halves fall. She handed me another DVD. Checking the date stamp, she shook her head, but we waited for the show to start. I didn't recognize this woman, but ejected and destroyed the DVD. We followed the process several times and the drawer was empty.

The next drawer resulted in a similar process and Heather's level of agitation was rising. I couldn't tell if it was what was on the DVDs, that there were so many different women, or that we hadn't located her DVD yet. Worse, before she would let me cut them, she had to be sure it wasn't her even if the date stamp didn't match. So far, other than Katie and Misty, I hadn't recognized the women. With her increased agitation, I felt less sorry for her and anxious again about my own safety.

We went back to checking DVDs as we found them. The first shot was usually of the woman alone, and in most cases dressed or covered with a sheet. I hadn't noticed Katie or Misty's initials, and neither could have afforded to pay blackmail, so maybe he just liked recording his escapades. I was thinking it was a good thing for Kim she opted to only see him at her place. She had exercised more control, and self-preservation, than she thought.

When we finished going through all the DVDs in the drawer, she looked about to panic. She started pulling books off the shelves and shaking them. If a photo fell out, she'd look at it and then move on. If it was a DVD, she'd throw it at me. At least once I glanced at the time on the monitor and was a little surprised at how quiet it seemed. Even when students should have been between classes, and were more likely to be on the floor, it was very quiet. I seriously wondered if Adam had somehow managed to soundproof his office. Around noon, her cell rang.

"We're fine. We found some photos, and lots of DVDs, but not the one of me," she said. Since she didn't have to give an explanation, I assumed it was her husband on the other end.

"We still have about six shelves of books. He hid the pictures and DVDs in the books," was her next comment. I looked around, and I was virtually surrounded by books thrown on the floor and peppered with half-DVDs. Even if she hadn't physically blocked my way to the door, the books were pretty much blocking the way out. To think we had cleared off this floor just yesterday.

"Yes, I know. We should be done in an hour and we'll come back over there." She closed her phone and went back to shaking and tossing books, a little more rushed.

I sat there and popped in DVDs, ejected them, and cut them. I couldn't come up with anything that might lessen her agitation, so I didn't say anything. Nothing in all my training prepared me for this situation. Thankfully, she didn't say much either. As one of the DVDs came to life, and she checked the date, she gasped. I took that to mean it matched. As the recording started, Heather was standing there in a Victorian style peignoir set. She was actually stunning. I hit the eject and waited. If there was only one DVD, we had just found it. I wasn't sure what the next step was.

I looked up at her as I pulled the DVD out and handed it to her. Tears were streaming down her cheeks. She took the DVD, and picking up the scissors from the desk, cut it into several pieces. She was so vicious in her attack on the DVD, I imagined she was seeing Adam's face. It made me wonder again if she hadn't killed him. She wiped her face with her sleeve and looked at the ledger. She handed it to me and went back to the book shelves.

There were only three more shelves of books, but there was another date on the ledger for her initials. Two DVDs later, no longer going beyond the dates on the ledger, we found the second date. The DVD played until it was obvious it was her. This time there had been no peignoir. She was beside herself as she cut up the DVD. Her anger at his betrayal was palpable. She definitely was angry enough to kill. I just hoped she didn't take her anger out on me.

Taking a deep breath, she said, "Okay. We're out of here. Kenneth is waiting for us."

"Heather, you don't need me anymore. The DVDs are destroyed," I offered quietly. I didn't move and hoped she would let me be.

"Kenneth said you were to come back to his office. Don't argue with me or I'll shoot you right here, now move," she demanded, no longer teary-eyed and in full angry mode.

"Okay, but I have to return the key and clipboard to Ali," I countered.

"I'm sure if you leave it here, someone will find it. Let's go," she said. She waved the gun in my direction. At the same time, she climbed over the books. She walked backward to the door, gun aimed at me. She stepped to the side to let me out from behind the desk.

I strained to hear if someone, anyone, was out in the hallway, but couldn't hear a sound. At the door, I looked at her. She had the hand holding the gun in her pocket now, and she nodded toward the door. I opened the door, and didn't see anyone at all. She came out behind me and we made our way to the stairway. Passing the ladies' room, I asked if we could stop and she pushed me forward. I took that as a no.

As we approached the stairway, I heard sounds. She grabbed onto me, spinning me around. I found myself staring at Brett and Chief Pfeiffe with Heather's gun pointed at me. They had their guns drawn and were pointing them at her. If I hadn't been so close, that might have made me feel better. Unfortunately, she moved so I was pretty much a shield for her. In effect, I had three guns pointing at me. Not a good feeling. Once again, I thought some self-defense training needed to be on my schedule soon. If I had a schedule, that is.

All at once, I felt myself jerked backward and heard a gun going off. I landed on the floor, and rolled to the side. In a daze, I watched as Officer Hirsch, Brett and the Chief managed to disarm Heather, and get her handcuffed. That accomplished, Brett came over to me and helped me up. I still wasn't sure who had jerked me out of the way.

"You had me scared to death! What have you been doing for the last three hours?" he said as he hugged me and kissed me. He paid little heed to anyone who might be watching. I didn't get a chance to answer before the Chief said into his collar mic, "All clear. Keep everyone out of the building until we clear the front door. Matthews, meet us at the administration building, and be sure the back entrance is covered as well."

I looked from the Chief to Brett, and Brett explained, "Terra called the Chief after you called in with the fish story. We were at a loss as to where to look for you. When you showed up with Heather, Terra called again. We evacuated the building as soon as we could without creating a panic. Possible gas leak. Officer Matthews has been watching the administration building since then." He rubbed my back, and then we walked toward the opposite stairway and out the back. I needed the ladies' room, but I wasn't going to say anything.

At the lower level, Hirsch went out first, and then came back with an "All clear". The Chief then propelled Heather out the door and into his car. Brett and I followed. Brett indicated we would walk over and meet them there. He kissed me again, and we walked around the building. We waited on the side, out of sight, while everyone entered at the front. We didn't want to run into anyone. We walked to the Administration building at a brisk pace. As we passed the fountains, Brett looked at me and asked, "Are you sure you're alright?"

I nodded and said, "Other than being in dire need of a bathroom, I am more than alright! Though with my shoulders jerked twice in two days I may also need a good physical therapist or chiropractor!"

He chuckled and rubbed my shoulders. The heat from his hand almost made me forget about the pain and the need for the bathroom. When we got to the administration building, our first stop was the restroom. Thankfully, there was no sign of Misty this time. I wasn't sure how

I would explain what was going on if she popped into the bathroom.

Then we walked upstairs. We went through the glass doors and after calling to check with the Chief, Brett knocked on the door and we went in. Chief Pfeiffe, Officer Hirsch, Heather and the Chancellor were waiting for us. I assumed Matthews was still outside.

"Dr. Hendley, I have already placed Mrs. Oakland under arrest for kidnap and attempted murder based on the behaviors we observed. I am assuming you will be pressing charges. The questions before us now are whether Mr. Oakland was involved in this morning's activities, and whether he killed Millberg or his wife did." The Chief looked from me to Heather to Oakland and back to me.

"Yes, I will be pressing charges. Yes, Mr. Oakland was involved. He was the one who grabbed me this morning and brought me here," I explained, my anger and indignation coming through.

"And the murder of Dr. Millberg?" the Chief asked.

"Based on his comments, I would say he did, but in fact, he did not at any point state that explicitly," I answered honestly. Judging from her anger, and the use of weights, it could have been Heather. After all the DVDs I had seen, even I had reasonable doubt. There were a lot of people who had motive.

"Thank you, Dr. Hendley," was the Chief's response, though I suspected he wished I had said Oakland had confessed.

Brett stepped forward, and began reading Oakland his Miranda rights. I assumed somebody had read them to Heather when she was arrested for my kidnapping. Brett then identified specific facts. He pointed out that Heather and Oakland were each other's alibis. He also pointed out that authorities had, through a search of financial records, suspected the blackmail.

He then pointed out the blackmail was now a given. He asked Oakland to explain how his wife's golf club, the murder weapon, ended up at the rec center. Heather gasped. When Oakland responded that obviously his wife must have been taking lessons there, Heather started screaming and rammed into him with her head. She started screaming, "You killed him! You killed Adam!"

He had not been cuffed yet, and he tried to contain her and hold her. Tears raked his face. Officer Hirsch pulled her off of him. Oakland looked at Heather with something like disbelief as she ranted how she hated him and she would never forgive him for killing Adam.

He shook his head. He still obviously did not quite believe her reaction. Brett pointed out that prints on the club were a match to both Oakland and Heather, her monogram was on the club, and that golf wasn't taught at the rec center. I wasn't quite sure how they had both sets of prints for comparison. Oakland would have had to get fingerprinted and have a background check in order to work on campus, but not Heather.

The Chief then asked him if he cared to answer the question. Oakland nodded and said he had agreed to meet Adam at the rec center to pay the blackmail. On impulse he grabbed one of his wife's clubs from the back seat. He didn't plan on using it at first, but Adam had looked so smug. Adam had asked him if his wife was as hot for Oakland as she was for him. He had used the club to kill Adam in a fit of rage and then returned home. He looked at Heather, and said, "I forgave you. I was willing to do anything to keep you safe. Even killing the scumbag."

She was hysterical, and she continued to sob while Hirsch cuffed her husband and took him out the back door. The Chief went with them. Brett took over the escort of Heather. As he proceeded to leave out the back door, he told me he would meet me in my office as soon as he transported her to the station. He gave me a brushing kiss and they were gone.

I left through the front door and walked back to the building. The sun was shining, and the air had a touch of fall. I realized I hadn't eaten and I was starving. I stopped at Georg's to get a sandwich and realized I didn't have a wallet. They let me charge it and I went up to my office. Then I remembered I didn't have keys and went to the front office. Terra and Ali were on me in no time. They asked if I was alright, told me how worried they were, and related how Kim had lit into Brett when it was suspected I had been abducted.

A master key opened my office and I fell into my chair. I was exhausted and hungry. The sandwich and another cup of coffee took care of the hunger. Thankfully, with the gas leak ruse, my afternoon class had been cancelled. I sat there for what seemed like forever. I went over the whole morning in my head. I didn't want to be alone, so I went back to the main office to sit with Terra and Ali.

Mitch came by and gave me a hug. He just kept shaking his head as I gave them all a condensed version of Adam's blackmail and how it had gotten him killed. While I told my story, Kim and Katie joined us in the office area. I left out all the details of how he was blackmailing everyone and the photos.

I didn't say what Heather looked for in Adam's office. Surprisingly, nobody was bold enough to ask. When I finished the story, Kim gave me a hug. She was teary eyed. Katie, other than looking a bit relieved, didn't seem to have any reaction. I wasn't sure she even knew she had been recorded or that Adam had immodest photos of her. I made a promise to myself to come back up over the weekend to finish cleaning out Adam's office. I wanted to dispose of all those pictures and the ledger, after clearing it with Chief Pfeiffe and Brett of course.

In the meantime, I went to Adam's office, and reclaimed the key and the clipboard. I closed and locked the door behind me. I walked back to the main office and let Ali know I was going to hang onto Adam's key until I could finish with his office. Back in my office, I seriously considered closing my door.

I wasn't sure how fast the grapevine worked or if the rest of the faculty knew that Chancellor Oakland had been arrested for Adam's murder. I hadn't seen Jim yet, and didn't know just how much more flack he would be getting from this. I pulled up the KCCX website to see if it was on there yet. Within in a few minutes, there it was in the late breaking news box:

Word just in that Kenneth Oakland, Chancellor of Cold Creek College, has been taken into custody and charged with the murder of Adam Millberg. Additional charges are indicated as pending. An unexpected conclusion to the tragedy that shook Cold Creek early last week, Chief Pfeiffe will be giving a statement later this afternoon.

It was about an hour later when Brett came by. We went out to the parking lot. Surprisingly, my car was there as well as his. He explained Hirsch had arranged to drive it there and Kim had my bag and my keys. It was about 3 when Brett and I stood by his car, and he took me in his arms and held me tight. It felt good, not only because he was big and strong, and my hero, but because there was a promise of more to come.

He kissed me thoroughly and the tingle went to my toes, warmth to my core. But then he stopped, and stepped away. He said he would call me over the weekend, and he would be back down on Tuesday for dinner. He got in his car and drove away. I went back up to find Kim and my bag and my keys. Besides, I just wasn't ready to head back home and be alone.

Kim came to my office to bring me my bag and find out more details about what happened. I filled her in on the fact that Oakland's wife had been Adam's first wife. It was their relationship that led to the altercation between the two men. She looked at me and wondered aloud if it was because they had renewed their relationship.

I could tell from her expression she realized that would mean he had been seeing both she and Heather at the same time. Somehow I sensed she'd decided any student relationships happened in the spring, before they had hooked up again. She asked more questions, and I answered as well as I could without mentioning the photos or the blackmail.

Before long, Terra and Ali also came by. They both seemed glad it was settled. Misty must have called them, because they mentioned she asked if I was okay. When they asked why Heather and Oakland came after me, I had to explain that somehow Oakland thought I was on to him. I also explained how he and Heather had been in the process of spiriting me away. I verbalized that I didn't see myself as very threatening. Mitch showed up in the midst of the story and just shook his head. Then he added, "Students sure see you as threatening!"

Despite Mitch's attempt at humor, we were all pretty subdued. Mitch again tried to shift the tenor of the conversation. Needless to say, my budding relationship with Brett was the fodder for the shift. It was all in fun and they all teased me and we all laughed in no time.

Max bounded in, all excited, and said, "You missed all the excitement!! A gas leak in the building, and now the Chancellor has been arrested. Can you believe it?"

We all looked at each other, and then I said, "I sure can, Max. And I sure hope the rest of the semester is a whole lot less exciting." None of us even thought about explaining the gas leak to him. For my part, I was just as glad he didn't seem to have a clue as to my part in the whole thing. After a bit, everyone gradually left my office except Kim. Kim suggested we get dinner at the Grill and catch the press conference to see what else they had to say, and we headed out.

We took our favorite booth at the Grill, with our favorite waitress. We had a great view of the television and the restaurant got pretty quiet once the news came on. The press conference began with a restatement of the arrest. Chief Pfeiffe spoke about how the Cold Creek police and State police worked together to bring this dreadful matter to a close. He said all of the College administration and trustees were quite surprised and dismayed at the results of the investigation. The lead trustee, Matthew von

Kroner, then announced that, at the behest of the board, he would be taking the position as interim Chancellor until someone could be vetted by the board on a permanent basis.

President Cramer then spoke in support of von Kroner. He also spoke of the need for the College community to be more vigilant and proactive with regard to monitoring each other's behaviors. The Provost then announced that one initiative in this regard would be a series of talks on sexual harassment, a problem only identified through this investigation. He went on to say that while they were sure this was a limited problem, a task force was being formed. He also announced that Dr. Sheridan Hendley of the Psychology Department would be asked to head this group.

I threw up my arms, eyes wide as Kim looked at me, almost as dumbfounded as I was. She wasn't the only person in the Grill looking at me all of sudden. I shook my head, and tried to sink under the bench to no avail. Kim chuckled and shook her head until I threatened to put her on the task force as well. As we got up to leave, a few of the other patrons congratulated me and wished me well on the task force. I just shook my head and decided that somehow a self-defense class was going to be included as an outcome of the task force.

CHAPTER 15

I slept well, and woke up Saturday morning a bit sore. Instead of prompting me to take it easy or relax, it motivated me to get the incriminating 'stuff' out of Adam's office. I realized that at some point the previous afternoon I had opted to ask for forgiveness rather than permission. I wasn't taking the chance of being told no when it came to destroying "revealing" photographs.

I grabbed a pair of heavy duty scissors to make cutting the DVDs a little easier and I was ready to go. I took Charlie with me for the company and drove to campus. It was pretty empty as I expected. I used my keys to get in the building and into my office. Then I took the key to Adam's office and went to work. I found an empty trash can and dragged it along with me. I left my door and Adam's open, and Charlie took up position closest to me.

I put aside any of the portrait style photos, along with the ledger on the side of the desk. The ledger should be all they needed to substantiate a blackmail plot. At least that was my rationale. I put the pictures that were the object of blackmail into an envelope. I picked up all the DVD pieces, cut them up some more and added them to the trash bin. I picked up loose papers and they went into the trash bin as well.

I filled the boxes with books from the floor after carefully shaking each one. It wouldn't do for something to be left in one of them. Getting the books off the floor, and finishing the books that had been left on the shelf was important. A few more DVDs and photos fell out.

I opened the cabinet and there wasn't much in there except some boxes for his speakers, and stacks of papers. I almost just left the boxes there, but thought better of it. I opened them, and there were more pictures and more DVDs. I emptied them and tossed the boxes. I carefully filtered through the stacks of papers, tossed the papers and sorted any pictures that fell out.

I almost had the office cleaned out, the trash bin was full, and I had run out of boxes. It was all I could do. I was at least sure I had found anything worth killing for. I took the envelope of incriminating pictures to the office and using the cross-hatch shredder made quick work of them. I then shredded some other papers as well.

Charlie was getting impatient and I was tired. I closed up all the offices. I left the key for Adam's office in my office. I felt better, and though I suspected I would catch hell from Chief Pfeiffe and Brett for destroying possible evidence, I figured that was better than the alternative.

I forwarded what I needed to prepare for Tuesdays classes since there were no classes on Monday. The Monday, Wednesday, Friday class would now be behind. I also grabbed all the papers and pretests I hadn't graded yet. I intentionally didn't access College email from home, so I decided to at least check and see if there was anything important.

I had an email from Jim that had gone out to everyone Friday morning. I looked at the time stamp and had a little trouble comprehending that so much had happened in the past 24 hours. The email was short, but included an attachment. Jim had assigned all of Adam's advisees. I pulled up the list and looked for Rachel's name first. She had been assigned to Mitch. That would be good. I scanned the list and it looked like I had been assigned three students.

I started to get a little miffed when I realized that Kim had also been assigned three, but Max and Priscilla had managed to only be assigned one each. So much for random and equal assignment. I reminded myself that given the circumstances of the past two weeks, Jim's approach to things was not anything to get in a tither about. I sighed and shut down the computer. I could wait until Tuesday to contact the students to set up advising appointments.

I took Charlie for a walk in the arboretum and then we went home. I no sooner got home and Kim texted me about the carnival. I agreed to meet her there at 5 and have dinner. In the meantime, I took a nice, hot bath to help with my aches and a short nap. Showered and in jeans and t-shirt, I was off to the carnival.

I was meeting Kim at the Grill and we were walking to the town center. It took a while to park but I finally found a space. I walked toward the Grill and waved to Kim. When I got to her she gave me a hug and told me I looked better. I laughed and we walked toward the crowds. She rambled for a while about her morning and then asked about mine.

"I took care of some stuff in Adam's office. I wanted that chore behind me," I answered. I sighed and she looked at me with a questioning expression.

"Worse than the box of condoms, huh?" she asked. When I nodded, she said, "Never mind, I don't want to know. Even my ex wasn't as sleazy as Adam turned out to be."

The carnival was the usual corny stuff. There were rides for kids of all ages, and some crafts and such. There were a couple of food tents. We grabbed a couple of burgers, fries and soft drinks and sat down on a bench to eat. There were lots of people walking around, including Wayne. He spotted us and came toward us a like a magnet. I sighed and made a show of eating.

"Sheridan, Kim, good to see you. I am so glad they finally made an arrest. Chancellor Oakland didn't think I was a good enough dentist for him. He and his wife used a dentist in Richmond. Guess they won't have a choice of dentists now," he said with a self-righteous expression. I just nodded and reflected on how quickly we are able to accept the dark side of the same people who the day before were our leaders.

"So are you enjoying the carnival?" he continued.

"Yes, Wayne, we are. Having a bite to eat obviously." I purposely kept my mouth full, so Kim carried the conversation.

"You know, Sheridan, there is a live band at 7. We could sit together," he offered.

I looked at Kim who about choked, and I explained, "You know, Wayne, Kim and I planned on spending time together tonight. But thanks, anyway."

Kim nodded, and said, "It's been a real hard week Wayne, and we need to decompress. Girl stuff, you know."

Wayne's face paled, though I am not sure what he thought 'girl stuff' was. We smiled and told him we hoped he enjoyed the carnival and the concert. He shuffled his feet and didn't move.

"Um, Mitch said you were becoming friends with that detective. Is that over now the investigation is over?" he asked, looking a bit too hopeful.

"Mitch was correct. We are seeing each other, and will probably see more of each other now the investigation is over." I smiled and waited to see what would come next. He nodded, looked at Kim as if evaluating her as a possibility, and wished us a good evening. Kim and I just looked at each other and then at him as he walked away, head down.

Once we finished eating, Kim and I walked around a bit and located the staging where the band would be playing tonight. It was a local band and neither of us had heard of them. We sat down and rehashed some of what hadn't come out. I shared a little of how much Oakland had been trying to protect his wife and his likening Adam to an addiction or a cancer.

Kim sighed and responded, "He got that right. There is something addictive about someone who is so charismatic and is constantly attentive and noticing the little things. He would mention when I got a haircut, or if I frosted my hair, or a new blouse. He complimented me in a way that didn't seem like it was exaggerated, but felt good. It wasn't hard sell, you know? I can see through that."

"It was just his way, I guess. He somehow had mastered the technique. Probably used a lot of subliminal messages and figured out what your weaknesses were," I suggested. "He used his knowledge of psychology to shape your behavior with consistent reinforcement," I added with a smile.

She nodded, and said, "Yeah, and there is no other person or setting that provides that level of consistent positive feedback." She sighed again and looked off. A minute later, she hit my leg and tilted her head to the side. I followed the direction and there were Max and his wife walking toward us.

They stopped, and Max said, "It's finally safe with the murderer behind bars, so Stella and I decided to stop by for a few minutes. I have the rest of the weekend to work on a grant I heard about." He continued to ramble about his research and his grant, while the three of us nodded our heads. Max was back to his normal self. He told us to have a good weekend, and they walked off. Stella hadn't said a word. Kim and I just smiled at each other. One of these days, he was going to get that job, and we wouldn't have him to make us crazy. We would probably miss him when he was gone.

As we sat there, other faculty members came by and said hello. The general theme was the same. It was so surprising it was Oakland. It was so good not to have this hanging over the college now. I guessed none of them considered there might be a trial and a lot of dirty linen aired.

I suspected Oakland had a good attorney who would easily get his confession thrown out. If we were lucky, his attorney would ask the trial to be held far away. Then again, the man had been so deflated in the face of his wife's anger, he might just throw in the towel. I hoped he was being kept on suicide watch.

Katie was the only other faculty member from our department who came by. She was civil enough and seemed to be hedging, trying to find out something. She finally just came out and asked, "Uh, did you find anything, uh, interesting when you cleaned out Adam's office?"

I half-smiled, and said, "There were some photos. A portrait of you from a few years ago."

Kim nodded and Katie said, "That's all?"

"No, Katie, there were lots of photos. I destroyed all but the portrait, professional type photos," I said pointedly. I looked her in the eye and hoped she got my message. She must have because she looked away, sighed, and seemed to relax a bit. It occurred to me that even if her initials weren't on the ledger, she knew what he was up to. I didn't mention DVDs and neither did she.

"Thank you, Sheridan. That was very thoughtful of you," she said and she walked off.

Kim looked at me and said, "What other kind of photos were there, Sher?"

I hesitated. Then I looked her straight on and shook my head. She put her head in her hands and stayed that way for a few minutes. I wasn't sure how public the blackmail aspect of the case was. I wasn't going to be the one to make it public. She did now have a sense that he had taken pictures that wouldn't be available for public viewing.

After a few minutes of letting her digest the inference in her own way, I prompted her we needed to move on. I felt some dessert calling. Chocolate may not be the answer to all things unpleasant, but problems sure seem to get smaller with it. We stopped at a couple of vendors until we found the frozen yogurt and loaded up with yogurt and fudge topping. That changed the tenor of the night back to the light.

We made it an early night, and I went home to Charlie. I decided to attack the third box in the closet. After much waffling, I kept the wedding album. I did toss a lot of the other stuff and I wondered why I had taken it to begin with. I did laundry and changed the sheets in the guest room that now smelled like Brett. Finally, I turned on the television to catch the news and started to grade papers. The news didn't say much about Oakland or Adam. Apparently Adam's murder was old news now.

The weekend continued in a relatively predictable manner. I took Charlie for a run, worked in the garden, and graded papers. Eventually, I even managed to get everything set for Tuesday classes. Kim called a couple of times and we chatted. My mother called and I brought her up to date on the murder. I conveniently happened to leave out my part in it all. Kaylie called, and I teased her about getting Kevin on my case. She asked about 'my detective' and I told her the relationship was progressing.

Late Sunday night, Brett called. It was good to hear his voice. He talked about decorating Madison's room and the shopping he had endured. Then he asked if I had plans for dinner on Monday. I agreed to dinner, and we talked a little more.

He was going to come straight from Richmond instead of going home and driving down on Tuesday. That sounded good to me. I didn't volunteer any information about the photos I destroyed. I figured I wouldn't say anything unless asked directly. In the meantime, I had dinner to look forward to and a man in my life whose kisses made me tingle. Life was good.

ABOUT THE AUTHOR

Christa Nardi is and always has been an avid reader. Her favorite authors have shifted over time, but mystery/crime along with romance are her preferred choices for leisure reading. Christa also has been a long time writer from poetry and short stories growing up to technical, research, and nonfiction in her professional life. With Murder at Cold Creek College, Christa is joining many other reader/writers in writing one genre she enjoys reading – the cozy mystery. Christa Nardi is a pen name for a real life professor/psychologist from the Northeast with those attributes.

The second in the series, Murder at Cold Creek Arboretum, is scheduled for release in July 2014. Sheridan will again get drawn into solving a mystery. You can stay up to date on the progress on the blog, Christa Reads and Writes (christanardi.blogspot.com). You can also follow Christa on Facebook or contact her at cccnardi@gmail.com.

Made in the USA
Columbia, SC
03 March 2019